FATED FEAR

ANGEL'S FATE: BOOK 3

TESSA COLE

Gryphon's Gate Publishing

Gryphon's Gate Publishing

550 King St. N.

PO Box 42088 Conestoga

Waterloo, ON

N2L 6K5

ebook ISBN: 978-1-988115-80-1

Print ISBN: 978-1-988115-79-5

AMIAH

ICE AND WIND AND SOMETHING ELSE, SOMETHING POWERFUL and foreign tore through my chest, overwhelming the fear of having sex in public as well as the exhaustion of having spent all my magic and some of my life force to save Hawk from a vicious poison.

Time stuttered and for a second my senses narrowed to the pain, the power, the bed's red silk sheet against my back, Sebastian's fingers digging into my hips with his furious grip, and his erection buried deep inside me.

He stared at me, his eyes wide with shock. Something in my soul clicked and my skin lit up again like it had the first time we'd had sex even though I was no longer a virgin.

His expression turned to horror. "Oh, fuck."

Then time lurched, yanking me back to the chaos erupting in the Winter Court's ballroom. People screamed and bolted for the exits, and Titus, now a massive red dragon, roared and snapped his tail at the Winter Queen sitting on her throne.

The queen stretched out her hand and a wall, half ice and half wind, stopped the strike, but exploded on the impact.

Cassius yelled, flames erupted over his body and poured from his hands onto the floor. He released his wings with a fiery burst and heaved free of the court's icy wind, while Hawk continued to wrench against the wind's control.

Titus jerked his attention to me and even with his face transformed, I could see the ferocious desperation in his golden eyes. He leaped toward me, his wings catching air, but Deaglan, the King of the Shadow Court and the man who'd held Titus captive for five hundred years and who'd tried to murder Sebastian, shot shadows from his hands and seized Titus's neck and legs and jerked him back to the floor.

"Fuck fuck fuck." Sebastian yanked himself from me and hurriedly secured himself back into his leather pants. "Amiah, are you okay?"

The court's wind blasted around us, filled with stinging ice that sliced my skin and Sebastian's and shattered against Titus's scales. It whipped open the front of my dress — a dress with a slit that went all the way up to my waist and barely covered my breasts — exposing my privates to anyone who might have been looking my way, but I couldn't get my thoughts to focus even to grab it and cover up. I should grab it. I should run. I should—

Cassius snapped a fire whip around the wind capturing Hawk in front of the queen's throne and freed him, and they both scrambled out of the way of Titus's tail as he smashed it against another wind wall while trying to break free of Deaglan's shadows.

"Amiah." Sebastian leaned over me and cupped my cheeks in his hands, dragging my whirling attention back to him.

I tried to focus on him, but the room kept spinning, and exhaustion weighed me down determined to drag me into unconsciousness.

If I passed out everything would go away, the fear, the pain, the shame, and the ice.

Everything was happening so fast. My worst fear had come true. Sebastian's mother had threatened to kill Hawk, Cassius, and Titus, and Sebastian and I had been forced to have sex in the middle of the Winter Court's ballroom with everyone watching.

"Amiah. Are you all right?" Worry tightened Sebastian's expression.

He'd hurt me, pulled my hair, bit my lip, and thrust himself into me before I was ready. Because I'd asked him to. Because I wouldn't have gotten through it if we'd actually made love and I'd connected with his life force. And because I was too weak to give his mother and Deaglan any other kind of show to please them and save the guys.

And then Titus had gone crazy and shifted, shattering the glamor hiding his identity and protecting him from everyone in Faerie... where we were... right now...

"Fuck. Amiah. Stay with me."

I dragged my eyes open.

"Atta girl." He glanced over his shoulder then captured me again with his pale blue, almost colorless gaze. "I can fight Deaglan long enough to get away, but you have to take control of the Winter Court from my mother."

His words tripped in my mind.

"But she's the queen." She'd already proven she could take away what little control I had of the court's wind with a flick of her finger.

"The Winter Court just claimed you as a rightful heir. I can feel its power rushing through you."

"I—"

Titus roared, drawing my attention to him as a pillar of ice shattered against his side, making him stumble, and sending massive shards shooting into the windstorm whirling around us.

Both the Winter Queen and Deaglan wanted him. Everyone wanted him.

Sebastian ducked close, protecting me from the shards with his body.

"I know you can feel it. It's like ice and power in your veins," he said, his breath strangely warm against my cheek when it was usually cool. "Amiah, take it, use your will to overpower my mother's and get us the hell out of here."

"But this is her court." *And yours.* Whether he wanted it or not, he was the next King of the Winter Court in Faerie, he would have a more powerful connection to the court than me.

Another pillar of ice shot toward Titus. He opened his mouth and blasted it with a stream of fire, melting half of it before the rest shattered on his scales.

I wanted to scream at him. We'd already decided there was no way we could fight our way free, but he'd shifted anyway, giving us no other choice. Now we had to escape or die trying... and the odds weren't good for escaping.

Faerie's Heart and its powerful magic had awakened and Titus, the last dragon and the only one able to find the keys to release it, had revealed himself to the entire Winter Court and the King of the Shadow Court. They would do whatever it took to keep him in their grasps.

"Bring me my son and his wife," the Winter Queen yelled, her voice carrying through the wind. "The queen's favor to whoever brings them to me."

Most of the men in her harem bolted toward us along with a few personal guards that were dressed only in leather pants like my guys — and likely worked for other winter court nobles or the few visiting nobles from other courts who'd come to the queen's party.

Hawk grabbed the long white hair of one of the queen's men, a stunningly beautiful high fae, and yanked him off his feet. Cassius blasted another in the back with a ball of fire, shoving him onto the floor and drawing a scream of agony before two more of the queen's men encased Cassius in ice. But liquid fire roared from his hand's melting it before my sluggish thoughts could fully register the danger.

Towering and bulky guards, beings constructed of ice and Winter Court magic, stormed in from the halls. They headed straight for my guys, and Deaglan threw more shadows around Titus's neck and his snout.

Titus heaved and jerked against the shadows and his

gaze, still locked on me as if not even fighting for his freedom mattered, turned desperate.

With a triumphant yell, the queen raised her hands. The frozen magic in my chest thudded like a powerful second heartbeat, and a barrier swept around all of us, trapping us in a magical icy dome.

"Amiah. I can't fight Deaglan *and* my mother. Take control of the court."

One of the queen's men, a bulky muscular werewolf, dove for me, and Sebastian rolled me out of the way, pulling me on top of him. But another man grabbed my hair and wrenched me off Sebastian with a painful jerk.

The sudden movement made the room darken and lurch and the ice inside me swelled. A blast of wind snapped out of the queen's storm and broke the man's arm.

With a scream, he released me and jerked back, and the wind, *my* wind, slammed him into another of the queen's men, knocking both of them over.

I staggered but managed to keep standing in my weakened condition, and my compulsive need to heal twisted in my chest. *Heal him. His arm is broken.* It didn't matter that he wanted to hurt me or the guys. God, I'd never been so grateful to be out of power.

Sebastian scrambled out of the way of a naga wearing the red leather pants of the queen's harem, his red scales — covering his chest and arms — protecting him from the flying ice. His thin prehensile tail flicked behind him, helping him keep his balance, but Sebastian activated a glyph on his left forearm and shot a force-wave at the man, and his tail wasn't enough to keep him upright. He staggered back and the windstorm threw him to his knees as three more of the queen's men barreled toward us.

Cassius snapped a fire whip around the neck of one of them and yanked him to the floor, but Deaglan shot a shadow spear at Cassius before he could stop the two others. The spear slammed into Cassius's shoulder, shoving him back and pinning him to the ice barrier.

"No." My pulse stuttered. How could they have been so stupid? They'd promised they wouldn't fight. They knew some or all of them wouldn't survive battling the queen, her men, her guards, and the Shadow King. Why had Titus shifted? He'd just had to control his beast a little longer and we'd have been free.

I'd been willing to sacrifice my body to save them? It had been the only option. It had almost been done. With the Winter Queen satisfied, we could have just slipped away. Why couldn't they have just let me save them.

Fire roared around Cassius, but the ice barrier behind him, keeping all of us captured, didn't melt, and the queen's men encased him in wave after wave of thick ice, rebuilding it as fast as he could melt it.

Hawk screamed, jerking my attention to him, and my pulse stalled altogether. One of the queen's guards had shoved his enormous ice spear through the center of his chest, and while the incubus could rapidly heal and take a lot of damage, there was still a limit to his powers. And if we didn't get out of the Winter Court soon, we'd find it.

"Amiah," Sebastian snapped. He held up his hands and shot light through the shadow pinning Cassius to the dome, freeing him. None of Sebastian's glyphs that I could see glowed which meant he could have been using his sorcerer's power — not the power of the many spells tattooed in his skin — and dangerously channeling the primal, raw power of Faerie itself, risking burning up if he couldn't control it. "Break the dome."

The werepanther who'd been by the Winter Queen's side since we'd arrived in court ran toward me. He shifted between one step and the next, his body melting into a sleek black cat with liquid effortlessness, and leaped at me.

I lurched out of the way, but the movement made the room whirl, and I tumbled back onto the bed. The werepanther's canines gazed my legs, slicing into my skin but not getting ahold of me, and the ice in my chest thudded again.

A blast of my wind shoved him a few feet away, forcing him to dig his claws into the floor to keep from tumbling even farther.

"Amiah, get us out of here," Sebastian yelled. His full-body glow had dimmed, his complexion was gray, and his breath was too fast. His light magic twisted and writhed with Deaglan's shadows while also tethering Deaglan's demon-vampire hybrid to the back of the dome to keep him out of the fight. Sebastian was stretching himself too thin and if he kept going, he was going to burn up.

The hybrid sliced at the light tethering him with his claws and jerked forward a step, but the tether quickly reformed and shoved him back again.

"How long can you hold both of us?" Deaglan called in a singsong. "You're not as strong as you were three hundred years ago."

"I can hold just fine." Sebastian's light surged, but Deaglan formed more shadows, catching the blast then shooting a flurry of spikes in my direction.

I tried to jerk out of the way but I wasn't going to be fast enough.

At the last second, Sebastian tackled me onto the bed and rolled us off the other side and my wind tore the shadows apart.

"Get us the fuck out of here," Sebastian snarled at me, before jerking up and throwing another blast of light in Deaglan's direction.

Titus howled and I glanced over the edge of the bed. Only a few strands of shadow still captured him. With a powerful flap of his wings, he broke free of the rest, but the Winter Queen seized his neck with a lasso of wind and wrenched him to the floor with a bone-rattling boom.

Icy fear roared through me and my wind tore the lasso apart without me trying to control it.

The Winter Queen's gaze, her eyes fully black with her terrifying power, jumped to me.

"This is my court." Her wind exploded into a hurricane that tore at my hair and dress and slammed me into the far side of the dome. My breath exploded from my lungs at the impact and the wind whipped it away as the room darkened.

"Amiah." That sounded like Hawk.

I forced my eyes open to see him barreling toward me. He'd broken free of the spear, leaving a large pool of blood on the floor, and had managed to draw closer.

But the queen's wind gusted and tossed him sideways

toward Cassius, who fought three more ice guards, as well as the queen's fae men. The wind tore at Cassius's fire, yanking it from his body and extinguishing it, and thick ice threatened to immobilize him.

With a guttural yell, he erupted in a ferocious blaze, radiating so much heat I could feel it halfway across the room. The ice encasing him shattered, and he snapped a massive fire whip around a guard's neck and tossed him at the Winter Queen. She wrenched her hand up, sending a blast of wind knocking the guard to the side, and the storm pummeling me stuttered.

The icy power inside me thudded again, and I mentally clutched at its cold slicing through my veins. I willed it, begged it, promised it everything if it would just give me control, just long enough to save them.

The hail and wind vanished and the room fell deathly quiet. Only Titus's snarls as he fought the wind pinning him to the floor and the crackle of Cassius's fire broke the silence.

I'd done it. I'd stopped the storm. Somehow I'd taken control of the queen's wind.

All eyes jumped to Sebastian who panted a few feet away, his complexion gray, his body trembling, then their gazes slid to me, their expressions filled with a mix of fear and horror and rage.

"I said," the queen hissed, her voice low, barely carrying across the room, and filled with a dark, deadly rage, "this is my court."

She wrenched both hands up and wind pounded into me. It stole my breath and crushed me against her barrier, cracking my ribs and sending a pain I was far too familiar with screaming through my chest.

Cassius yelled and shot a fire whip at the queen, but both of her fae men encased it in ice and the two remaining ice guards stabbed at him with their spears.

The wind's pressure grew. I heaved against it, strained to regain control, but couldn't breathe and could barely think.

Deaglan sent a flurry of shadows at Sebastian, wrenching him off the ground and slamming him into the floor before he could defend himself.

One of my ribs snapped, exploding agony through my chest, and then another.

Hawk leaped toward me, but the werepanther dug his claws into his side and yanked him around with a wild spray of blood that was whipped up into the queen's reawakened storm.

Another *snap*.

I screamed and the wind tore the cry from my mouth and devoured it.

Titus wrenched and spat fire. His wings wildly flapped and his claws dug rents into the floor as he fought to break free of the queen's hold.

All of the guys fought, desperate, panting, and bleeding. Cassius's fire stuttered, and Hawk staggered as the werepanther raked his claws against his back. Light snapped from Sebastian's hands burning through some of Deaglan's darkness but the demon-vampire seized him by the throat and pinned him to the floor.

Another *snap* and darkness swept over me, promising blissful nothingness. I struggled to stay conscious, to regain control of the wind, do something, anything. I had to do something.

It didn't matter that I didn't have any power of my own. Everything within me screamed that I had to save them. Somehow. Whatever it took. I would pay it. Whatever the cost. *Please. Someone, anyone, save them.*

AMIAH

My soul screamed, *save them, save them,* but it was more than just my compulsive need to heal. It was deeper, more consuming, and it twisted with the ice in my chest.

I have to save them. I have to find the power.

I couldn't let the Winter Queen kill them and I couldn't let her or Deaglan imprison Titus. He'd suffered too much already for too long. He'd already lost everything, his whole species, what he'd thought was a friendship with Deaglan, and five hundred years of his life.

He didn't deserve that. No one did.

Sebastian screamed and blasted light into the demon-vampire, breaking free of the hybrid's grasp and tossing him to the dais at the back of the room. Cassius barely held his own, his inferno ripped from his body by the queen's ferocious wind, and Hawk tumbled out of the way of the werepanther's teeth, blood gushing from his wounds.

The Winter Court's magic thudded in my chest, my

veins, my soul, an overwhelming second heartbeat, and I gasped in an agonizing breath.

Whatever the cost? it asked.

"Yes." *Yes yes yes.*

The ice thudded again and locked in. The court's cold swept through my cells and wove into my essence, and frost crackled over my skin. There was no going back. The Winter Court had claimed me and I'd let its wild magic in without restraint.

A small part of me screamed, desperate to take back my consent. I was trapped. I'd let myself be trapped in a permanent bond, the very thing I'd been trying to avoid, the very thing I'd begged Sebastian to help me avoid when he'd helped remove my mating brand. Worse, I'd enslaved myself to a magic I didn't understand.

And the rest of me didn't care.

It was the only way out, the only way to save everyone. And I *was* going to save everyone.

I seized the ice inside me, willing it, begging it to obey my command and only my command. I was stronger than the Winter Queen. I had to be stronger than her. The guys weren't going to survive if I wasn't.

I. Will. Save. Them.

I forced everything I had into one powerful command to the Winter Court. Mine. Right now, it was mine. The wind would stop. The dome would break. And the court would help us escape.

The ice inside me shuddered, not because it wanted to resist me, but because the Winter Queen still possessed its power.

"Mine!" I screamed, releasing all of my fear and determination into that word and seizing control of the court.

Ice tore at me from the inside out and the queen's storm vanished, taking all the air in the room with it for a gasping, heart-stopping moment and making my world whirl.

The Winter Queen howled and the dome shattered with a sharp *crack*, showering us with massive chunks of ice.

A piece slammed into Sebastian, knocking him to the floor and drawing a cry of pain. Hawk twisted out of the way of another piece, barely managing to dodge it, while Cassius shoved one of the ice guards into the path of another chunk.

The queen raised her hands, blocking the ice falling on her with a wind shield then tossed the pieces at me.

I jerked my hands up and threw myself to the side as my wind battered her ice out of the way, but another piece from above crashed against the side of my head and sent me reeling.

Titus wrenched free of the Winter Queen's wind, leaped across the room for me, and snatched me up in his large front claw.

Without waiting for the others, he shot straight up and smashed through the skylight.

"Stop that dragon," the queen screamed.

Cassius extinguished his flames, grabbed a barely conscious Sebastian, and slung him over his shoulder, while Hawk scrambled to join him. With the incubus clutched against his other side, Cassius took off as well, but with the extra weight he couldn't fly as fast as Titus and we were leaving them behind.

"Titus, the others," I gasped, my teeth chattering with the cold inside me.

Titus snarled and rose higher into the freezing night sky, strangely lit not with stars but with a shimmering, opalescent barrier.

If his beast had fully taken over there was no way I'd be able to reason with him. He'd be working purely on primal instinct, and I could only pray that after having been forced to deny his beast for five hundred years Titus the man hadn't been locked away in the deepest recesses of his beast's mind for good.

"Titus, please."

He jerked around, pulled his wings back, and dive-bombed Cassius, whose eyes flashed wide. The wind of our fall whipped my hair and dress around me, stung my bare skin, and made the world whirl. Fire snapped over Cassius's hands, drawing a yelp from Hawk and a moan from Sebastian, and Titus seized Cassius and Sebastian in a large claw — Hawk managing to jerk out of the way at the last minute and cling to Titus's leg.

With a roar, Titus shot fire in ferocious defiance into the ballroom. Then he flapped his wings with powerful strokes, gusting the air around us, and soared away from the heart of the Winter Court.

Below, ragged snowcapped mountains stretched as far as I could see in every direction, and above, thick storm clouds started to rush in around us. They brought a vicious, freezing wind, filled with ice shards, and I knew in my heart this was the Winter Queen's fury.

The wind tossed us, adding nausea to my spinning vision and I fought to control the icy magic freezing my soul and regain my hold of the Winter Court.

But the queen's fury was too strong and I'd been exhausted and weak to begin with and getting weaker and it didn't seem to matter that I now belonged to the Winter Court.

Titus roared, fighting the wind, his grip around me — and most likely Cassius and Sebastian as well — tightening, while Hawk, with his fingers locked together, clung to his leg.

You thought you could keep the dragon for yourself, the wind howled. *Too impatient to wait for me to fade to inherit my court.*

A blast of wind slammed against Titus's back, dropping us toward the jagged mountain spikes. He twisted, narrowly missing crashing into the stone and shot through a crevasse barely wide enough for his body.

"Mother, please," Sebastian gasped pinned against Cassius's body. His full-body glow flickered and disappeared for a terrifying second then stuttered back to life, but it was barely visible.

I won't let you leave my court. I won't let you take my dragon. I will kill him before I let you or anyone else possess my Heart.

An enormous vortex roared to life in front of us. Titus jerked, trying to avoid it, but it seized him and wrenched him in.

The air was sucked from my lungs and the world went frigid and dark. Wind stung my skin and we spun around and around and around making my stomach heave.

Titus roared and fire sparked from Cassius but the flames were whipped away the second they appeared. Hawk wrapped his legs around Titus's and locked his ankles, desperately trying to hold on.

Winter court, please, I begged.

Not. Your. Court, the Winter Queen's wind howled.

Command me, the court said inside me, its ice snapping and cracking as if it tried to keep hold inside me but the queen's control kept breaking it. *Command me.*

Let us go.

A massive blast of wind slammed into us and we were tossed out of the vortex and through the opalescent barrier protecting the Winter Court from the Wilds, the magic of the barrier painfully tearing at my essence as we tumbled through.

For a second we were suspended in a cold, clear sky filled with glittering stars above a barren, mostly flat landscape stretching as far as I could see, then Titus faltered and plummeted to the ground.

He tossed me and the guys and started to shift — using the magic that changed his shape to partially cushion the impact. But I hit the cold, hard-packed cracked earth, agony screaming through my chest, and tumbled over and over again before I could see if he succeeded.

My shoulder hit something hard, bringing me to a jarring halt lying face down, and my stomach immediately heaved. It threatened to expel the little bit of food I'd managed to eat during the party, and my uncontrollable shivering with the Winter Court's ice inside me and the agony of my broken ribs didn't help.

"Amiah," Cassius groaned.

I struggled to not throw up and raised my head, but that only made my stomach clench tighter and my world darken.

"Amiah, answer me," Cassius said, his tone sharp. Footsteps pounded toward me, smoke enveloped me, and burning hot hands rolled me over, making me cry out in pain and straining my mental hold on my stomach's contents.

Cassius's striking blue gaze met mine and for a second I was floating in brilliant blue, embraced by angelic light, home and safe. I'd felt that way when he'd rescued me from that faith healer. I hadn't thought I'd ever see the familiar glow of a fellow angel's eyes again, had believed that I'd be alone until the faith healer had drained me of all my power and I'd died.

Then Cassius had found me and looked into my eyes like he was doing now, his gaze filled with fear and rage and... something else, something I couldn't quite place, something stunned... or was that awe... desperation? Need?

My stomach clenched tight and his eyes widened.

"Crap." He jerked back, fire erupting over his body as I threw up, barely managing to avoid his boots.

"Jeez, Amiah," Hawk gasped.

Cassius staggered farther away, his fire pouring onto the ground around his feet, hissing and snapping as if he couldn't control it. Smoke billowed around him, and every muscle in his body tensed.

Hawk scrambled to my side and brushed my long blond locks, tangled and windblown, out of my face, keeping the ends out of my vomit.

Heat radiated from his body in massive, suffocating waves, burning down my nose and throat with every breath. Sweat burst from my skin even though my insides remained frozen, and I inched away from him making him frown.

"Are you okay?" he asked, his voice tender, his usual blue-gray gaze filled with concern and a barely smoldering prick of hellfire.

"Are you?" I asked back through chattering teeth despite the heat coming off of him and fighting to keep my breath shallow. I wasn't okay. I didn't know if I'd ever be okay again. I was exhausted, in pain, out of power, freezing cold on the inside, and possessed by the Winter Court.

"You," Titus snarled, dragging my attention past Cassius and Hawk to the enormous naked shifter — the magic that transformed him having consumed his clothing. He stormed toward Sebastian who had barely managed to get to his hands and knees. "You hurt her."

"Titus—" Sebastian started to raise his head, but Titus grabbed the back of Sebastian's white leather jerkin and slammed him back into the ground.

Everything within me froze, unable to fully comprehend what I'd just seen.

"You made her cry." Titus jerked Sebastian back up again and smashed his fist into Sebastian's face with a sharp crack that resounded through the quiet darkness.

"You rammed your cock into her and made her cry, you fucking bastard."

Blood gushed from Sebastian's nose and he opened his mouth but Titus punched him again. Another sharp crack that snapped Sebastian's head to the side.

My mind jerked into motion and my heart leaped into my throat. After all that, Titus was attacking him?

"Titus, stop." I staggered to my feet. Pain sliced through me, and the barren landscape lurched along with my stomach. Cassius reached for me but jerked back at the last moment and Hawk grabbed me instead, pulling me into a blazing hot embrace, searing my skin and making me whimper in pain.

"You weren't supposed to have sex with her," Titus roared, his voice booming in the stillness.

"Titus, stop." I pushed against Hawk's grip, but I was too weak to fight him, and he wouldn't let me go. "It's not his fault."

"How could you do that, Seireadan? She cried. In pain." Titus smashed his fist into Sebastian's face again. *Crack*. Sebastian's full-body glow flickered, his eyes rolled back, and my compulsion to heal twisted in my chest, adding to my nausea, even though I barely had any healing magic left.

Fear quickened my pulse and I weakly heaved against Hawk's grip. I had to stop this. Didn't he know it hadn't been Sebastian's fault? I would have cried if it had been any of them.

"Stop. Just stop," I begged, the ice in my chest swelling, numbing the agony of my broken ribs, and making me shiver despite Hawk's burning body temperature.

But Titus smashed his fist into Sebastian's face again. "She cried." Another crack even though Sebastian's head lolled to the side, his eyes barely open. "Because of you."

My need to heal twisted tighter. God, Titus was going to kill him. He might have shifted back into a human, but his beast still had control and he was furious that Sebastian hadn't been gentle when he'd been forced to have sex with me... because I'd asked him to.

Titus snarled, wrenched Sebastian close, nose to nose, and bared his large, wickedly sharp canines. "You even think about touching her again and I'll rip your heart out and eat it."

"I said stop!" I commanded, letting my fear and frustration and pain harden my voice, but Titus wrenched his hand back to hit Sebastian again.

AMIAH

"Just stop!" I screamed again. *Please, God, stop.* Sebastian wasn't going to be able to take much more. I could feel his life force stuttering even though I wasn't touching him and I was supposed to need contact to sense someone's life force. And while I also wasn't fully connected and had no idea how serious his injuries were, I knew a few more blows would kill him.

"Please, Titus."

Titus jerked to face me, a wild fury blazing in his golden eyes, making his body shake.

Blood filled with sparkling flecks of white light gushed from Sebastian's nose and a cut along his cheek. It splattered onto the hard earth and was instantly absorbed. His breath was ragged and he hung limp in Titus's grip.

"Please." I pushed against Hawk's embrace but he still wouldn't let go, and to be honest, I wasn't sure I could stand without his help, but I had to go to Sebastian. Even if I couldn't heal his injuries, I had to check on him, prove to my magic there wasn't anything I could do. *But please, God, let there be something I can do.*

"Let me go," I said.

"You're not going anywhere near him," Titus snarled. "Not after what he did to you."

"I said let me go. You don't get to tell me what to do. None of you do," I snapped. *Not after what I'd just been through.* "I *need* to check him," I added, putting emphasis on need hoping Cassius would understand that I was too tired to ignore my compulsion to heal even if I barely had any power. "And you certainly don't have the right to hit him for something I told him to do."

"You what?" Cassius asked, smoke billowing from him, his fire a molten pool around his feet, bright in the darkness. "You told him to assault you?"

"He didn't assault me." How could they possibly think Sebastian had assaulted me?

"Yes. He did," Cassius spat out. And now *he* looked like he wanted to pummel Sebastian into the ground, too.

The light in Cassius's eyes flared, revealing a hard, furious expression in bright angelic light. I wasn't sure if I'd ever seen him that angry before. The last time I'd seen him let his fire pour around him like that had been when I'd been kidnapped by Balwyrdan, and that fae had seriously beaten me.

Oh, God. Did he think Sebastian was as bad as Balwyrdan? Had it really looked that horrible? It couldn't have. Yes, Sebastian had been rough, but Balwyrdan had been brutal.

"That was hard to watch," Hawk said, his grip tightening, burning against my skin, "especially knowing you weren't enjoying it." Which was something I couldn't deny. Not that I wanted to. With his ability to sense sexual energy, he knew exactly how I'd felt about what had happened and could probably guess that the reality of it hadn't fully hit home because I was still too exhausted and stunned.

"It had to be done," I said.

"Not like that," Cassius growled.

"She was going to kill you. If we didn't put on some kind of a show, she'd make us do it again, and I was too weak for anything else."

My throat tightened with the fear that I'd felt — still felt, because now all of Faerie knew we were with the last dragon and was coming after him — along with a rapidly growing rage. The Winter Queen had threatened whatever had been building between me and Sebastian by forcing that on us. And now it looked like she'd threatened his relationship with the other guys as well.

"I wasn't going to do it again. I just wanted it over with. Hurting me, making me cry, getting it over with fast was the best way to satisfy her so we could get out of there."

Wild sparks snapped from Cassius's body and the smoke billowing around him thickened. "He could have built up the hybrid's magic."

"Do you honestly think Sebastian could have done anything to make me enjoy that?" I shot back, my eyes burning with tears I didn't want to cry. Yes, I'd had the seductive magic of the demon-vampire's bite coursing through my veins, but it would never have been enough. I would never have relaxed enough to even partially enjoy it, not with everyone watching, not knowing the guys' lives hung in the balance.

"Amiah—" Cassius took a step toward me then jerked back as if he remembered he was still on fire.

"The only way I could have gotten through anything else was if you'd enthralled me," I said to Hawk. "And you weren't in a position to help."

He, Cassius, and Titus had all been trapped at the foot of the queen's dais and while an incubus's magic could affect someone from a distance, he needed to touch a person to fully enthrall her.

I shot a glare at Hawk and Titus. What was wrong with them? Didn't they know Sebastian would never do something like that to me? I'd had to beg him to do it. "You know him. Do you honestly think he'd have done that without my consent?"

The muscles in Hawk's jaw flexed. "Just because you agreed to it, doesn't make it right."

"Don't you think that hurt him as well? Didn't you see our first kiss?" I pressed. I hadn't known Sebastian very long, and even if I'd only met him that night, that first kiss had been so gentle, so caring it had broken my heart. He might wear a cocky overconfident demeanor the rest of the time, but in that moment, he'd revealed his true heart, someone who cared deeply for others, who didn't want to hurt others because he'd been horribly hurt himself.

It all made perfect sense now why he flirted with everyone and had a reputation for sleeping around — which he probably did. If he kept the same lover for too long, he'd become emotionally involved, and I was willing to bet the last time he'd been emotionally involved with someone was with his fiancé who'd slept with his best friend and then tried to kill him.

Sebastian groaned and his glow flickered and went out again. His muscles clenched tight and his breath picked up, making my pulse trip.

I *had* to check on him, had to use what little magic I'd managed to recover in the short time since I'd pushed everything I had into Hawk to help Sebastian.

"Now let me go." I heaved again against Hawk's grip, shooting agony through my chest and gritting my teeth, refusing to cry out in pain. "Don't make me fight my healing compulsion on top of everything else.

"Fine," Cassius growled. He gave a tight nod and Hawk released me — which made me furious because Hawk had done what Cassius had said and not what I'd wanted. "Titus, back away from Sebastian."

Titus snarled at Cassius and didn't release Sebastian.

"Titus," Cassius snapped.

"He won't hurt me," I said, staggering to them.

"Amiah—" Cassius started, but I jerked my head back to glare at him, making my stomach heave and the world lurch.

"He's beaten Sebastian to a pulp because of me." I sucked in a steadying breath, shot agony through my chest, and ended up panting. "He's not going to hurt me."

A flurry of sparks exploded from Cassius's blaze and flew into the night sky,

I turned my attention to Titus. "You're not going to hurt me," I said, keeping my voice soft and trying to look confident and in control while hiding my shivering body and chattering teeth.

"No," he growled as I reached him and placed my hands on his massive muscular arm, praying that the flesh to flesh contact would help calm his beast. As much as I really wanted to tend to Sebastian — now now now — I needed to deal with Titus and his beast first. If I didn't calm him down more and steady his soul, he could break down and attack Sebastian again.

"For fuck's sake, Amiah," Hawk hissed.

"Back away from the dragon," Cassius demanded.

Titus tensed at my touch and turned his golden gaze on me, his pupils fully slitted and a hint of red-gold scales curling over his neck and jaw.

"If there'd been any other way, you know he wouldn't have hurt me like that," I said, pressing my forehead against his biceps, adding another point of contact, and letting a whisper of my magic connect with him, just enough to gage through his vitals when he'd gotten his beast under control.

A shudder swept through him and he growled low in his throat.

"Amiah, please," Cassius begged.

"He could have fought," Titus said, but his pulse and breath were already starting to slow, my contact helping to steady his soul and let his human side regain control.

Oh, thank God. Because I had no idea what we were going to do if he remained furious with his beast in control. We needed him. *I* needed him. I needed all of them right now... and I wasn't going to think too hard about what that might mean.

"We barely escaped," I murmured back. And we'd only escaped because I'd given myself to the Winter Court. Something else I didn't want to think about.

Sebastian moaned and I strained to stay with Titus, my need to heal twisting, its pressure mixing with the pain and cold in my chest.

"Titus, I'm okay."

"You're not," he said, his voice a low rumble. "I smell your blood. I smell sex from him and the incubus."

My pulse stuttered and I prayed Cassius was too far away to hear that. I wasn't ready to tell him I was having sexual intercourse with both Sebastian and Hawk... which was silly given everything that had happened. What he thought of me, how he saw me, was nothing compared to what I'd just gone through.

"The light in your eyes is gone. You've spent all your power and I wasn't there to protect you." Titus dropped Sebastian, drawing a grunt of pain. He embraced me, curling his massive body around me — thankfully without putting pressure on my ribs — and a part of my soul sang at the physical contact, the closeness. And not completely because I was being held by a ruggedly handsome naked man. No, part of my satisfaction was because of the strong, ferocious pulse of his life force caressing my senses and the knowledge that all of his injuries, all the lacerations and contusions he suffered during the fight, were melting away with his unusually fast healing.

But instead of the embrace calming him, his breath picked up and he started to tremble, his beast suddenly struggling to take over again. "I should have protected you. You're fragile. You're hurt—"

"I'll be okay," I insisted. Just as soon as we got some-place safe and I could recover some of my magic and heal Sebastian and myself... and Cassius. Jeez, I hadn't even thought to check on Cassius, and with his fire blazing, any injuries he might have gotten during the fight weren't easily noticed.

"You. Were. Hurt," he growled, his muscles bunching around me.

"Titus, please." He was losing control again, the contact wasn't enough to calm him, and I had to get him calm. If Sebastian was out of commission, Titus was the only one who knew Faerie well enough to get us to safety.

I reached up and cupped Titus's cheeks, urging him to look down at me, hoping eye contact would help him regain control, but it wasn't Titus the man who looked down at me. It was Titus the beast, his eyes filled with a wild, ferocious intensity that stole my breath, half in awe and half in fear.

"You were hurt. I should have protected you. *He* should have protected you, not hurt you," he snarled. "He doesn't deserve you."

"Titus, please. Control your beast. Just for a little longer." I knew what I was asking might be impossible. He'd spent five hundred years in captivity and had only shifted one other time since. His connection with his beast had to be strained, and I could only hope it wasn't completely broken because that wasn't something I could heal.

"He hurt you." Titus heaved in a ragged breath, his nostrils flaring, and bared his teeth at me.

I met his glare without flinching, not in a fight for

dominance — there was no way I'd ever be dominant to Titus — but in earnestness. There'd been no other way and his beast knew that, had to accept that. "I told him to."

His battle with his beast raged in his eyes. He wanted to protect me, wanted to support me, wanted to believe me. His primal instincts had to be tearing him apart because he'd denied half of his soul for far too long. And all I could do was press my body against his and pray that even though I wasn't a dragon or his mate my essence was enough to calm his and help him regain control. It was the only thing I could do.

"We thought it was our only way to keep all of us alive." *Please believe me. Please calm your beast. Please don't hurt Sebastian anymore.*

His eyes narrowed and his gaze dropped to Sebastian, who moaned in agony, more flecks of light sparking from his body, now not just from his blood but his skin as well, all of it sucked into the hard, barren earth.

"He was your best friend. You know him."

"I do," he spat out, pain tightening his expression, his whole body trembling.

"You know he wouldn't hurt me on purpose." Well not physically. He'd tried to hurt me emotionally to get me to turn my desires to Cassius when I wasn't at all certain I was in love with Cassius. But then he'd confessed that he wanted to continue having sex with me when we'd saved Hawk... and if I thought too hard about that right now with my whirling unsteady thoughts, I'd make myself crazy trying to figure out what that had meant. All I really wanted was to have sex with him, to explore what I'd denied myself for too long. And he'd been perfect because he didn't want a relationship.

More sparks exploded from Sebastian's skin and his full-body glow stuttered and went out again for a second.

My need to heal clenched around my heart. "You know we did what we had to in order to get out of there," I said, forcing my voice calm.

"I do." He yanked away from me. For a heart-stopping second, I thought he was going to attack Sebastian. His hands curled into tight fists and he bared his teeth. Then he jerked away. "I need a minute. Faerie is already ripping out his magic. We can't stay here."

He stormed a few feet past Cassius, his whole body tense with his beast's fury, stunning me at his sudden change of mind. He released a wild, ferocious howl, dropped to his knees, and punched the earth again and again as if he could scream and beat out his rage and regain control.

I sagged to the ground beside Sebastian, my magic connecting with him before I'd even touched him. His nose was broken, his cheek fractured, and his right orbital bone shattered. But more than that, a different kind of pain tore through him, turning his breath into shallow, desperate gasps. Except I couldn't find the source. It was everywhere and nowhere. In his veins, igniting his nerves, and consuming his fae light from the inside out. This had to be Faerie taking back its magic.

"Holy fucking hell." Hawk scrambled to my side and drew me back into his too-hot arms, sending agony screaming through my chest and making me gasp in pain, while Cassius stayed where he was, fire pouring off his body as if he'd given up on trying to control his magic.

"Don't you do that again," Cassius snarled. "God, please." He sank to his knees, his fire undulating around him in a ferocious burning pool.

The eyelid of Sebastian's one good eye fluttered open, and his gaze instantly met mine, making my pulse stall. There wasn't even a glimmer of the power in his eye that I'd seen before, only writhing painful darkness.

"Fuck man, you need to get that dealt with," Hawk whispered.

"Sure, find me a demon in Faerie that can pull it out." Light sparked from Sebastian's body and sank into the earth. He bit back a strangled moan and raised a trembling hand to my cheek, his skin strangely warm. "I'll fix this. I promise."

"We did what we had to. Titus will understand that. Cassius will too." A whisper of my healing magic sank into him, but it wasn't enough to knit any of his broken bones back together let alone mend all the lacerations he'd gotten from the ice in the queen's storm. "I don't have enough power to heal you. You're going to have to hang on for a while."

"I wasn't talking about that." Another spark snapped from his body and he panted in quick shallow breaths. "I'm talking about the court, about this." He drew my hand up. My skin still glowed like it had the first time we'd had sex as if I'd still been a virgin, except now I could see threads of white shimmering magic trailing through my skin like veins. "I'll get the court to release its claim on you and take back its magic. I promise."

"What? The Winter Court claimed her?" Hawk's grip around me tightened, making me whimper and he quickly eased up on his embrace. "That's why she's lit up like the sun and is freezing?"

"Yeah," Sebastian huffed then groaned as more light sparked from his body. "Guess what Amiah, you're now high fae. Soon you too will get the pleasure of having Faerie's magic ripped out of you if we stay here much longer."

"I'm what?" I must have been too exhausted and sore and cold to have heard that right. "How can I be fae. I'm an angel."

"You've Faerie's magic running through your veins now," he gasped.

"Because you two had sex on your mother's magic bed?" Hawk demanded.

"Best guess," Sebastian said as Cassius, his fire pulled under his skin with what had to be an extraordinary force of will — his frigid hard expression proof of his effort — drew closer. "Titus somehow gave her the first key to unlocking Faerie's Heart without killing himself and the Winter Court latched onto its magic inside her soul."

AMIAH

My thoughts stuttered. "I have a key to unlocking the Heart? When did I get the key?" Wouldn't I have known I had the key? In my soul? "How did I get the first key?"

Then my memory jumped to the kiss with Titus on the balcony when we were being attacked by the ice men.

Heat had filled me and I'd thought, since it hadn't been my mating brand awakening — the brand I no longer had, thank goodness! — it had just been a rush of adrenaline and desire. Because I did desire Titus. I'd been drawn to him from the moment I'd met him, and I wasn't sure anymore if that was just because he was a shifter and could give me the physical contact I craved or not.

"I don't know how I gave it to her. It just happened," Titus said, stepping up beside Cassius. His pupils were still slitted, but he was no longer heaving in giant breaths in a desperate attempt to calm down.

Another spark snapped out of Sebastian's skin,

drawing a moan and making his good eye roll back for a second. "You didn't think that was something we should have known? The power of the key mixed with the court's power and my mother's will to make us conceive a supposedly impossible child. It connected Amiah to Faerie. If I'd known, I could have stopped it, woven a spell to lock Faerie out, something. Then Amiah wouldn't have a permanent glow."

"So you're not glowing because that was your first time?" Smoke billowed from Cassius's hands and he blew out a heavy breath. "Oh, thank God."

"Why?" I snapped suddenly irrationally angry. "Because fragile little me wouldn't have been able to handle it if I had?"

Jeez, I had no idea why I was so angry. But my sex life was none of Cassius's business... unless I wanted it to be—

Not the point.

I was sick and tired of him trying to protect my virtue when it wasn't his to protect and looking at me as if I was still that weak, pathetic angel he'd rescued all those years ago — even if right now I was weak and pathetic.

"I'm allowed to have a sex life. Just because I've never told you about it doesn't mean it doesn't exist. You've been keeping your distance from me ever since the war ended. For all you know I've been having wild, crazy sex for years and I can't wait to get back home and pick things up where I'd left them with my lover."

"Oh, really?" Cassius glowered at me, fire rolling up his arms, his control starting to slip again. "So you didn't just spend the last four years pining over a man who didn't love you and never would. You've been fucking every Tom, Dick, and Harry that came along."

"You really want to take that back," Hawk said, tightening his grip around me.

"All you really know is that I haven't been fucking you," I said to Cassius, the curse word flying out of my mouth like it had his.

His angel glow flared, but I didn't know if his reaction was at me swearing or if I'd hit my unintended mark. Sebastian had said Cassius was in love with me and if I'd stopped to think about it, I'd just said the most hateful thing I possibly could.

"Not sure this is the best place for this conversation," Hawk said.

Sebastian moaned, jerking my attention back to him and the sparks snapping from his body.

I turned my glare back to the guys. "Just to make things perfectly clear, my sex life is no one's business but mine and whoever I choose to sleep with. Sebastian did what he did because I asked him to, and he barely had a chance to do anything so no one has to worry about a half angel half fae nephilim abomination baby making their life complicated." If conceiving had even been possible... which it shouldn't have been. He hadn't ejaculated and even if he had, he'd said he was shooting blanks because we hadn't completed the fae marriage ritual where he became fertile for his wife and only his wife.

Cassius heaved his smoke back under his skin. "Amiah—"

"We're *not* having this conversation again. We're *not*

breaking anyone's bones about it. And we're not discussing how all of you made my sacrifice pointless," I said, my voice turning shrill, my breath short, desperate pants that sliced agony through my frozen chest.

Oh, God. It hadn't meant anything. Letting myself be exposed and hurt like that hadn't meant anything.

No. Stop thinking about it. Just stop.

But I couldn't focus my thoughts. Everything was whirling, the world around me, all my thoughts, even my soul. I spun, encased in ice and pain, and I was never going to be free.

God, I'd been beaten by a monster, I'd been forced to have sex in public, I'd begged a kind man to do something horrible to me because I hadn't been strong enough to handle it, and I'd lied to Cassius.

I was weak. So horribly weak. I couldn't handle any of it.

No. Not true.

I'd given myself to the Winter Court to save the guys and I'd do it again in a heartbeat.

Okay, so I was trapped. Again.

I bit back a sob.

Fine. I could handle this. I *would* handle this.

I'd pull myself together and get through this. We weren't safe. The Winter Queen could still send men after us into the Wilds not caring that it risked their lives, and I had no idea how far we'd been flung away from the Winter Court. I couldn't see its barrier, but for all I knew that didn't mean it wasn't close, since I knew next to nothing about the fae realm.

I clamped down on everything, all the desperate

panic screaming through me, and heaved my professional doctor's persona in place. It would get me through this. It had gotten me through the war, and through watching the man I thought was my destiny fall in love with someone else. I clung to the persona, praying, begging, that it would hold me together until there was a more convenient — and private — time to have a breakdown.

"I've got you," Hawk murmured, his lips pressed against the back of my head. "Whatever you need."

And with just those few words some of the tension eased from my body. Hawk had my back. He didn't want anything from me and didn't need me to be anything to him. I could be who I was with him and not have to worry.

"Okay." I drew in a shallow, steadying breath that still sliced agony through my chest. "We have to get someplace safe. Sebastian? Titus? Where should we go."

"My ancestral nest," Titus said, his voice gruff, and he marched a good twenty feet away and shifted into his massive dragon.

I loved watching a shifter change, loved the magic that was woven into their very cells that allowed them to melt apart, multiply or merge their cells and transform into something beautiful. And this close, Titus in his dragon form, was stunning — and I suspected he'd be more beautiful when I saw him in daylight when I could see the different shades of red and gold in his scales that I'd only really caught a glimpse of in the ballroom.

"Before we go," Sebastian gasped, drawing my attention back to him. "Knock me out. You're fae now, you've

Faerie in your veins, so you should be able to power my glyphs." He took my hand and placed it over the sleep glyph on his right shoulder. "Put your other hand over my heart, imagine pushing power into the glyph, and say ignite. The glyph will do the rest of the work."

My throat tightened. God, I wanted to be able to knock him out. Anything to help him get through the pain while he waited for me to regain my magic. But— "Even if I could power your glyph, I'm out of magic."

Fire popped inside me, shockingly hot against the ice, and a brilliant white spark exploded from my body with a sharp pinch and was sucked into the ground.

"Faerie disagrees." He quirked a ghost of his wicked smile, making my throat tighten even more because of what we'd just gone through. Then he groaned, his expression shifting back to pain, and more sparks exploded from him and were sucked away. "You've more Faerie magic than me right now. The less you have, the more painful losing it will get."

"Which means we need to get going," Cassius said, not meeting my gaze. His expression was harder and icier than I'd ever seen it and I knew my words had cut him. Well fine. He'd hurt me too. His overbearing protective-ness constantly implied I didn't know what I wanted and couldn't handle my own life. "If you're going to power his glyph, do it now, since we have no idea what other effects Faerie will have on you."

And as much as I wanted to argue that there wasn't anything else Faerie could possibly do to me that was worse than claiming me and filling me with frozen magic, he was right. There were probably hundreds of things this realm could do that I couldn't even imagine. I was a being from the Realm of Celestial Light. I wasn't supposed to have Faerie's magic in my veins ever.

I wasn't supposed to be trapped here.

I shoved that back.

"Okay." *Focus on what needs to be done. Focus on staying in control.* I had no idea if I would be able to activate Sebastian's glyph — very few angels had the ability to use glyph magic and they were rarer than angels with healing magic — but if Sebastian said I could do it, I had to try.

I pressed my free hand over his heart and imagined pushing power into the glyph on his shoulder. Ice thudded in my chest, misting my breath as if we were outside at wintertime and sending thick frost rushing over my hands. Power flooded me, frozen, biting, overwhelming. It was just me and the ice... no me and the Winter Court.

Then its power exploded out of my hand, ignited Sebastian's glyph before I could even think the word to activate it, and kept going, pouring into his body, blazing through the thick, painful darkness, and flooding his heart.

He sat up with a strangled scream, his full-body fae glow suddenly bright. "What the fuck—?"

Then his non-swollen eye rolled back and he collapsed, unconscious, his body radiating more light than I'd ever seen before as if I'd just imbued him with Faerie magic.

I jerked my hands back, terrified that I'd hurt him even as that whisper of healing magic inside me connected with him, assuring me he was fine... still injured with lacerations and broken bones and still filled with that strange consuming darkness, but I hadn't made things worse.

"Is he still alive?" Cassius asked, but his tone was so cold I couldn't tell how he felt about his question.

As if in response, a spark snapped from Sebastian's body and he groaned in his sleep.

"I just hope he's asleep long enough for me to regain some power."

"And to heal yourself," Cassius said, squatting to pick up Sebastian. "You're the priority. We lose you and we lose our healing."

He heaved Sebastian over his shoulder and marched to Titus before I could respond.

"Because that's all I'm good for I guess," I said to Hawk as he gathered me against his too-hot body.

"You hurt him. He's gone into soldier mode and shut his emotions down. I saw it all the time during the war."

"You were in the war?" I didn't know why that surprised me. After Michael's first few vicious attacks that had decimated some of the largest cities in the world, millions of people had volunteered to join the newly formed Angelic Defense. Humanity's survival as well as the survival of all supernatural beings depended on winning the war and very few souls were willing to sit back and hope for the best.

"Yeah." His voice turned soft and I sensed a great sadness in that one word, one that spoke of a grief deeper than the usual grief I'd seen in other vets. Whatever he'd gone through, it had really affected him. "Maybe someday I'll tell you about it."

"You don't have to." I leaned into him despite the heat radiating from his body. "I'll listen if you want to tell me, but I don't need to know."

He pressed a kiss against the top of my head and carried me to Titus. We climbed onto his back, and with the guys clinging to his spine ridges, Titus leaped into the air, flapped his wings with a powerful stroke, and took off into the cold night sky.

If Faerie is kind, Titus said, using the telepathy all shifters had in their shifted form, *it'll reveal the aerie sooner rather than later.*

"God, I hope so," Hawk said. Guess Titus had said that in everyone's head, not just mine.

No one else said anything and I, finally getting used to Hawk's hotter-than-normal-even-for-a-demon body temperature, gave in to the pain and exhaustion and let myself drift.

I dreamed of ice. Unending frozen, consuming ice. Wherever I looked, wherever I went, there was only ice. It groaned, massive pieces grinding against each other, and squeaked when I walked on it like a heavy snowfall or snow that was bitterly cold. It froze my blood and replaced my heart with a ball of ice. I belonged to it. I was it.

There was no escape.

I was trapped. The one thing I desperately didn't want. I'd voluntarily accepted agonizing pain and had a part of my soul ripped out to eliminate my mating brand in an attempt to remain free, and now I was trapped.

Trapped trapped trapped.

Because I made a choice.

Mine.

And if it kept the guys safe, I could live with that.

I jerked awake, shooting agony through my chest and crying out in pain, despite the determination that had filled me in my dream. I'd made the right choice. I had. I'd chosen my destiny and while I didn't like it, everyone was alive and free... except for me. What was one soul compared to four others or even all of Faerie?

"Hey." A seductive curl of magic unfurled inside me, Hawk's magic, muting but not completely getting rid of my pain.

Hawk still held me, his bare chest against my mostly bare back still uncomfortably hot. We were still on Titus's back, the wind rushing past us, and I was still out of magic... or rather out of my *healing* magic — I was still frozen inside so I guessed I was still brimming with Winter Court Faerie magic. Regardless, low healing magic meant I mustn't have been out for very long.

Ahead on the horizon loomed a flat-topped mountain that got bigger and bigger the closer we approached, a giant, jutting protrusion reaching out of the barren wasteland below as if an enormous rock had been dropped and left there.

Titus flapped his wings, picking up speed, and hurtled toward it. His pulse picked up and a new energy sang through his life force. This was home. This was a place he hadn't been to in over five hundred years.

He banked, soaring around a solid, sheer cliff face, climbing almost to the top and into a wide cave. For a second we were flying in absolute darkness then magical red flames burst to life along the ceiling, revealing a wide passage that quickly opened up into an enormous cavern as if the inside of the mountain had been hollowed out.

Only part of the cavern was closed off from the sky, and on the cavern floor, a dozen stories below us, was a small lake — its water lapping against the far side of the cavern — as well as a small forest and a meadow in the middle. Outcroppings jutted from the cavern's sides, big enough to hold one, two, or three dragons — if all dragons were Titus's size — and the walls were riddled with passages, some of which were dragon size while others were closer to human size.

Titus landed on an outcropping halfway down with a human-size passage, and, with Hawk's help, I slid to the ground where he promptly picked me up again and cradled me against his chest.

I leaned into him. Yes, he was still too hot, and yes, his life force was weak from all the injuries he'd taken during the fight, but he had me. I was safe with him. I could give in and trust him to take care of me... something I used to feel about Cassius.

The human quarters "are this way," Titus said, half in our heads as he shifted and half out loud once he was done.

Cassius adjusted Sebastian's unconscious body on his shoulder and we followed Titus down the passage. More flames burst to life as we walked, but the light couldn't ease the growing sense of dread squeezing my chest. We were heading deeper into the mountain, farther away from any open space and sky. I was going to be trapped inside a mountain again, just like when I was trapped in the Winter Court.

We passed dozens of doorways, none of which had doors, until we reach the doorway at the end of the hall. Without hesitation, Titus led us into a large sitting area filled with pillows of all different shapes, sizes, and colors, along with low, intricately carved wood and stone tables, all in perfect condition and arranged into a number of conversation areas. Flecks of white light shimmered in the air, mixing with the dancing magical flames near the ceiling, and with a soft *pop* the musty smell of age and decay vanished and the room felt fresh and clean as if it hadn't been abandoned for half a millennium.

And directly ahead of us, stood a window — or rather opening since there was no glass — that stretched from one side of the far wall to the other and from the floor to ceiling with only a waist-high spindly stone railing to stop someone from a terrible fall.

The weight in my chest vanished at the vast open expanse stretched before me.

Oh, thank goodness.

"I won't trap you underground," Titus said, his voice gruff.

I guess I'd said that out loud.

"I'd never do that to you." He shot a dark glare at Sebastian then hopped over the railing, shifted, his body turning to liquid flesh and changing from one second to the next, and took off.

"Shit," Cassius hissed. "He shouldn't be out there alone."

"Then go after him," I said, "Hawk and I can take care of Sebastian."

"Fine." Cassius set Sebastian on the floor and leaped

over the railing like Titus had. With a burst of fire and white angelic light, he released his wings and glanced back at us, his expression still hard and frozen, before he soared away.

It broke my heart and made me furious at the same time. He didn't have a right to tell me what to do, and yet he was— *had been* my best friend for over a hundred years. I missed him. I'd been missing him since the war ended. I wanted the thoughtful, warm angel who'd been by my side, supporting and encouraging me, back. Even if he'd driven me crazy by being overprotective, I wanted that Cassius back.

CASSIUS

SHE'D TOLD BANE TO DO IT. OF COURSE SHE'D TOLD HIM to do it. I was an idiot to think she hadn't thought of the horrible plan for Bane to attack her because she'd do anything, sacrifice anything to save people. So she'd done the biggest, stupidest thing she could think of to save us.

The God damned idiot. The God damned fucking idiot.

I screamed, shooting fire into the sky, doing little to ease the inferno burning through my veins, an inferno that shouldn't have been there because of all the magic I'd used during the fight.

How the hell could I protect her if she kept doing things like that? How could I keep her safe? God, I had to keep her safe. She'd already been horribly beaten because I hadn't been paying enough attention. For her to think having Bane assault her like that had been her only option—

I screamed again and fire poured off my wings and showered onto the wasteland below.

He'd shoved inside her and she'd lit up and I'd thought I was going to die. I'd thought she was a virgin and that this had been her first, horrific time having sex.

And now I didn't know if I was furious because I'd been horrified or furious that she'd been angry at me for having feared that. And for her to have pointed out we weren't having sex! To have shoved it in my face—

She had no idea how much it hurt to know I couldn't be with her, couldn't show her how I felt because I'd burn her, and yet she'd cut straight into my heart. She'd zeroed in on the one thing that could truly hurt me and struck her blow.

But worse was the fact that she'd been right, that I didn't know her anymore, not really. I'd withdrawn from her after the war because I knew I was going to hurt her, and while I hadn't burned her, she'd still been hurt. She'd fallen in love with Marcus and I hadn't been there for her when his soul mate had come along and broken her heart. What kind of protector was I? What kind of friend? How could I tell her I didn't think she was weak when my actions, my need to keep her safe, belied those word.

Except the thought of letting go, of trying to prove that I thought she was strong by holding back my protective instincts made my heart pound. I couldn't lose her like I'd lost Dominic. I couldn't fail her. I'd told Dominic to take that mission to infiltrate Michael's army, told him he was perfect for the job with his dual magic. Angels rarely had two powers and with his light magic, Michael would never know Dominic could also read minds. But somehow Michael had known and had killed him.

Because of me.

I'd sent my youngest brother to his death.

My fault.

And now Amiah was in danger.

All of Faerie was hunting us and I had to keep her safe. I couldn't fail her. Not like I'd failed Dominic. And now wasn't the time to hold back my protective instincts just to make her feel better.

I released another scream and blast of fire, lighting up the night sky.

If I wanted to keep her safe in all of this, I couldn't be her friend. I'd rather she hated me for being overbearing than her being dead. Like Dominic. The only thing that mattered was that she got through this mess alive and unharmed, and I'd already failed on the unharmed part of my mission.

Once again she was hurt and out of power, and the moment I managed to calm down and Bane was awake I was finding out why the hell her power had been spent when Titus and I had found her, Bane, and Hawk being accosted by Deaglan and his hybrid in that hall.

Something serious had happened and I needed to know what. Not because I needed to know everything that might have happened between her and Bane — although a part of me feared I did want to know — but because I needed to know if whatever had happened was going to continue to be a problem. It took a major injury for Amiah to fully drain herself by healing someone... unless, of course, she was the one who'd been hurt.

My pulse picked up again at the thought of someone hurting her and me not being there to protect her. I couldn't lose her. God damn it. I just couldn't.

Except I'd already lost her. I couldn't touch her, not even to carry her now. It took everything I had to hold back my fire and it was getting harder and harder to do so. From the moment she'd risked her life by taking in that massive blast of Hawk's power when he'd been ODing on sexual energy and saving him, I'd been burning up, my heart and soul on fire. I couldn't release enough fire to ease the inferno inside me, and I couldn't turn it back into the small waiting flame that it used to be in my heart.

And now every time I opened my mouth, I upset her, and I had no idea why. She no longer trusted me and that hurt more than not being able to carry her out of danger.

Now she turned to Hawk. She let Hawk hold her like she used to let Marcus as if she needed physical touch for comfort like a shifter did. She leaned into him, was comforted by his words, and I had no idea why she was demonstrating such unangel-like behavior because I knew she was smart enough to know Hawk would never fall in love with her.

Except she'd already broken her heart over a man who hadn't loved her.

God, she was doing it again, and there was nothing I could do about it.

Not a God damned thing.

And right now it didn't matter. Hawk might eventually break her heart, but at least he was comforting her, something she desperately needed right now and apparently on a more physical level than a typical angel. Her world had been turned upside down, she'd thought she'd needed to make Bane hurt her to save our lives, and now she had a foreign magic inside her.

And I was *not* going to think about her having sex with Hawk, because eventually his nature would get the better of him and he'd use his magic to seduce her or she'd sacrifice her body again to feed him and they'd be intimate.

And she'd made it clear that was her business and absolutely none of mine.

Except I desperately wanted it to be mine... which it could never be...

Fuck!

More fire exploded from my body.

Fuck fuck fuck. God damn fucking shit.

And fuck Bane, because it had to be his influence turning me into a foul-mouthed angel. I didn't think I'd ever sworn this much in my life, not even during the war.

Stop following me, Titus growled in my head, his massive form a dark shadow on the edge of a horizon just starting to lighten with a golden dawn.

None of us should be outside alone, I growled back.

I can take care of myself.

Right, I said, filling my mental voice with as much sarcasm as I could, *that's why you risked Amiah's life by shifting in the middle of the Winter Court.*

He was hurting her, Titus snarled, turning and flying toward me.

Yeah. The asshole had been hurting her, and I should have known he wouldn't have done that because he'd wanted to. He'd propositioned her and every woman I'd ever seen him come in contact with every chance he'd gotten and had business dealings with a lot of unsavory people, but he'd proven time and again that he'd never have purposely hurt her. Push her buttons — definitely push mine — and make her blush, but never hurt her. Hell, he'd willingly suffered by taking on Titus's half of the leash spell so we could rescue her from Balwyrdan.

You nearly got her killed by revealing yourself to the Winter Queen and Deaglan, I said. *She asked Bane to hurt her to save us. What do you think she would have done to save you from another five hundred years of captivity?*

Which was the truth I despised. I'd been relieved when she'd stopped doing fieldwork during the war because her compulsive need to heal, to do whatever it took to save someone, made her take terrifying risks. She had realized that too, thankfully early on, and had been smart, getting herself stationed in the Angelic Defense's main hospital, far away from the front line.

She used to have so much common sense. So much control. When had she lost it? When had she decided risking herself was better than protecting herself so she could continue to heal people?

The blaze inside me surged. She'd lost it when she'd had her control taken away, when Balwyrdan had proven it hadn't mattered what she did, or how hard she tried, she'd never be completely safe. She could be taken like she'd been taken by that faith healer all those years ago.

More fire burst from my body. *We only got out of the Winter Court because of a miracle.*

Because the Winter Court claimed Amiah, Titus said, his mental voice filled with regret. *She broke the Winter Queen's hold on the court and now everything is worse for her.*

He swooped past me, soaring back to the flat-topped mountain towering over the wasteland.

I trailed after him, releasing one last burst of fire, hoping I'd used up enough magic that I could pull the rest of my flames inside my body and regain some semblance of control.

She can't stay in Faerie, he said, lightly landing on a narrow ledge jutting from the top of the mountain as if he weren't a thirty-foot dragon who likely weighed thousands of pounds. *The minute Seireadan can find a portal, you all have to leave.*

I heaved my flames back under my skin, revealing all the bruises I'd gotten during the fight and the angry burns I'd seared into my body to cauterize my wounds. At least with my fire blazing through me, I couldn't feel much of anything else, even the pain of my injuries. *She's not going to let you stay here by yourself,* I said, landing on the ledge beside him.

Make her. Titus snorted fire and curled his front claws over the edge of the ledge. *She's not safe here and the rest of you are not safe with me.*

What does that mean? Except I had a feeling I already knew. He was barely keeping hold of his beast. One flight across the Wilds to his ancestral nest wasn't going to be enough to erase five hundred years of not shifting.

My beast would have killed Seireadan if Amiah hadn't stopped me. It still wants to kill him. You have to take her back to the mortal realm and leave me.

One, she wouldn't leave you, not knowing there are people still after you and that you're struggling to heal the connection between you and your beast. No matter how practical it was to leave, it was clear she was committed to helping Titus, and even though her magic couldn't help his connection, she was still going to use the rest of her extensive medical knowledge to help. *And two, can she even leave with the Winter Court's claim on her?*

I had no idea what being claimed by a Faerie court really meant. Bane, heir to the Winter Court's throne, had left and lived in the mortal realm for who knew how long, but had the court claimed him?

She has to. She has one of the keys. If she leaves, the Heart can never be freed.

But that only complicated the matter, because if anyone figured out she had a key, all of Faerie would be hunting her as well.

That thought made my fire boil my blood and filled me with a desperate need to see her.

Are you going to fly off again? I asked. God, I hoped not, because I had to see with my own eyes that she was still okay. The compulsion was overwhelming and shocking and infuriating, and I was too tired to fight it.

No. I think I'm okay if I'm not near Seireadan.

When they wake, we'll need to come up with a plan, I said, stretching out my wings and straining to hold back my flames. *And as much as I'd love for her to return to the mortal realm, I'm not sure we'll be able to convince her of that.*

Then don't convince her, Titus said, his mental voice gruff. *Just take her.*

Which would make her furious. But it would keep her safe... or rather safer... until someone in Faerie figured out she had a key and then we were back where we started.

I stepped off the ledge and caught the wind with my wings. She'd never forgive me if I forced her to return home. If she even could return home. But she would be safer there for a little while longer at least.

I glided around the side of the mountain, looking into dark caves and crevasses, and other sitting rooms magically frozen in time waiting for someone to enter until I found our sitting room.

Bane had been shifted to a thick rug and pile of fluffy pillows a few feet from where I'd left him, and Amiah and Hawk lay on another pile of pillows beside him, Amiah curled half on top of Hawk with his arms wrapped around her.

Seeing her didn't comfort me, and my compulsion to protect her grew stronger.

Her whole body glowed a soft white light, a reminder that I'd failed her again and she had a foreign magic inside her that could be hurting her in unimaginable ways, and she was splattered with blood, some of it ours from when it had been swept around in the Winter Queen's storm and some hers from all the little cuts all over her body from the ice in that storm.

I should have kept her safe. I didn't know how, but I should have.

And here was Hawk, holding her like a lover, like how I wanted to hold her as if it were nothing to just wrap his arms around her and let her use his body as a pillow.

Ice and snow and God damned frozen things. Thinking of the cold had barely worked when we'd been in the Winter Court, but it was all I had. *Just keep it frozen. Keep her safe even if she hates you.*

I quietly landed on the far side of the window, determined to not disturb them, and was about to turn my attention to the half dozen doorways at the back of the room when Hawk's eyelids cracked open.

"Hey," he said, his voice soft, his hellfire small flickering flames in his eyes, not fully banked but not fully released either. "Find the big guy?"

"Yeah. That's more or less under control." And was the best it was going to get for now.

"Good. He's angry now, but I have a feeling he'd never forgive himself if he killed Bane."

There was that, too.

Amiah whimpered and snuggled closer to Hawk, and my fire surged.

Ice. Frozen ice. I could hold my fire in. I would hold my fire in.

"You should hold her," Hawk said. "I could use a stretch and she seems to need body heat."

"Seems to? I doubt you tried to avoid holding her," I snapped, my tone a hell of a lot sharper than I intended.

"Actually I did after she fell asleep. I wanted to explore a little, but she wouldn't let me go." His gaze dipped, sliding down the length of her body.

She'd been stunning in that dress. Showing so much skin it had embarrassed her — and I'd never make her wear it again if she didn't want to — but God, I was grateful I had the memory of seeing her in it. Just thinking about it— hell, seeing her now with it bloody and torn, made me yearn to touch her, kiss her, give her pleasure. Would she let it all go? Would I finally get to see her without worry or struggling to stay in control? I wanted to give her that moment, those sensations, fill her with bliss. I wanted—

My fire surged and smoke billowed around me.

I wanted things I'd never have. I'd never be her mate and she'd never want me to be her mate. The most I could do for her was keep her safe.

I would not fail her like I'd failed Dominic. I'd die first.

"Take my place," Hawk said, tugging the slit in her dress closed and covering her up a bit more. "I want to look around, find her a bathroom so when she wakes, she can clean up a little."

More smoke curled from my hands.

There was no way I'd be able to hold her and keep my fire inside. I'd probably set the whole room on fire.

"No."

"Come on, man. I'm pretty sure with your fire magic you can run your body temperature as hot as a demon's."

God, I wanted to. Wanted the incubus to stop giving her what I wanted to give her, but— "How do you think she'll react when she wakes and finds me holding her instead of you? She's made her position clear."

"That you two aren't sleeping together?" Hawk asked. "Doesn't mean that's the way it's going to stay." He huffed a soft laugh. "Of course, if you keep yelling at her and telling her what to do, she'll never invite you into her bed."

"Like she's invited you?" *Shit. I shouldn't have said that.* Because it was none of my God damned business.

"Just take my place. When she wakes, apologize for

being an asshole," Hawk replied, not answering my question. "That'll go a long way toward getting into her bed."

"I can't."

Hawk's hellfire flared and his eyes narrowed. "Apologize or hold her?"

"Both." I clenched my hands, fighting my fire, but smoke still curled from my skin. "I'd rather she hate me and be safe than like me and be hurt again. I won't lose focus and let her be hurt again." I glared at Hawk. "That includes her heart."

Whatever it took. I wouldn't fail her.

AMIAH

I WOKE COMPLETELY CONFUSED ON A SOFT BED IN A DIMLY lit room, snuggled against a blazing hot body, and my chest screaming in pain. Cassius had left Sebastian on the floor and flown after Titus, and Hawk had moved all of us to a thick rug and a pile of pillows and I'd passed out in his arms. I had a vague memory of Cassius returning, but that could have been a dream, and then sometime after that Hawk had picked me up. I guess he'd carried me to this bed and I'd fallen back asleep.

Beneath me, Hawk's chest slowly rose and fell, his breath deep with sleep, and his life force thrumming against my senses. He was alive but his magic was low and he hadn't been able to fully heal all the lacerations, fractured bones, and bruises marring his beautiful body. If he was going to finish healing, or worse survive another fight, he was going to need to feed.

The thought made my pulse quicken. I really liked the idea of that, of having sex with him again without the fear of losing him. Except we weren't going to be able to do much until I'd healed my broken ribs. Which I wasn't going to do until I'd healed Sebastian's broken face. And as much as Cassius had said I should heal myself first there was no point in Sebastian suffering. Yes, only five of my ribs had been broken this time, but I was still going to need to drain myself twice to mend them.

At least my power was mostly at full again, which meant I had to have been out for at least eight hours.

My heart pounded faster, and the ice in my chest sank and churned into a stone in my stomach. I'd drained myself because someone had poisoned Hawk and my power had locked onto him. The queen had threatened the guys. Titus had shifted. I'd yelled at Cassius that we weren't having sex. And, oh God, I'd been claimed by the Winter Court.

I shoved those thoughts deep down, straining to ignore the ice and fear, and concentrated on Hawk. He was too hot... because of the ice now permanently frozen in my soul.

No. Well yes, but don't focus on that. Focus on his life force, on its thrum.

I drew in a steadying breath, shot agony through my chest, and gritted my teeth, determined to keep my focus. The sense of simmering hellfire crackled through the energy of his life force. Fiery and dark, because he was a being from the Realm of Celestial Darkness. Surprisingly, it slid against the light inside me, caressing my essence instead of grating against it and easing the freeze of the Winter Court.

As if thinking about it made it stronger, the Winter Court's power swelled. But it wasn't painful and wasn't consuming. It just was. Neither good nor bad. Merely a miniscule flicker of power now embedded in every cell in my body and woven into my essence. In my mind's eye, it sparkled, like snow in brilliant sunlight after an icy storm, and it connected with another life force behind me. A life force surging and straining against an oozing, consuming darkness.

I turned my head, trying not to aggravate my ribs or wake Hawk.

Sebastian lay beside us on the bed, his swollen bruised face tight with pain, his breath fast and shallow. Yes, his injuries were hurting him, but there was something more, something dark sliding through his veins, fighting the thread of ice from the Winter Court and the shimmering radiance of Faerie's raw magic. I'd felt the pain when I'd connected with him last night and now, somehow, I could also feel the power staining his life force.

My healing magic swelled in my palms, thick and sticky, determined to burst free, compelling me to heal him — although thankfully not locking onto him — and I eased my hand out from under my body.

Just moving made my power surge stronger, and it fully connected with him before I'd even gingerly pressed my fingers against his temple, forcing me to strain to hold it back and turn its flow into a soft trickle. I didn't have to heal him quickly, there was no reason for the healing to hurt or to even wake him.

He groaned and my power oozed into his face, immediately splitting three ways and sinking into his shattered orbital bone, fractured cheek, and broken nose. It flooded

his cells, knitting bone back together with an effortlessness that it wouldn't have when I healed my ribs, and
struggled to blast into the rest of him, sealing every laceration, even the smallest cuts, shut.

I kept the flow down to a steady, warm stream even as
my power burned hotter up my forearms and past my
elbows, and I reveled in the feel of his body mending
until there was no evidence that he'd ever been in a fight.
Not even a scar. He was still in some pain, his life force
still struggling against the darkness my magic couldn't
even recognize, but the agony of his shattered face was
gone.

He murmured in his sleep but didn't wake and I
turned to lie back on Hawk's chest, still at half power but
ready to go back to sleep.

"He could have lasted a little longer," Hawk
murmured, stroking my hair back from my face. "You
could have gotten started on yourself."

"I'm going to take longer than just one healing
session," I said, carefully easing my weight back onto him
and waiting the few seconds it took for my cheek and
chest to get reaccustomed to his body heat. "The Winter
Queen broke a few of my ribs."

"You've got to stop doing that."

"Oh," I said with an eye roll he couldn't see, "because
I planned on having my bones broken again."

He tensed beneath me and for a second I thought he
was going to bring up Sebastian hurting me, then he
pressed his lips to the top of my head and a whisper of
seductive heat unfurled inside me. It mingled with the
ice, also not grating against it like it hadn't grated against

my celestial light essence. It eased some of my pain and a slow, gentle throb pulsed in my core.

"Is that better?" he asked.

"Yes," I breathed. God, I could get used to having an incubus lover. "A little more and we could get some of your magic restored as well."

"But not just a tease." His tone turned wicked, reminding me of the last time I'd woken in bed with him, my body burning with pain and I'd begged him to not just tease me. "I know how much you hate being teased."

My insides squirmed, my desire building at just the thought of Hawk's magic bringing me to a climax again. "If you do more than just tease, you'll get more power back."

"True, that." He eased me into my back and captured my lips in a soft tender kiss that made my heart flutter. It made me feel safe and cherished... and loved. And I wasn't going to think too hard about that because Hawk couldn't love me, it wasn't in his nature. I was just going to enjoy the feeling and pretend it was real for the meantime.

"But you've got to remember to lie there and enjoy it like last time," he said.

"And we've got to keep it subtle and quiet." I glanced at the open doorway. There wasn't even a door we could close.

"Titus is far below us, probably at the bottom of the cavern," he said, trailing kisses along my jaw and down my neck. "And Cassius..." he murmured against my collarbone, his hot breath feathering over my skin, sending a shiver of desire racing through me. "He's a good hundred feet at least to our left, so not outside our bedroom door."

"I didn't know incubi could sense where people were."

He brushed his lips along my dress's plunging neck-line, teasing the inner swells of my breasts, and another seductive curl of magic unfurled in my chest, easing away more of the pain of my ribs.

"We usually can't get so specific," he said, inching lower and lower down my body, his heat sliding away letting the Winter Court's cold grow stronger. "But I'm a Sensitive too and we're literally the only people here so there are no other sources of desire to muddy the waters. That and both of them could use a release. Their desire is particularly strong at the moment."

"Have they not gotten over being influenced by your magic?" I asked, my pulse picking up with the memory of Hawk's power raging out of control when we'd been in the Winter Court and how it had affected all of us.

He pushed a hot hand under the hem of my indecent dress and slowly slid his fingers up the inside of my thigh, urging me to open for him. Oh, yes.

"They're probably still thinking about you in this dress."

I huffed a bitter laugh. "I believe that was the Winter Queen's plan with the dress. To embarrass me and make all the men in the room want to sleep with me." I didn't know if the latter had worked, but I'd certainly been embarrassed. I'd never worn anything so revealing before and I'd never wear anything like it again.

"Well it certainly made four of us want to sleep with

you." He pressed a kiss to the inside of my knee. "And I really enjoyed it. You know, after you and Sebastian saved my life and all."

He trailed his lips up my thigh, his breath caressing my skin drawing closer and closer to where I really wanted him.

Oh, that felt good.

Okay, so I might consider wearing something like that again. It certainly gave Hawk easy access and if I didn't think about the panic of trying to save him, having Sebastian push into me from behind and pinning me between him and Hawk had been incredibly... stimulating.

"Yeah, like that," Hawk purred, nudging my other thigh with his elbow and settling his gorgeous, muscular, shirtless body between my legs. "Are you thinking about Sebastian satisfying you or me?"

"Does it have to be one or the other?" I asked, my voice deliciously breathy.

"Nope. I'll never make you choose, gorgeous." He brushed his tongue against the inside of my thigh at the crux where my leg met my torso.

I gasped at the feel of him against my skin and the sudden breath shot agony through my chest, but Hawk's seductive heat swept through me before I could even whimper.

"You're going to spoil me." I ran my fingers into his sandy-blond locks, curled them around his horns, and rubbed my thumbs against their base. It was one of the most sensitive spots on an incubus and a major erogenous zone, like the base of an angel's wings, and if he was going to stay down there, I was going to explore just how erogenous they were.

He groaned at my touch.

"I like spoiling you," he said. "And I like the sounds you make."

He brushed his tongue through my folds, making me softly moan.

"I love how you taste."

Another slow, drawn out brush that spiraled heated desire in my core. *Oh, yes.*

"I love the feel of your body."

He slid his hands up the outside of my thighs and captured my hips, stopping me from squirming against his mouth and hurting myself.

"And I love the feel of you letting go, that you'd even want to share something like this with me."

He pushed his tongue inside me, my nerves suddenly hyperaware of his slick heat against my cool insides, and my eyes rolled back with the sensation.

Oh yeah, I could definitely get used to having an incubus lover.

I rubbed my thumbs harder against the base of his horns. His breath grew faster, his sculpted muscles rippling with every shift of his body, mesmerizing me like he was supposed to. And I fully gave into his allure as he carefully built up my desire, licking and sucking and adding whispers of heated magic to soothe my pain.

The pressure inside me grew, and I fought to keep my moans quiet so I didn't wake Sebastian, but with my desire spiraling tighter and tighter, it got harder and harder to remember to hold it all in.

Then Hawk sucked on my clit and pushed a soft swell of power into me. My orgasm swept through me, a glorious, gentle wave, and I released a breathy, satisfied moan.

"Well, that's one way to wake up," Sebastian said, his voice gruff.

I let my head roll to the side to look at him and met a stunning, pale blue, almost colorless gaze, his eyes filled with heated desire. The look sent another soft ripple of orgasm through me and Hawk's fingers dug into my hips and he moaned against my folds.

"Guess having me present wasn't just a dirty little necessity to save his life." Sebastian slid his gaze down my body as if he didn't know where he wanted to start first, and the still-swirling heat of Hawk's magic swelled.

"You're just going to frustrate yourself," Hawk groaned, rising up on his forearms and giving me a look just as heated as Sebastian's. "She's got broken ribs. She can't do much for you. But if you want to get her off again, I won't stop you."

Concern bled into Sebastian's eyes and he reached to caress my face but hesitated. "Would you want me to? After I hurt you like that?"

I slid my hand up to his and interlaced our fingers, his self-doubt scaring me. While I didn't know him that well, I'd never seen him be tentative about propositioning anyone.

"That didn't count. I told you I like the way you make me feel," I said. "I thought I'd made myself clear. I don't want a relationship right now, I just want sex. With you."

"But you're free now. Your reason not to commit is gone." His gaze dipped to my left hip where my partially formed mating brand used to be but thankfully didn't say anything in front of Hawk who, like everyone else, didn't know I'd been cursed with an angel's most sacred mark.

"And when I'm ready to commit to someone I'll commit." It was the first time in my life that I had the freedom to love how I wanted to, and I didn't want to just jump into a committed relationship. I wanted to explore my sexuality, who I was, and what I desired. Hawk and Sebastian — if he was interested — were perfect. "My reasons for having sex with you haven't changed. You don't want me to fall in love with you and you're not going to fall in love with me, and you've plenty of experience."

"So I'm just a good fuck then?" he asked, but he didn't sound upset about that.

"Hmm, I don't know." I gave him my wickedest smile, which was probably terrible since I had no experience with that kind of thing. "I've had sex with an incubus now. Do you think you can rise to the occasion and match his prowess?"

"That's quite the challenge," Sebastian said, his tone turning seductive and thoughtful. "You've had a quick fuck against a wall. You haven't had the full incubus experience yet. And while I'm good, Hawk *is* a professional. He's going to blow your mind when you finally get down to it."

I pursed my lips and Hawk, with a Cheshire cat grin, crawled back up beside me and gingerly tugged me into his embrace, using his magic to ease the spike of pain caused from moving me.

Sebastian's eyes widened. "Holy fuck. You've already

slept with him. That's why you didn't bat an eye when you had sex in the alcove."

"And yeah, it was mind blowing." My pulse picked up with fear. God, I was actually going to say it. I was going to proposition Sebastian for a *ménage à trois*. "But there are things I'm curious about that I can't do with Hawk alone."

His eyes widened even more. "Oh, fuck me," he groaned.

"Not yet, her ribs are still broken," Hawk replied with a chuckle.

"Who the hell are you and what have you done with the annoying as hell, uptight angel I first met?" Sebastian asked me.

Jeez. I was not going to beg for this. "Are we going to keep having sex or not?" I asked, my fear of rejection making my tone sharp.

Sebastian's face lit up with a glorious, heart stopping grin, reminding me of the Sebastian I'd first met, the one who'd relentlessly teased me about sex.

"There she is," he said, and he captured my lips in a breathtaking kiss that made the remnants of Hawk's magic surge inside me.

God, I wanted to get started now, and yet I was going to have to wait until my ribs had healed. How had this become my life? How had I suddenly become free of the nightmare of a forced, permanent soul bond? And how had I ever ended up in bed with both Sebastian and Hawk?

Of course, we were also on the run from all of the Faerie courts, the Winter Court had claimed me, and my relationship with my best friend had somehow been torn to pieces.

I leaned into Sebastian's kiss, determined to let the feel of his mouth against mine, his desire for me, and the residual heat of Hawk's magic make me forget.

"Hey," Hawk murmured, gently tugging me away from Sebastian's lips. "Your ribs are still broken and Cassius is coming our way... Unless you've changed your mind about him knowing about this."

I bit back a heavy sigh, managing not to shoot agony through my chest. "I should rub this in his face given how he'd reacted to the idea of me having a sex life."

"Please don't," Sebastian said, rolling onto his back and staring at the ceiling, but he interlaced his fingers with mine again and I wasn't sure if he was conscious of the act or not. "I was barely conscious last night and even I know he's barely holding his shit together. I swear to God he's in love with you."

"So that makes trying to slut shame me okay?" I snapped back. "I should be able to have sex with whoever I want and however I want it."

"Which is why I didn't turn you down," Sebastian said.

"Gee thanks. You make it sound like having sex with me is a chore." Except while I hadn't wanted him to feel like it was a job, I also hadn't wanted his emotions to get involved. Which was the whole point of having sex with him and Hawk. They weren't going to fall in love with me.

"That wasn't what he meant." Hawk hooked a stray lock of my hair behind my ear, the motion softly stroking his hot fingers across my cheek and sending a shiver of desire racing through me that shot agony across my chest.

"It's okay," I said, trying not to show my pain. I squeezed Sebastian's fingers and he glanced over at me. "This isn't an emotional arrangement. I understand that. When it stops being good for any of us, we stop."

A strange expression flashed across Sebastian's face and disappeared before I could figure out what it meant. "Deal. But you have to promise to mend things with Cassius. If we're going to survive what's coming, we're going to need him thinking clearly, and he's eventually going to figure out we're having sex."

"I'm sure both you and Hawk have experience being discreet."

Sebastian gave me a look so heated it made my heart skip a beat and my insides throb with need. "It's not us I'm worried about giving it away."

"You don't think I can be discrete?"

"What he's saying, gorgeous," Hawk whispered in my ear, his hot breath teasing me, "is that a man, even an uptight angel like Cassius, can recognize a thoroughly satisfied woman, and you, my dear, are going to be thoroughly satisfied."

AMIAH

OH, MY GOD! I WANTED TO GET STARTED ON BEING thoroughly satisfied. Right now. To hell with my broken ribs... although a part of me was terrified I'd taken on more than I could handle with the two of them.

Sebastian, however, was right. Not about me letting Cassius know we were having sex, but about mending things with Cassius. Even if we hadn't been hiding from all of Faerie, I still should at least talk to him.

But he just made me so angry. It didn't matter that his belief that I was weak and unable to defend myself was right. He needed to stop barking orders at me like I was an agent under his command and he certainly had to stop protecting my virtue as if we were in the Dark Ages.

"He's just about here," Hawk said and Sebastian slid his fingers from mine and moved to the far side of the bed.

I felt Cassius's fiery life force blazing across my senses before I heard his soft steps to the doorway. His life force was so strong, so determined, stronger than Hawk's or Sebastian's, but it was as if a part of him was struggling to break free and he was desperately trying to hold it back, as if he weren't in harmony with himself, which heightened my sense of him.

"You healed Bane first, didn't you?" he said, his tone icier than the ice inside me.

Of course that would be the first thing he said to me.

"I have broken ribs again. There's no point in Sebastian suffering for days while he waits for me to heal myself," I said as Hawk helped me sit up.

Cassius's eyes narrowed and smoke curled from his hands. He'd cleaned up and found a change of clothes, and while he still wore leather pants, they were now brown instead of dark blue and looser fitting. He'd also found a loose cotton shirt, the soft beige fabric covering up most of his honed muscular chest, but he'd rolled up the sleeves to his elbows as if he were too hot even in the thin material. Dozens of scabbed-over lacerations covered his forearms, and more marred his neck as well as the hint of chest I could see through the V of his shirt. His angel glow was bright, indicating he was brimming with power, but his eyes and expression were that of a man running on too much stress and too little sleep.

"Did you get any sleep?" I eased myself over Hawk's legs and got off the bed, the Winter Court's chill swelling and growing stronger the farther I got from Hawk. My teeth were chattering and my whole body shivering, shooting agony through me by the time I was within arm's reach of Cassius, and while his body heat was a fraction of Hawk's, it still drew me inappropriately close. "How bad are your injuries?"

"I'm fine." The muscles in his jaw flexed.

"Let me check." I leaned toward him, even knowing he wouldn't want me to snuggle up to him, and reached to press my palm against his chest.

"Heal yourself first." He grabbed my wrist, but my magic connected with him anyway, and I instantly knew he had three cracked ribs and half a dozen nasty burns where he'd used his fire to cauterize his wounds.

"You're not fine." I released a thread of magic into him, using his hold on my wrist to gain entry into his body, and it rushed straight to his ribs.

"I said, heal yourself first." He jerked away from me, but my magic stayed connected and surged. It roared through him, using up almost everything I had left, even though mending that amount of damage normally wouldn't have. With one sudden, agonizing blast, it healed his ribs and burns and drew a strangled, pain-filled scream.

Gasping, he dropped to his knees, his chest heaving and his body trembling. Smoke billowed from his hands and his life force snapped as if I could somehow feel his fire through his life force. "God damn it. I said heal yourself first."

"Don't tell me what to do with my magic," I snapped back, even though I shouldn't have healed him like that. I certainly shouldn't have spent all my magic, and I had no idea how I'd done it without touching him.

The room darkened and lurched, and the exhaustion at using all my power swept through me. I sagged against the doorframe, my shivering growing stronger, and didn't even bother trying to look strong. What was the point? They'd all seen me at my worst. No point in hiding the truth. Besides, just being myself wasn't nearly as exhausting as putting on an in-control strong demeanor. Especially since none of them would have believed me anyway right now.

Hawk picked me up in his too-hot arms before I collapsed on the floor, and his heat seeped into my skin. "We need to do something about your body temperature."

"If you can hold out a little longer for me to get some power back, I'll see what I can do." Sebastian rubbed his face and sighed. "And I need to finally deal with the leash spell as well."

"Well, first we all need to eat," Cassius gasped. He staggered back to his feet and glared at Hawk, the light in his eyes flaring. "Do you? You took some serious damage during the fight."

"My options are somewhat limited," Hawk said, not giving away that I'd just given him an influx of sexual energy.

"I'm aware of that," Cassius forced out refusing to make eye contact with me. "I found a stocked kitchen and some food for the rest of us," he said, jerking away and heading toward a low table in the middle of the room. "Let's eat and figure out how the hell we're going to get out of this mess."

A platter with strange looking fruit, a small wheel of cheese, a knife, and a pile of dried meat sat on the table.

Cassius took a seat on one of the cushions in front of it and grabbed a piece of meat.

"Hunh," Hawk said as he approached and sat cross-legged. He set me in his lap but kept me close, letting me press my barely covered torso against his bare chest. "Where did the fresh fruit come from? And do we honestly think that cheese and meat is safe? How old is it? I'd hate for Amiah to have to use her magic to deal with food poisoning on top of everything else."

It's safe, Titus said in our heads, and his massive dragon form hurtled toward the window, his life force wild and ferocious, mixing with Cassius's burn, Hawk's darkness, and Sebastian's ice and pain inside me.

Titus shifted as he reached the threshold, his body shrinking and melting in the blink of an eye, and he transformed into a ruggedly handsome, completely naked man.

He'd broken the glamor changing his appearance when he'd shifted in the Winter Court's ballroom, and now he was back to the man I'd first met with his stunning powerful musculature, dark red shaggy hair, square jaw dusted with red-gold stubble, and mesmerizing golden eyes.

Those eyes met mine for a second and the world stood still. The intensity of his gaze was breathtaking, powerful, predatory, and I was his prey. Except that didn't terrify me like it probably should have and reminded me of the sudden ferocious kiss we'd had when we'd been attacked. I shivered at the thought of all that passion and power directed at me, embracing me, filling me, thrumming against my senses.

He jerked his gaze from me to glare at Sebastian as he dropped onto a cushion on the far side of the table.

Sebastian met Titus's glare for a second then lowered his gaze, wisely giving Titus dominance. I had no doubt if Sebastian was at full power Titus wouldn't stand a chance, but Sebastian was also smart enough to know Titus's hold on his humanity was still tenuous, and challenging him right now would only cause problems.

"Faerie always magically preserves the aerie while it waits for occupants," Sebastian said. "That's why none of these pillows, the clothes Cassius found, or the bedding has rotted into nothing even though there hasn't been anyone here in over five hundred years."

"And the fruit comes from the trees in the cavern." Titus grabbed a piece of meat and tore a chunk off with his teeth. "This morning the Wilds were a jungle instead of a wasteland so I stayed close to the mountain and did a bit of hunting. There's fresh meat in the cold room so we won't have to just eat this."

"How long do you think we can be here?" I asked, reaching for a dark blue, apple-like fruit, sending agony screaming through me, and making me gasp.

Sebastian grabbed it for me and Titus's glare deepened.

"It all depends on how much Faerie wants Seireadan," Titus growled. "The aerie can only protect you for so long."

"Painfully aware of that," Sebastian replied, grabbing his own apple-like fruit. "I'll eventually need to get into a court or get out of Faerie."

"So we find a portal and get the hell out of here,"

Hawk said. "Your realm won't eat you alive and I'll be able to properly feed."

"We'd either need to use a portal in one of the courts or try to find one hidden in the Wilds," Sebastian said. "So neither option is easy. I've got at least a few days before Faerie breaks through the aerie's defenses and comes after me. We've got time to catch our breath. Not to mention, only a dragon can find the aerie so we're safer here for now than anywhere else, including my apartment in the mortal realm."

"Great, so we're staying at least until Amiah heals herself," Cassius said, cutting off a piece of cheese and not sounding happy about staying. But it was the most logical plan, especially if it was going to be dangerous getting to a portal to return home. He turned his gaze to Hawk. "Can you manage?"

"If everyone has a few really sexy thoughts, I'll be able to get by." Hawk slid his hand up my thigh, nudging the slit of my dress open a few more inches, not even enough to be considered indecent by my — old — standards. Every eye dropped to my leg, and Hawk hummed low in his throat, the sound only audible to me. "God, I love this dress."

Cassius stiffened and his attention jerked up to my eyes, dipped again to my cleavage then back up to my eyes. He cleared his throat and a layer of emotional ice settled over his expression.

"We also need to discuss what happened last night," he said, his voice gruff.

Titus stiffened and the memory of the fear and pain

of everything that had happened heaved against my mental barrier.

"No." I shoved those emotions further down. I was doing just fine as I was. I didn't need to have a breakdown, I could pretend none of it had happened... except for some amazing sex. *That* I was going to remember. "I said we weren't going to bring it up again and you're not."

"Not that." Cassius raked a hand over his blond buzz cut, his angel glow flaring. "You were out of power. What happened between the Winter Queen pulling us away to discuss her plans for the Heart and us finding you in that hall?"

Heat seeped across my cheeks. One of those amazing sex moments.

"Someone poisoned Hawk," I said. "My magic locked onto him and it took everything I had to save him."

"Actually one of the queen's men who I saw making out with your sister by the way," Hawk said to Sebastian, "tried to stab Amiah with a poisoned knife."

My thoughts stuttered at that, then realization hit me and panic squeezed my chest. That poison had nearly killed Hawk with his extraordinary healing. There was no way I would have survived, even if I'd flooded myself with my magic.

"That was Padraigin?" Sebastian asked. "Well, shit. I'd thought if there was anyone at court we could trust it would be her."

"Amiah stands between her and the throne," Titus said.

"No, I don't." But as soon as the words came out, I knew I was lying. The Winter Court had claimed me and

I'd taken control of its power from its current queen. I might have more claim to the throne now than even Sebastian.

Sebastian pursed his lips, confirming what I feared.

My pulse picked up.

I was trapped.

And I would handle it.

I. Would. Handle. It.

"Come on," Hawk said, drawing me tighter against his chest as if he could sense my fear. "It's been obvious since the beginning that your return pissed Padraigin off."

"Yeah. I know. I'd just hoped—" Sebastian rubbed his face, his glow flickering and his complexion sliding back into that unsettling gray for a second. "It doesn't matter. I don't care who's sitting on the throne of the Winter Court so long as it isn't me."

"Or Amiah," Titus growled, his canines extending and his beast straining to break free.

Sebastian's gaze jerked to him. "I said I'd fix the court's claim on her and I will. Just give me a minute to catch my fucking breath. It takes longer to restore magic ripped away by Faerie."

"Hey." I reached out for Sebastian's hand before realizing what that might look like then decided I didn't care and interlaced my fingers with his. "I know you will."

Surprise flashed across his expression and his gaze, filled with concern and something else, something softer, captured mine. For a second I was drowning in a vast universe of power and yet writhing in a painful darkness.

"I promise," he said, his voice soft, and he slid his

fingers free, taking with him the power and pain and dimming my connection with his life force.

"Okay." The Winter Court's ice swelled, as if filling in the emptiness left when Sebastian pulled away. "Sebastian and I need to regain our power with more rest, and the three of us still need to clean up and change clothes."

"Right." Cassius's gaze jumped from me to Hawk then Sebastian. "Who's helping you?"

"I can clean up on my own." Sure, I wouldn't have minded a shower with Sebastian and Hawk, but later, when my ribs weren't broken and I wasn't freezing and I could do all the things I wanted to do.

"You're still dizzy and you still need body heat," Cassius said, his posture getting more rigid by the second.

"I can manage by myself long enough to clean up and get back into a bed."

He opened his mouth, and I glared at him. "This isn't a discussion." I turned to Hawk. "You go first, then I'll meet you back in bed."

"There are other bathing rooms in all the other suites," Titus said. "Just go back into the hall and pick a doorway."

"I'll go change the sheets on your bed." The muscles in Cassius's jaw flexed. "The last door on the end is a bathroom and I put a variety of clothes for everyone on a rack with the towels just inside the door." He jerked to his feet and strode from the room, a wisp of smoke curling behind him.

Hawk carried me to the last doorway, down a short hall with a sharp ninety-degree turn so no one could just look in and see into the bathroom. It was almost identical to the one in my room at the Winter Court with a stone sink and toilet, a waterfall shower, and a tub carved into the stone floor.

He set me on my feet at the edge of the tub while Sebastian grabbed a towel, a washcloth, and a change of clothes from the rack and brought them over.

"I'll meet you back in bed," Hawk said, his hot breath washing across my cheeks and down my neck. Oh man, I couldn't wait to be healed.

"But *I* won't be waiting in bed for you," Sebastian added, "not until you talk to Cassius."

The two of them left, and I sank to the floor shivering uncontrollably with the Winter Court's cold, agony screaming through my chest. But I wasn't going to call them back. I wasn't sure I could resist either man's allure at the moment if I was naked and I'd just end up frustrating all of us and hurting myself.

And I was going to think about that and only that. How they made me feel. How I ached just thinking about having sex with them again. How I could just let go of everything.

I untied the hidden laces at the side of my dress, pulled off the bloody and ripped fabric, and dipped my foot into the tub's cool water.

God, if you'd asked me about having sex with them a week ago, I would have said it was the most terrifying idea ever.

The water in the tub started to warm up, and I eased into its soothing heat.

I'd never have given someone else control over me

like that, let alone them, and I'd never have let someone see me without my rigid hold on my body and my emotions. Now I couldn't wait to let go with Sebastian Bane of all people and an incubus.

And I really wasn't going to think about how everything would change the moment we returned to the mortal realm. I'd have to go back to my real life and both Hawk and Sebastian would remember who I really was.

TITUS

I STARED AT THE BATHROOM DOORWAY, MY BEAST STRAINING to regain control. Seireadan and Hawk had left with their changes of clothes and towels and now it was just me and my angel in the suite.

Except she wasn't mine, no matter what my beast wanted. The Winter Court had claimed her so Seireadan had to have lied and married her and Hawk had her scent and arousal all over him. And I'd have believed just her scent being on him because he'd been holding her since we'd crashed into the Wilds, but the scent of her arousal could only mean one thing.

In fact, both he and Seireadan had smelled of sex when Cassius and I had found them in the hall off the ballroom facing off against Deaglan. The scent had been so strong and her angel glow so weak it had taken everything I had just to hold my beast in.

Then seeing Seireadan kiss her like he hated her and then ramming himself into her making her cry on top of all of that had been too much. My beast had torn free of my mental hold and the only thing I could think of was getting to her, protecting her, and making Seireadan pay.

I sucked in a heavy breath that did nothing to calm my beast. Fuck, I should have stayed in my dragon form and not joined her and the others for that meal. She'd spent the entire time cuddling with the incubus, which only pissed my beast off more. And while logically I knew she needed his heat — she'd been freezing when she'd leaned into me in the Wilds and stopped my beast from killing Seireadan — my beast didn't give a fuck. She needed to be cuddling with me. Using me for comfort. Using me to satisfy her sexual desires and not them.

Not fucking them.

My beast snarled, heaving inside me.

She was only a few feet away and naked. *I* was still naked. It was perfect.

My fantasy of sliding into her hot tight sheath, of her stunning radiant gaze capturing mine, and the look of pure pleasure when she came could come true.

Except she was hurt and exhausted. Now wasn't the time to have sex with her... even if the incubus had... although I hadn't smelled *his* arousal on her, not this time, which meant he'd just pleasured her.

Which I was just as capable of doing.

Really.

I jerked forward but managed to stop myself just before I reached the ninety-degree turn and saw into the bathroom.

My beast was wrong. I hadn't had a sexual touch from a female in over five hundred years. There was no way I'd be able to control myself let alone my beast if she was naked and in my arms. Hell, that barely-there dress the Winter Queen had made her wear had strained my control even with the fear that she was going to get hurt by the night's events.

If I was smart, I'd fly around the nest again and try to mend the connection between me and my beast. Except my beast didn't want to shift. That would mean it wouldn't be able to hold Amiah, and it *had* to hold her, be comforted by her soul, bring her pleasure.

I dug my claws into the wall and sucked in another breath.

Leave. Just turn around and jump out the window.

Go into the bathroom and comfort her. Neither Seireadan or Hawk can comfort her like I can. They aren't her soul's mate.

And yet the Winter Court had claimed her with a connection strong enough to take away the queen's control. That spoke of a deeper connection between her and Seireadan...

Except Seireadan had said the connection had happened because I'd given Amiah the key.

So he wasn't her mate.

She was still mine.

I bit back a roar and clawed chunks from the wall. Damn it. She wasn't mine, not until she'd chosen me... or whatever it was that angels did to recognize their soul's mate.

"Hey," she said, jerking my attention to her as she eased to my side and pressed her freezing hands against my forearm.

She was fully dressed now in a pair of loose, soft

cotton pants and a cotton shirt that was too big for her, the open V-neck exposing a glorious amount of cleavage. My beast shuddered with pleasure at the sight as well as her touch, and my soul rang with the truth.

Mine.

With a growl, my beast captured the back of her head with my free hand and smashed my mouth to hers before I could stop it. And the moment our lips touched I was lost.

My cock went rock hard and all of my senses locked on her. The rightness of connecting with her, the thrum of her soul against mine reassuring my beast, the feel of her lips, her soft sweet scent, her too-cold body, and her shivering even though she was fully dressed.

She gasped in surprise at our sudden connection, and I seized the opening created by her breath, raking my tongue into her mouth and deepening the kiss. This kiss was going to be so much more than the desperate locking of lips when I'd somehow given her the key. I was going to show her with my mouth — and my mouth alone — how she was mine, how it didn't make sense to choose anyone else but me, how I could satisfy her.

I slid my arm free of her hands, shifted closer, and gently captured her delicate body against the wall with mine. She was so small, so unlike any female dragon, and yet absolutely perfect. My erection pushed against her belly, letting her know in no uncertain terms how I felt, and I slid my hand under her shirt and softly — oh so softly so I didn't hurt her — brushed my fingers up to her breast.

She moaned into my mouth, the scent of her arousal

thickening and her breath coming faster, but also sharper.

Somewhere in the back of my mind, I knew I was hurting her. I needed to stop, to pull away.

Except this might be my only chance to show her how I was her mate, how we were meant to be together.

Shit.

I heaved against my beast, but it snarled back at me and rubbed the pad of my thumb against a nipple pebbled and begging for my mouth.

She moaned again and arched her fragile perfect body into my hand, making my beast growl with pleasure.

"Titus, please," she gasped, cupping my cheeks in her small freezing hands, her voice tight with pain. "I can't."

Because she was Seireadan's—

No, because she was hurt, her ribs broken, and each breath had to be agonizing.

Shit.

Her hands on my face trembled, her breath sharp and shallow. "Titus."

Shit shit shit.

I wrenched myself away from her and pressed my back against the other side of the hall, fighting my beast and holding myself there. The loss of our connection, even just that few feet of distance, made my soul cry. I needed her, needed her soul to steady mine.

Her gaze dipped to my cock, painfully hard and standing at full attention. Heated desire dilated her pupils and her arousal taunted me.

My beast clawed at my insides. She wanted me. Why

the hell was I holding back? It could be steadying her soul — and it wasn't going to recognize that she wasn't a dragon and didn't need her soul steadied — and it could be making her feel good. It would protect her for as long as I had breath. It would do anything to see her smile, to feel her soul, to be with her. It would die to protect her.

"Be my mate," I blurted out. I wasn't going to be able to hold it back much longer. She had to know how I felt, had to know what I wanted. If I didn't say anything, she'd keep sleeping with Seireadan and Hawk, and I didn't know how much longer I'd be able to hold my beast back before it challenged them for her.

Shock swept through the desire in her eyes. "Titus."

"Be my mate."

"Titus, you don't know me."

"I do. You're powerful and kind and you calm my beast." Just being near her settled me. She felt right, more right than my mate before the Heart had awakened.

Because she's mine, my beast growled, heaving against my control.

"Can't you feel it?" I asked. "When you touch me, we connect."

The light in her eyes weakly flared, barely a glimmer of what it should have been because she was low on power. "You've just gone without for too long. You haven't been able to completely calm your beast and he rules your primal needs. You're mistaking lust for love."

"I'm not," I snarled back. How could she not see we belong together?

"Titus." She raised her hands, palms up toward me.

"Take my hands, let me help you calm your beast. You're not in love with me. You just need to have sex, that's all."

"Is that what you're doing with Seireadan then?" I glared at her hands and dug my claws into the wall behind me. If I took hold of her, my beast would take over and I'd hurt her. "Just having sex? He's not your mate?"

"I'm having sex with Hawk too. Also not my mate." She took a step toward me, her hands still extended as if she weren't afraid of my beast like she should have been, proving all the more that she was mine.

"If they're not your mates, then be mine." If they truly weren't her mates then I didn't have to win her, my beast wouldn't have to hurt them.

"I don't want a mate."

My beast heaved inside me. Of course she wanted a mate. She wanted me. She just hadn't realized it yet. She was my soul's mate. We were destined to be together... unless my beast was wrong and she was right. What if it was just my damaged connection with my beast making me think there was more between us than there really was. Surely if we were soul mates she'd feel it, she wouldn't reject me.

"You really don't want a mate? You don't feel anything between us?"

My beast howled and wrenched against my mental grasp. It had to break free, had to claim what was his—

It was going to hurt her.

How can she so easily calm me if she isn't my soul's mate? How? How?

"Titus." She inched closer and the cold radiating from

her body swept over my skin. She was trembling, shaking from the cold and yet still trying to calm me.

Damn it. "If there's nothing between us, why aren't you afraid of me?"

I jerked toward her and snarled, trying to get her to back off before my beast grabbed her and hurt her.

But she pressed her hands against my chest instead of stepping away. "Because you *need* someone. You need another soul to stabilize yours. I'm not going to let you suffer with a damaged connection. You don't deserve that."

My beast shuddered again at her touch, its tension melting away, and it leaned in. It couldn't do anything else.

Mine. She's mine. She has to be.

And yet another part of me was so certain she was Seireadan's because the Winter Court had claimed her. But both her and Seireadan had said I was wrong about that. She was claimed because I'd given her the key. Maybe I was wrong about us.

"You don't love me?"

"I don't really know you. I don't love Sebastian or Hawk either." Her weak angel glow flared again and her gaze dipped to her hands. "All I know is that I need this too. With you. With them. I don't know how to explain it. I'm not a shifter. I shouldn't *need* this. And yet it's like a part of me that I didn't know was asleep comes awake when I connect with all of you."

She raised her brilliant blue eyes to meet mine and my pulse stalled. This time instead of holding me captive like she'd done before, it was like she'd pulled back a veil and I could see into her soul. There was a rawness there, a soul-deep need that she didn't understand and feared. It was as damaged as my connection with my beast, and was so much bigger than a connection with a single person. And I wasn't even sure she realized all of that, only that there was something wrong with her.

Mine.

But my beast was mistaken. It was confused. If she felt a connection with all of us then she couldn't be my soul's mate.

And even knowing that, I still wanted her. My cock was still hard.

Because I hadn't gotten laid in over five hundred years, and because I understood the desperate need in her soul for a connection.

Even if she wasn't my mate, I could still give that to her like Seireadan and Hawk... if I could keep my beast at bay... and if she'd still accept me... which she did. Her arousal still filled my nostrils and her pupils were still dilated. Her desire for me hadn't diminished because I'd begged her to be my mate, and that desperate need to heal a connection within her that she didn't understand still filled her eyes.

She was already giving so much to help me calm my soul, the least I could do was give her my body to help calm hers. I just had to figure out how to get my beast to shut the fuck up and not hurt anyone.

AMIAH

"I can give you what you need," Titus said, his voice gruff, surprising me.

That wasn't what I'd expected him to say at all.

"I just need time to get my beast to settle." He jerked back a step and stroked a heated gaze down my body. "And you need to heal."

Desire shuddered through me even as my thoughts stuttered over his words.

"I don't want you to be with me if you have to fight your beast. I don't want it to make you hurt the others." How had this suddenly turned into us discussing a sexual arrangement?

"I won't. It understands your situation." He turned before I could respond, strode to the window, and jumped out.

In the blink of an eye, he shifted into his magnificent dragon, caught a wind current, and lifted out of sight.

I sagged against the hall wall, exhausted from having used all my magic again and shivering not just from the Winter Court's cold. There was something broken inside me, something as an angel I wasn't supposed to have and didn't understand. And it hadn't just been years of ignoring my desires that made me crave sex, it was the years of denying something deeper inside me.

My life force *needed* to connect with someone else's life force. It was the foundation of my magic, why, if I didn't use it often enough, a pressure would build inside me, and why, if I was pulled away before it was done or resisted its compulsion, I'd suffer a debilitating backlash.

Denying that needed connection for so long had damaged it just like Titus being unable to shift had damaged his connection with his beast. Now we both had to figure out how to heal ourselves.

And much to my surprise, I believed Titus when he said his beast understood what I needed. Which was good, because I ached to connect with Titus physically, but I also knew, especially now that I was aware of my broken connection, that I needed more than just his touch. It was why I still wanted to have sex with both Hawk and Sebastian, why my soul thrilled at the idea of connecting with both of them at the same time. Just like someone else I knew, I was *supposed* to have multiple lovers. Not because I was destined to have multiple mates like her but because my soul needed the strength of multiple connections.

"Amiah?" Hawk asked, hurrying across the living room toward me, his fiery dark life force sliding against my senses and sending a thrill through my soul. "You okay?"

No. I needed to connect with him, to have him inside me.

He'd changed into clean leather pants like Cassius but hadn't put on a shirt and I had a perfect view of his stunning sculpted body. A body made for sex... which I was in no condition to have, and was going to have to wait for.

I just needed to hold out until I'd healed my ribs.

I could do that. Really.

"Just cold and tired," I said.

His eyes narrowed.

Yeah, I wouldn't believe me either.

"Titus just jumped out the window again." He picked me up, cradling me against his too-hot body, and I leaned into him, not waiting to grow accustomed to his body temperature before trying to get as much flesh to flesh contact as possible. "He looked upset and you're both horny as hell."

"Can't hide anything from you." I slid my hand over his pec and savored the feel of his hard, honed muscle as well as the gentle snaps under my skin of his life force responding to mine.

"Is he going to be a problem?" he asked, carrying me back to the bedroom and laying me on the bed. "You keep putting your hands on him and I get the impression dragons are like wolves and they have trouble sharing."

"We've worked it out."

"You sure?" Hawk settled in behind me and pulled a heavy blanket over top of us.

Mindful of my ribs, I carefully snuggled against him, letting his heat melt the cold inside me and the physical contact strengthened my connection with his life force. All of it relaxed me, dragging me closer and closer to sleep. "He understands what I need."

"Doesn't mean he won't be a problem," Hawk said, his hot breath feathering across the back of my neck.

"He won't." Because once again Titus was the one most likely to understand my situation. Just like being held against our will, we were the only ones in the group with souls that needed a connection with another soul.

"Okay then," Hawk replied without further argument.

Which struck me as funny. If it had been Cassius, we'd still be arguing. We'd argue about it all night long because he didn't trust my judgment—

Not true.

He couldn't let even the slim chance of danger threaten me... because I was weak and he saw me as his responsibility.

That thought twisted around my heart. I didn't want to be his responsibility. I wanted my friend back, wanted the easy relationship we used to have before the war, wanted more. If my stupid brand hadn't gotten in the way, I'd probably be married to him now.

And then I'd never have had sex with Sebastian or Hawk or realized the truth about my soul. Angels, compared to other species, were distant with each other, even with their lovers. Unless they were soul bonded, they never opened their souls to anyone, and without a doubt, Cassius would never open his to mine. He certainly wouldn't open his now.

Which twisted my grief tighter. The war had torn a hole in his soul, and it wasn't just because of his youngest brother's death. All I wanted was to heal him. Except I couldn't heal souls. His other brother's mate could with her empathic healing magic, but it was going to take a lot of convincing to get him to even consider seeing Essie. And first, we'd have to get out of this mess and find our way back to the mortal realm... if I could even leave Faerie now with the Winter Court's claim on me.

My eyelids slid shut and my exhaustion pulled me into a strange sleep. I dreamed of ice again and also fire, twirling around and around inside me, trapping me, freeing me, filling me with power and life and something else I couldn't find the words for. It crushed and pulled and threatened to consume my soul and there wasn't anything I could do about it.

Because I was trapped.

Trapped.

I woke with a start, gasping for breath, my power full and burning in my palms. My body ached, but it wasn't screaming in pain, and a whisper of Hawk's sensual magic pulsed in my chest and throbbed between my thighs. I still lay under the blanket in his arms with my back against his chest, but now his hand had slipped under my shirt and was cupping my breast and his erection was hard against my rear.

My thoughts instantly jumped to him pushing inside me, and his magic swelled. He murmured, still asleep, and started kneading my breast, making my nipple harden in anticipation.

A soft moan escaped my lips and he shifted his hips forward adding a delicious pressure to the press of his erection. His life force crackled against my senses with the promise of so much more if I just took him inside me, and my whole body throbbed with need at the thought.

Which was a terrible idea since I really needed to heal my broken ribs first.

I shifted so I could touch his face, wake him, and look him in the eyes. The movement slipped his hand from my breast, and with a throaty, masculine groan, he slid his hand inside my pants, his fingers going straight for my clit.

His touch shot sensation through me, stealing my breath, and his power curled tight in my core.

Oh, wow.

"Hawk," I said, my voice breathy.

"Just let it go," he murmured still asleep and he slid two fingers inside me. "I've got you."

My eyes rolled back and my breath picked up, spiking only a glimmer of the pain that I should have felt. Which didn't mean my ribs were healed, just that Hawk's power was growing inside me and I couldn't feel them.

"Hawk, wake up." I caressed his cheek with what I knew was a freezing cold hand to his naturally hot demonic body temperature and his eyelids fluttered open, capturing me with his unusual blue-gray eyes, his hellfire blazing.

"We should probably wait," I said.

He frowned. "We should wait?" he asked his words slurred with sleep.

Then his eyes widened and I guess he realized where his hand was.

"Oh, well," he said his expression turning wicked. "You want to finish?"

The thought sent a sudden rush of desire racing through me. "You have to ask?"

He shrugged. "Not really."

With a swell of magic, he quickly worked me up and over the edge. It wasn't the deep, connection that I craved. His fingers inside me didn't fill me with his life force to the same degree as his erection did, but it still felt amazing, and I wasn't an idiot. I'd never say no to him making me feel like that.

"God, I love how that feels," he said, pulling me back into his arms and wrapping me in his heat.

"That makes two of us, and you'll be able to get a lot more power once I heal my ribs."

"With all the sexual desire in this group, I'm already at full." He kissed the divot behind my ear. "That was purely for the pleasure of it. But yes, heal those ribs. There should only be pain during sex if you're into that."

The memory of Balwyrdan with sexual pleasure gleaming in his eyes as he slammed his fist into my face rushed into my mind's eye chilling my desire.

"Yeah. Didn't think that was your thing," Hawk said. "So what do you need me to do to work your magic and heal yourself?"

"Just keep holding me. You're not injured so there's no chance my magic will slip into you, and it takes a lot of concentration to heal myself. I'd rather not have to try to do that while I'm also freezing." I gathered my power, hot and sticky, in my palms and gave him an apologetic smile. "It's going to look like I'm asleep and it's going to take a while, so it might get boring."

"Gee, holding a sexy woman in my arms." He flashed me a wicked grin. "I think I can manage."

"Just holding. As much as I'd love something else, I can't."

He pressed his lips to my cheek and said, "I've got you." Just like he'd said in his dream.

I closed my eyes and dragged my power from my hands and into my chest, pushing it into my broken bones and agonizingly slowly knitting them back together.

God, it was such a waste. This was why I needed to be more careful. All this magic could have saved someone's life, could have healed all the guys — except Hawk — of serious injuries. If I was supposed to be using it on myself, healing me would have been as easy as healing everyone else.

And as much as staying out of trouble was the ideal, it wasn't the reality. Especially now. I was in the middle of all of it just like the guys and I knew, even if I had a chance to get some place safe, I wouldn't leave them. Getting hurt was a risk I was more than willing to take if it meant I was nearby when one of them needed me.

I pushed power into my ribs until only the small spark in my palms that I could never use up remained. Three of the five ribs had been healed, good as new, and much to my surprise, the fourth's break had been healed into a hairline fracture.

Exhaustion weighed down my body and once again the room was slowly spinning, even with my eyes closed. I drew in a breath not nearly as painful as before in an attempt to ease my dizziness and opened my eyes.

Hawk's gaze locked with mine and worry clouded his expression. "Jeez. I hate seeing your glow that dim."

"I hate feeling it," I replied.

"I'll get you something to eat." He pushed back the covers and eased away from me. "Be back in a minute."

I grabbed his wrist. "Help me into the living room so I can see the sky before I pass out again." There weren't any windows in the bedroom and while Hawk was an amazing distraction, seeing the sky would also help me steady myself and make it easier to regain my power.

"Deal." He picked me up and we stepped into the living room.

Sebastian was the only one around, lounging on a pile of cushions staring out the massive window at a clear blue sky. His icy life force surged against my senses, connecting me with him even though he was halfway across the room and filling me with his pain, the source still invisible to my magic.

"Set her right here," Sebastian said, opening his legs and shifting so he was sitting instead of lying. "I've got enough power to ease the Winter Court's cold. I think that, and not the leash spell, is our first priority."

"Agreed." Funny how the leash spell was no longer the top priority. Sure, Sebastian had lengthened and eased its deadly side effects, but we were still bound together. I was still trapped. And yet that no longer terri-fied me. Maybe because I knew eventually we'd deal with it, there was a way to be free.

The Winter Court, however, was a different matter.

My gaze dipped to my still-glowing hands. The light had dimmed a bit, or perhaps I was just getting used to it, but I still glowed. I still had Faerie's magic woven in my cells, impossibly making me a high fae and it wasn't just going to go away.

"Can you get rid of all of it?" I asked, even though I suspected I knew the answer. He'd said he'd fix it when we been in the Wilds but he hadn't mentioned that when we'd all discussed our situation.

"No." Sebastian's expression darkened, confirming my fears. "That's going to take a lot of power and I'm not up for that right now. Best to deal with the cold and make things manageable for you until I'm strong enough."

"Are you up for even blocking the cold?" Hawk asked.

Sebastian patted the cushion between his thighs again. "I'm fine. Let's just do this."

I rolled my eyes at him. "You're not fine. You're in pain and it's getting worse."

"Because every time he casts a spell the demonic magic trapped inside him gets stronger," Hawk said, still not putting me down. "You channeled a lot of magic when we escaped the Winter Court."

"No shit. And our other options were...?" Sebastian patted the cushion again. "There's nothing I can do about it and Amiah shouldn't have to spend who knows how long freezing."

So that was what their strange conversation in the Wilds had been about. Sebastian, a being from Faerie shouldn't have been able to connect with the Realm of Celestial Darkness let alone take its magic into his body. If he somehow had demonic magic in him, he might not be able to get it out, which would explain why he'd mentioned needing to find a demon.

Except if he wasn't able to connect with demonic magic— "How do you even have demonic magic in you?"

"Long story." He sighed and patted the cushion again. "It involves teleporting too many people at once, a crazy hellfire queen, and an archnephilim newly awakened to her powers."

And he'd dumped everyone into the middle of the cafeteria in the Joined Parliament Operations building. He'd saved everyone's lives with that spell, and it had torn up his insides, nearly killing him. Thankfully my fellow healer, Priam, had gotten to him first and stabilized him, stopping my magic from locking onto him, but once we'd all gotten to a safe location, I'd still had to drain myself to heal him.

"Why didn't you say anything?"

"Because it was none of your business." Sebastian glared at Hawk.

Hawk glared back. "Given our situation, I think she has a right to know."

"I don't see how me being infected with demonic magic influences us being fuck buddies," Sebastian snapped. "It's not like it's contagious."

"Because she's counting on your magic to keep her safe and it's going to fail and soon." Hawk's grip on me tightened. "I've been watching it eat you from the inside out since you walked into my tent."

"And again I say, find me a fucking demon in Faerie who can pull it out." He slapped the cushion between his legs. "The sooner I ease up Amiah's chill the sooner Cassius will feel it's safe to move and we'll get back to the mortal realm. Problem solved."

"Fine," Hawk said, setting me on the cushion between Sebastian's thighs. "I'll go find you something to eat."

He stormed out of the living room and with a groan Sebastian tugged me back against his chest. His life force pulsed against my senses, cold and uneven, and his pain slid through my veins.

"How bad is it?" I asked.

He wrapped his arms around me and the heat from his body — the temperature not as hot as Hawk's but still warmer than mine when it shouldn't have been — slowly seeped into my skin. "It used to just hurt when I cast something. Now I hurt all the time."

"Then don't ease the Winter Court's cold. I can manage."

He snorted and lifted one of my softly glowing hands. "Your fingernails have already turned blue again. You've been snuggled up to a natural furnace for hours and you've only been away from him for a minute. Your body isn't made to handle the Winter Court's magic."

"Then why would it claim me?"

"I have no idea." He tensed and his icy magic prickled over my skin then sank under it, rushing in a freezing wave to my heart.

I tensed, anticipating a pain similar to the agony of changing the leash spell, but instead, it filled me with bliss. An icy version of Hawk's seductive magic. It flooded around my heart, making my pulse pick up, then sank lower into my core.

"But fuck if it doesn't like you," he said, his voice husky. "I've never felt my magic do that before."

"If it likes me, will it even let me leave Faerie?" The seductive chill swelled and I breathed out a soft moan.

"Let's just deal with one problem at a time," he groaned back.

Which meant he didn't know... or he did and the answer was no. Meaning even if we got to a portal, the Winter Court wasn't going to let me leave. Ever.

HAWK

Fucking hell.

I wrenched open a cupboard looking for a bowl. Just plates. Great. So now I'd found serving platters and plates. Where were the damned bowls?

I'd stormed down the hall to the last doorway where Cassius had said there was a kitchen, finding it attached to a massive dining room.

The kitchen part was constructed from a mix of stone carved — likely magically carved — from the mountain itself and wood. Stone counters ran from the doorway and along the walls in a long L, broken only by a large old-fashioned metal stove and a sink, and jutted out from the wall marking the boundary between the kitchen and the dining room.

Someone had left a pot of stew simmering on what I could only assume was a magically heated element because there was no electricity in Faerie that I'd seen and no fire heating the stove, and I'd decided that something warm would be good for Amiah even if Bane did manage to ease the Winter Court's chill.

God, I hoped he had enough power for that. As much as I loved holding her in my arms, it was clear the constant cold was taking its toll, and she was either putting on a good face or was too worried about everything else to notice.

And now I'd given her something else to worry about.

What the hell was wrong with me?

I shouldn't have said anything about the demonic magic consuming the magical channels in Bane's body in front of Amiah. I should have kept my damned mouth shut.

But it was clear from the way she looked at him that she cared for him more than just for the sexual pleasure he could give her. Sure, she'd made a point of saying love wasn't going to be involved in our arrangement but that didn't mean we couldn't care for each other, and she was going to be shattered if Bane killed himself trying to free her from the Winter Court.

Every time he used his magic the demonic magic got stronger and his connection to Faerie got weaker. Eventually, he was going to be completely cut off and he'd die since a high fae couldn't survive without a connection to their realm.

She had a right to know the danger he was putting himself in for her. Hell, the others did, too, but they wouldn't blame themselves like Amiah would, and I couldn't live with her blaming herself.

Fuck. I couldn't live with her being cold or in pain, and I wasn't sure I wanted to live without her when she finally decided to fall in love with someone and have a committed relationship.

I didn't want to give up the feeling of her desire rushing through my veins, or her body moving against mine, or the sounds she made, and certainly not the look of absolute pleasure when she came. I'd even been dreaming about making love to her and had woken with my fingers buried inside her and my hard-as-hell cock pressed against her butt.

I'd never woken like that before.

I was supposed to have more control than that.

But there was something about her, about the way she looked at me, connected with me. It wasn't love. It couldn't be love. But there was something there, something so deep I'd dreamed about it and had felt so fucking good when I'd woken with her desire rushing through me and her body aching for a pleasure I was more than happy to give her.

Fuck.

We'd only known each other a short time. I'd only slept with her twice and while the hard fuck in the alcove to save my life shouldn't have counted, the look in her eyes, that sense that she was seeing into my soul and embracing all of me not just my body, had been even stronger than before. She'd closed her eyes when her orgasm had swept through her, but just before that there was that perfect moment again where she saw me. All of me. It had stolen my breath and left me stunned. Again.

Fuck.

I wrenched open another cupboard.

Bowls.

Finally!

"Is she awake?" Cassius asked from behind me, making me jump and drop a bowl.

The pottery shattered on the stone floor, sending chunks flying in all directions.

"Jeez." I knelt and started picking up the pieces. "Yes, she's awake."

"And her ribs?" Cassius picked up a piece halfway between us. His aura snapped and heaved, an angry red nimbus around his body, and his expression was hard. If I hadn't known from the turmoil in his aura how much he was struggling to keep his fire inside him, I'd have mistaken his expression for bottled up rage.

"I don't know. She spent a couple of hours healing herself, but when I moved her to the living room, she still looked like she was in pain."

"She's in the living room? Good," he said, surprising me since I was sure he'd want her to stay in bed until she'd fixed all her broken bones. "Seeing the sky will help her recover her magic faster."

"An angel's need for open spaces is that strong?" I'd known angels liked open spaces and claustrophobia was more common in angels than any other species, but I hadn't known the need was so strong it affected their magic.

Cassius's aura flared and a wisp of smoke curled from his right hand. "Amiah's is. She needs to know she's free, that she can escape. I suspect the need wasn't as strong before she was taken." Another *snap* in his aura and the wisp of smoke thickened. "Before the *first* time she was taken."

Right. Which had been the first time they'd met. A part of me wondered if that had been when he'd fallen in love with her, while a selfish part of me was glad she hadn't fallen in love with him then too. I'd never have met her if she had.

Except now that she was allowing herself to feel, I suspected she'd eventually fall in love with him too.

She and Cassius had been friends for a long time and he was completely dedicated to her. Even if he hadn't told me, it would have been clear in how they interacted. They behaved like two people who'd known each other for years, comfortable — for the most part — in each other's company. They had a lot in common, had shared a lot of experiences, and I suspected when he got his head out of his ass, they had fun together... a stuffy angel kind of fun, but still fun. They were perfect for each other.

And yet the part of me that didn't want to lose her to a committed relationship was getting louder and louder. If she committed to Cassius, I'd lose her. She needed to commit to someone who'd accept me as well — since if she committed to me and me alone, I'd end up killing her or starving, because if she committed herself to me, I wouldn't want to sleep with other people outside of our relationship.

Hell, I wasn't sure I wanted to sleep with other people right now.

My pulse stuttered at that.

Fuck me.

It wasn't supposed to be possible, but in that instant, I knew Amiah was going to break my heart.

The realization stunned me.

"Hawk?"

I wasn't sure if I was in love with her yet, but I would be. Even if I'd never been in love before and wasn't supposed to be able to fall in love, I just knew I was going to fall in love with her. With how she made me feel, what I wanted to give her and show her, how I wanted to take care of her... it was inevitable.

"Hawk."

If I was smart, I'd pull away from her and protect myself. I had no idea how a broken heart was going to affect me. Incubi weren't supposed to be able to fall in love, and there were only a few recorded cases of it happening... and ending very badly. Falling in love was akin to a mental illness in any other species.

But the thought of ending what I'd started with her made my heart race.

It wasn't even a matter of want. I *couldn't* do it. Not even to protect my sanity.

I'd always known my time with her would come to an end, no way was I going to be an idiot and end it sooner than absolutely necessary. I'd rather have more time, a bigger broken heart, and end up locked up in a psych ward, than less time and centuries of regret.

"Hawk!"

I jerked my attention to Cassius.

"What is wrong with you? You've cut yourself three times on the same shard."

My gaze dropped to the half dozen blood drops on the floor by my knee and the bloody shard — my finger perfectly fine because of my rapid healing, although the blood drops on the floor indicated at least one of the cuts had been deep.

"We need to get Amiah out of Faerie." The words rushed out of me. She wasn't safe in Faerie. What little time I had with her was going to be cut short because someone was going to kill her.

"We need a plan first," Cassius said, tossing his pottery pieces into the sink, not sounding happy about that at all. "The aerie will protect Bane, and I guess Amiah now too, from Faerie ripping its magic out of them for a few days, but we can't just return to the mortal realm. We're seriously vulnerable there."

"Bane's place has spells hiding it. Balwyrdan only found us because Mavis told him."

"And how much do you want to bet one of Deaglan's assassins didn't get that information too?"

Fuck. "What about the JP Operations building? It has protections and agents." I dropped my pieces in the sink with his. "And an arsenal. God, what I wouldn't give for a rifle right about now."

"You honestly think I haven't already thought of that?" He gripped the edge of the counter, his aura writhing and smoke billowing from his hands. "That's the last resort. I don't want to get any more people involved in this mess than necessary. Amiah has one of the keys. That means Titus got a key while he was Deaglan's prisoner. Once Deaglan figures out Amiah has it, he'll be coming after her whether we like it or not, wherever she might be. We need a better plan than just holing up at Operations."

"Well we're going to need to think of something."

"I said I was going to keep her safe and I will." Cassius's eyes narrowed and his angel glow flickered, shockingly bright for a second. "Back in the Winter Court you said I shouldn't doubt your resolve."

"And I'd meant it." I'd been pissed when I'd said it. Cassius had pressed me for details to prove I was actually a vet and I'd told him about the horrible thing I'd had to do in the war. I should have lied, just said I was a canary for a reconnaissance unit or something, but that would have meant getting my story straight with Bane who'd been with me during that nightmare, and there were more important things to worry about.

"What are you willing to do to keep her safe?"

Anything.

Everything.

I was already going to happily lose my mind and heart to her. I'd give up my soul too if it meant protecting her.

I was so completely fucked.

"What are you asking?"

The light in Cassius's eyes flared again and for a second his expression was filled with heartbreak and resignation before his icy mask slid back into place. "Are you willing to have her hate you if it means protecting her?"

He was. He'd told me so. And yet it was clearly tearing him apart.

Was I? Could I withstand losing her because of something I did and not because it was time for her to move on to someone else?

God, I didn't even want her to move on to someone else.

Except I wasn't supposed to care. Not like that. And if I didn't want Amiah worried about my sanity, I couldn't let her or anyone else know the truth that I was impossibly falling in love with her.

AMIAH

Much to my disappointment, I woke alone, my magic at full indicating I had to have slept for about eight hours, and once again I pushed my power from my palms into my chest to finish healing my broken ribs.

Back in the living room, Sebastian's magic had caressed my insides, turning me on but also making me drowsy, and I'd floated, propped up against him, watching puffy clouds drift across the sky.

Hawk had brought me a bowl of stew, his body not nearly as hot as before — which a far-off part of my brain knew that meant Sebastian had managed to ease the Winter Court's chill inside me — then they'd put me back to bed, each man stealing a breathtaking kiss before I passed out.

Now I lay in the bed, a little too warm under the heavy blanket and fully dressed, trying to figure out what I wanted to do first: eat or take a pain-free shower.

Cassius would have said eat, "you can survive if you're dirty," but the more I thought about it, the more I liked the idea of having a long hot soak. Just lounge in the tub and let my thoughts wander—

To all the things I was trying not to think about...

Best to have a shower.

Unless I could find Hawk or Sebastian and invite them to join me in the bath. That was something I definitely wanted to try. Of course, we'd have to do it in a different suite. It would be best to avoid an embarrassing situation with Cassius walking in on us.

Just the thought heated my cheeks with embarrassment... but also desire.

Jeez. What was wrong with me—

No. There was nothing wrong with me. I had to stop thinking like that. I wanted to connect with all of them because that was who I was, what my soul needed.

Except, did I want to connect with them because I needed to feel their life force and anyone would do, or because they were them?

And the minute I thought that, I knew it was because of who they were. I'd never craved Marcus like I did Hawk, Sebastian, Titus, or even Cassius. Now that the part of my soul that had been asleep had awakened, I knew there was something about them, about their life forces, that resonated with me.

They weren't my soul mates. Or at least Sebastian and Hawk weren't. As much as they weren't the men I thought they were, it was still crazy to think either man was my perfect match. So it couldn't have been my partially formed brand drawing me to them. That, and the draw was stronger now that my brand was gone and the part of my soul that could create a bond had been permanently removed. No, it had everything to do with the power in their souls.

Connection and desire aside, however, I still wasn't prepared for Cassius to walk in on me having sex with Hawk or Sebastian or both of them together. In fact, right now, I didn't want to have anything to do with Cassius. I was still furious about him thinking he had any kind of say in my sex life.

Except Hawk and Sebastian had said I needed to have a conversation with Cassius, and they were right. But it wasn't to clarify who I could and couldn't have sex with. That was none of his business. What I really needed was to figure out how to get my friend back and not the icy soldier who seemed to think he could tell me what to do.

I pushed the blanket back and got out of bed, praying I wouldn't run into Cassius. I wasn't even close to being ready for our much needed conversation and he'd probably make me eat something which meant the shower — or sexy bath — would end up waiting. And, God, I was just so tired of waiting. I was tired of being patient and denying myself something I hadn't even realized was a fundamental part of myself.

For too long I'd forced myself into a tight little box: Amiah the healer who was waiting for her soul mate. I'd tried to ignore everything else, because everything else couldn't be controlled. Everything else increased the risk of making a mistake, of being hurt and held captive again, of feeling things for someone I wasn't supposed to have feelings for because he wasn't my soul mate.

But squeezing into that box hadn't kept me safe or protected my heart. The man I'd thought was my soul mate had been destined for someone else and the brand that I'd thought was beautiful was a nightmare. And the man who I'd thought was infuriating and selfish was a generous lover who was hurting himself to help me.

I hadn't really known anything.

I stepped into the living room and my attention instantly jumped to Cassius. He was the only one in the room and stood at the railing staring out the open window at the clear afternoon sky. He'd released his wings from his body and extended them, letting the gentle breeze caress his feathers, and was absolutely breathtaking. The perfect image of the perfect angel.

For a second he looked like the man I used to know. The thoughtful warm angel who'd saved me, made me laugh, and kept me company without even knowing I was foolishly waiting for a love I now no longer wanted.

Then he turned, his gaze locking on me, and ice swept across his expression, turning him back into the hardened soldier.

My throat tightened and tears pricked my eyes. God, I wanted the old Cassius back. But just like me, he'd learned things that had fundamentally changed him, which broke my heart because it wasn't anything I could heal.

"Hey," I said, unable to think of anything else to say and yet unable to turn away from him.

"Are your ribs healed?" he asked, his voice so cold it made me shiver.

"Yes." Was even a glimmer of the man I used to know in there anymore? I desperately wanted him to be. I needed *him,* not the soldier determined to keep me safe whether I liked it or not.

"I'll get the other guys so we can discuss our next plan of action." He pulled his wings back into his body and started to storm off.

My heart clenched and everything within me screamed that I couldn't let him leave, not with this anger between us. He'd made me so mad and if I thought about it, I'd said something hateful back. If he really was in love with me like Sebastian said, rubbing it in his face that we weren't having sex would have really hurt.

"Cassius, wait."

But he didn't stop, didn't even look at me.

Jeez. I scrambled to the door leading to the hall and put my body between him and the exit, pressing my palms against his chest. The sense of his life force flared, snapping with a burning heat just under my skin, even as he froze, his body going rigid.

"Amiah—" he said, his voice gruff, smoke curling around his hands. "Let me get the guys."

"Let them rest or whatever it is they're doing for a minute." We needed to have this conversation. I needed to get back what was left of *my* Cassius.

I drew in a steadying breath, determined to gather my thoughts and say the right thing but I couldn't pull my attention away from the feel of his firm pecs beneath my hands, only a thin cotton shirt separating our flesh. He didn't have the sleek sculpted physique that Hawk and Sebastian had, but his musculature was just as stunning, just as developed only a little bulkier. What would it be like to have him moving on top of me, those powerful arms holding himself up, his broad chest—

My thoughts stuttered and I realized I'd just stroked his chest.

I lifted my eyes and our gazes locked. For a breathtaking moment, I saw a desperate desire that ignited a matching desire within me.

He wrenched his gaze away, grabbed my wrists, and put more than an angel-appropriate amount of distance between us.

"Amiah, please. If you're still cold, grope someone who'll like it, like Hawk," he said, his tone implying that grope meant sex because of course now that he knew I was having sex I had to be incapable of touching someone without having sex with them.

How dare he!

"Oh, so I do get to have a sex life," I snapped. "Or am I only allowed to *grope*?"

"Don't be ridiculous." More smoke billowed around him and his palms grew painfully hot around my wrists. "I didn't say you couldn't have sex."

"No, you just think it's disgusting that I am."

"Of course I don't." Fire snapped from his hands, stinging my skin, and he wrenched away from me.

"Right, because you weren't appalled at the idea of me having sex with anyone and everyone?"

"No," he growled back, "I was shocked because I didn't think you'd sleep around while trying to win Marcus. I thought you were in love with him."

"I was in love with him." The words leaped out before I could stop them. Crap. I shouldn't have said that, because I hadn't really been in love with Marcus. I knew that now. I'd been in love with the idea of being in love, of his shifter's passion, of how wonderful having a completed mating brand would be. "I *thought* I was. I was wrong."

God, I'd been such a fool. How could I have ever thought what I felt for Marcus had been love? I wasn't in love with Hawk, Sebastian, or Titus, and what I felt for them was so much stronger than what I'd ever felt for Marcus even after four and a half years of being near him.

Because I needed something in their life forces, something that Marcus didn't have.

Something that Cassius also had.

"You know you're not in love with Hawk, either," Cassius said. "He can't love you back."

Jeez. I wasn't stupid. I was well aware Hawk couldn't love me back.

"It's just his magic," he added. "It's influencing you because he can't be bothered to pull back all of it."

Oh, for the love of—

"What does it matter?" I asked. "So what if his magic is influencing me."

Cassius rolled his eyes at me. "So if you have sex with him, you're going to regret it and I'll have to help you mend another broken heart."

I stared at him, stunned. I hadn't just heard that. I couldn't have. "You'll *have* to?"

"That's not what I meant," he huffed, not looking at all like he regretted his choice of words.

"No, that's exactly what you meant." God, I had to

stop. I had to shut my mouth and walk away. But I couldn't. I was so angry at everything, and I was furious at Cassius for looking at me like he wanted me, like maybe there could be something between us, then pushing me away and acting like he had the right to tell me who I could and couldn't have sex with. "So I'm some kind of chore? A duty you're stuck with because you pulled me out of that faith healer's tent? Protect poor weak little Amiah from everyone, from life, from herself? She doesn't know what she wants. She's too fragile. She can't possibly make the right decisions, especially about sex."

"That's not what I said at all." Fire rolled over his arms and he glared at me. "Things have happened to you and you're not thinking straight right now."

"I'm thinking perfectly fine."

"Right, that's why you risked your life by taking on all of Hawk's power, why you keep getting close to Titus when he's about to lose control of his beast, and why you had Sebastian practically rape you in front of the entire Winter Court ballroom." Sparks exploded from his hands, catching in one of the cushions and it burst into flames. "Fuck!"

He heaved his fire back under his skin, taking the flames consuming the cushion as well, and stormed back to the window.

"You are *not* fine," he growled at me. "You can't possibly be fine."

"Well neither are you."

"I'm not going to do something I'll regret, like sleeping with Hawk."

"I'm not regretting it," I yelled back.

Shock flashed across his expression.

"I see." He released his wings with a fiery explosion and dove out the window.

Crap.

I'd just yelled at him that I was having sex with Hawk, the complete opposite of the conversation I was supposed to have had with him. Just great.

AMIAH

I DIDN'T EVEN KNOW HOW THE CONVERSATION HAD GONE SO wrong. The argument hadn't even made any sense. He'd told me to go grope Hawk and then turned around and told me he needed to protect me against having sex with Hawk and falling in love with him.

I released my wings and screamed out the window even though he was out of sight and I didn't really want to fly after him. I wasn't the one who wasn't thinking straight.

Where was *my* Cassius, the man I could lean on, who I'd thought trusted me to make good logical decisions? I hadn't even been arguing with the hard as ice soldier who'd come back from the war.

I had no idea who that had been.

Except I had no idea who I was. I hadn't been thoughtful or logical in that argument. I wasn't sure I'd been logical since this whole mess started.

Now Cassius was flying around somewhere so angry

he hadn't wanted to stay in the same room as me and I'd pushed him further away.

And there wasn't a thing I could do about it.

Swell.

Well, since the cat has been yelled out of the bag, I might as well go find Hawk and grope him.

I yanked my wings back inside my body and checked all the bedrooms and the bathroom.

No Hawk or Sebastian.

Just great. The aerie was huge and I didn't want to aimlessly wander around with the hope that I'd find one of them. I could run into Cassius again and as much as a part of me wanted to continue yelling at him, the smart thing to do was just avoid him until both of us had calmed down.

Which brought me back to my original plan: have a shower and then get something to eat.

I grabbed a towel from the rack in the bathroom and stared at the ninety-degree turn. One of the guys could still walk in on me, and I wasn't in the mood for an awkward anything or not being able to move on my desires because I was worried someone in the living room might hear us or walk in on us.

That was a frustration I just didn't want, so I decided to use the bathroom in the suite at the very end of the main hall. But when I left our suite, I ran into Sebastian.

He leaned against the wall in the doorway of the second suite down, watching me approach with his arms crossed and his lips pursed, and not at all looking like he wanted to have a sexy bath.

"Well," he drawled, "that was one way to tell him you and Hawk are having sex."

"I'm aware of that." I didn't want to have an argument about my argument, and that's what it looked like Sebastian wanted. "And I'm not talking about it," I said, marching past him.

He grabbed my wrist, tugged me into the shadows of the suite's long hallway, and captured me against the wall, his palms on either side of my arms, boxing me in, making my pulse pick up in anticipation. Except his expression remained concerned, not even a hint of sexual desire.

"There are a lot of things you don't want to talk about," he said.

"Because there's no point in talking about them." My throat tightened and all the things I didn't want to think about threatened to break free. I leaned in and brushed my lips along his jaw so he wouldn't see I was about to have a breakdown. "There are so many better things we could be doing instead of talking."

"Sex will only be able to distract you for so long," he replied, nipping at my ear.

"It just needs to get me through this mess."

"And then what?" He slid his hands into my hair, capturing my head, and pressed his forehead to mine. "What will you do when this is done?"

His life force tingled against my senses, his icy brightness writhing against the demonic darkness. I didn't want to give up whatever it was that I needed from him, but he'd made it clear he'd never make a commitment to anyone. Ever. And given that the last person he'd been committed to had tried to murder him, I couldn't blame him. Which meant at some point I'd have no choice. I'd have to give him up.

And I'd deal with that when we got there.

"I don't know." I slid my hands under his shirt and ran them up his washboard abs. "Is this really what you want to be doing? Talking about the things I don't want to talk about? I'd rather you were doing me."

He snorted. "Jeez. You have sex a couple of times and all your angelic propriety gets thrown out the window."

"Would you rather I ask you primly for sexual inter-course?" I asked. "Or how about..." I dropped my towel, reached for the laces of his fly, and slowly sank to my knees.

I'd been curious about this, about what it would be like to hold a man's erection in my hands and feel it slide between my lips. It had felt amazing when Sebastian and Hawk had put their mouths on me, I bet it would feel just as amazing for them.

"Amiah," he huffed. "You've made your point. You don't have to do this."

I freed him from his pants, wrapped my hand around his full thick erection, and gave him my answer by slowly running my tongue over his tip.

"Fuck, Amiah," he groaned

His skin was softer than I imagined, a velvety layer over a steel shaft that I knew could bring me immense pleasure, and I slowly licked his tip again, drawing another groan.

"If you're teasing, just stop." He tangled his fingers back into my hair and started to tug me up, but I slid him into my mouth and he froze, his fingers digging into my scalp.

"Fucking hell."

My heart skipped a beat. I was pretty sure taking him in my mouth was how it was done, but he'd gotten tense, his body trembling.

Well, maybe I could convince him to give me some instruction so it felt good for him.

I glanced up at him through my lashes, ready to pull him out and ask for his help, but my words stalled at the look in his eyes.

Desire. Smoldering, dark, hot-as-hell, barely contained desire, that made the muscles in my core clench in anticipation at the possibility of wild, passionate sex. While I hadn't enjoyed what we'd had to do in the Winter Court ballroom, that didn't mean I wasn't excited at the idea of less restraint. It made me wet just thinking about the first time we'd had sex. I'd thought he'd been barely controlled before, but this, from the look in his eyes and the tension in his body, was what it really looked like.

Keeping our gazes locked, I drew him out until just his tip was in my mouth and slid him back in.

"Oh, fuck." He pressed a palm against the wall.

I did another slow withdrawal with my hand sliding up his length following my lips, my eyes still on his, and his breath picked up.

There was something so incredibly erotic about watching him struggle to hold himself together, not because of my oral sex prowess — I was sure it was just adequate at best — but because it was clear he thought he'd never see this. Me, on my knees, with my lips around him, and now I knew he'd been fantasizing about it.

His grip in my hair tightened and his hips rocked forward, pushing him back in, and I freely took him, my own pleasure an insistent throb, growing hot and wet between my thighs.

He rocked his hips back and I let him take over, showing me the pace he liked, never looking away because I couldn't get enough. God, the look in his eyes, the sound of his breath getting faster, the noises he made when he pushed into my mouth, and softly, on the edge of all that, the pulse of his life force teasing my magical senses.

Feeling him slide between my lips and against my tongue was just as stimulating as feeling him pushing in between my legs. It was amazing the things the body could do, the pleasure it could take or give, and my guess that me giving someone this kind of pleasure would turn me on as much as receiving it hadn't been wrong.

What I hadn't expected was the added thrill of maintaining eye contact, watching his need build, his hand in my hair, his pace getting faster as his restraint started to crumble. His sounds got louder too and with a groan, he pressed the sound blocking tattoo on his hip.

A flicker of pain swept through his expression, and his life force snapped against my senses, but he pushed back into my mouth and his burning need returned, inflaming my own.

God, like everything about sex so far, this was so much more than I imagined, the sensations more intense, the surprising desire building inside me even though I was the one stimulating him.

His breath grew ragged, his thrusts almost more than I could handle, but I could see he was getting close and I wanted to feel his release in my mouth, feel his erection pulse between my lips and against my tongue, and taste him.

"I'm going to come," he warned.

I moaned my pleasure in response.

"Jesus. Fuck." He jerked out of my mouth and tugged me up to my feet by my hair.

"Why did you stop?"

"Because— Fuck." He yanked me into the bedroom across the hall from us and smashed his lips against mine in a searing kiss that made me dizzy.

My back hit a wall and, with his hand still in my hair, he angled my neck to deepen the kiss and shoved his other hand up my shirt. The kiss was a lot like the kiss in the ballroom. Hard and wild, but there wasn't anything angry about this one. It was passionate, an overwhelming need that I'd inflamed by taking him in my mouth, and it made my pulse race and my body ache to be filled.

His fingers went straight to my nipple, making me moan, and he pushed his tongue deeper into my mouth. All breath and thought vanished, there were just the sensations of his hard body pressed against mine, his mouth taking what he wanted, his fingers rubbing and pinching my sensitive nipple, and God, I loved it. I was pretty sure I would have loved what we'd done in the ballroom too if we hadn't had an audience and he hadn't forced himself in me before I was ready.

"Take your pants off," he breathed against my lips.

Absolutely!

I fumbled with my lace-up fly, loosening it enough so I could push the soft fabric over my hips and rear. They hadn't been very tight and they easily slid down my legs to pool around my ankles.

"Step out of them and turn around." Sebastian stepped on the pants' crotch so I could step out, but I only managed to get one foot free before he spun me around and pressed me into the wall again.

My pulse stuttered, and for a second I was afraid being pinned like this, my face against the cold stone and his erection hard against my rear, would make me panic. I had no control in this position and I wasn't strong enough to break free. But I pushed my worry aside. I'd had to beg Sebastian to hurt me in the ballroom. He'd never hurt me during sex unless I asked for it, and even then, he might not.

He pulled off my shirt and ran his hands over my back.

"Is it true?" he asked. "Are the bases of an angel's wings sensitive?"

He teased his tongue along the invisible seam beside my left shoulder blade where my wing would emerge. It was just a whisper of a touch but it made my breath stall, the sensation rushing hot and heavy straight to my core. I'd never had anyone touch me there before, not like that, and while I knew academically that the base of my wings were an erogenous zone, I hadn't expected it to feel so good.

"Yes," I moaned.

"Show me."

He stepped back and I pushed a glimmer of power into my back and released my wings. They unfurled out of me with a flash of light, and before I could even stretch them out, Sebastian was close again, his hands roughly caressing the outer curve of my rear and slowly sliding up my back, ratcheting up the anticipation of his touch.

God, he had to be driving himself crazy as well. His breath was still wild, his erection hard as steel against my rear, and his body trembling.

Then his fingers skimmed the base of my wings and the hot, heavy need inside me thickened and all thoughts of Sebastian's amazing control disappeared. It was like his touch on my wings was a direct connection to my core, and every brush of his fingers and—

He leaned in and traced the path of his right hand with his tongue. *Oh God!*

Every tease with his mouth made my desire throb stronger.

He swept his tongue over the base of my other wing and reached around to cup my breasts.

I moaned low in my throat, leaned back, and pushed out my chest, not knowing which way to go, my body begging for more, for all of it. I'd already been turned on by having him in my mouth, feeling him tremble and tighten with something I was doing to him, now I was on fire and quivering.

His licks grew more insistent, his tongue rasping against the base of my wings and his fingers roughly kneading my breasts, and he quickly worked me up until my breath was as ragged as his.

"God, you react to this like I'm sucking your clit." He tugged me away from the wall, pushed me forward onto the bed, grabbed my hips, and pulled my rear tight against his pelvis, sliding his erection through my folds. "And you're as wet as if I was too."

He rubbed his thumbs against the base of my wings and the tremor of a climax clenched my muscles. Gasping, I ground myself against him, seeking the final connection between us, and with a shuddering groan, he pushed inside me.

Oh, yes.

The sense of his life force surged inside me, aligning with that thing in my soul that needed to feel his energy, and my desire surged with it.

SEBASTIAN

I PUSHED INTO HER SLICK TIGHT SHEATH IN ONE SMOOTH slow move and nearly came at the sexy as hell moan that fell from her lips. Fuck. She was going to make me come before I could make her. I'd barely held it together when she'd been sucking me off, and had no idea how I hadn't with her brilliant blue, glowing eyes staring up at me through her lashes. Her gaze had never left mine even after I started to lose control and began fucking her mouth as if this wasn't her first time sucking cock.

It had taken everything I had to pull out, but I'd been fantasizing about pushing back into her and being exactly where I was now since she'd asked me to join her and Hawk in our new sexual arrangement— hell, since she'd told me she loved the way I made her feel back in that alcove when we'd fucked to save Hawk.

A part of me was seriously disappointed that I hadn't been able to see her face and watch her desire build as I rubbed her wings, but I'd needed to get her wet fast because the rest of me had been screaming to get inside her, and had been screaming since I'd almost come in the hallway. And she would have gone the distance too. I'd given her fair warning, thought she wouldn't go so far against her angelic sensibilities to finish the job, and instead she'd doubled down in response. She probably would have swallowed too.

Holy fuck, how the hell did I get this lucky?

I could only pray she wouldn't change her mind about this or at least change it anytime soon, and not because she'd swallow — I could have cared less about that — but because I liked the way she made me feel, too, the way she trusted me and the connection we always seemed to make when I entered her. I'd felt it that first night, but I'd thought it was because she was a virgin and it was her angelic magic affecting me. But then I'd felt it again in the alcove, and again when I'd hurt her in the ballroom, and now here, even stronger.

The connection couldn't be because we were married. It wasn't possible for me to have accidentally married her that first night. But the Winter Court hadn't seemed to care if we were or not. It had treated her like my wife, claimed her body and soul—

And that was a problem I wasn't going to think about right now. I was balls deep in an amazing woman, barely holding myself together, and I needed to focus and make her come first, ideally screaming, because I loved the way she cried my name when she came.

I pulled out to the tip and slowly pushed back in, fighting to stay in control, but she moaned again and my balls tightened at the sound, making me rush the thrust and sheath myself with more force than I intended.

Except that only made her gasp and an amazing shiver rushed over her, a tremor in her physical body and a ripple in her unnatural full-body fae glow. A glow that emanated from every inch of her skin and feathers.

God, she was beautiful. Inside and out. There was something mesmerizing about her glowing wings, the swell of her butt, and the way her hair veiled her face as she tried to watch me fuck her. But what made her really beautiful right now was that she was being herself with no persona, no need to be in control of this, and no worry about what I thought of her or the incredible sounds she was making or the fact that I had her ass in the air and her face on the mattress.

Fucking hell.

I rubbed the base of her wings again and started to pump into her slow and steady purposefully straining my control to build her up as tight as possible. I might not have the magic, or hell, the experience Hawk did, but I still had the skill to make her feel really good.

She arched her back, her wings stretching and contracting with our movement, and her fae glow undulated under her skin like gently disturbed water.

I'd seen the fae glow undulate during sex a few times a long time ago — not all high fae glowed like that during the act — but I'd never had sex with an angel before and her wings were astounding. It didn't matter if I brush them, rub them, or held on for dear life, she reacted. A gasp, a groan, a rippling of her muscles around my cock promising her release.

It drove me crazy and it was getting hard to hold back when I sensed Hawk's essence drawing close. A hot pressure that filled the air, vibrating with the struggle to hold his power in as much as possible. Which was surprising, since he never used to care whose head he'd turned and he knew he was going to walk in on me and Amiah mid-act.

He stepped into the doorway, casually holding a pair of boots — not his because he was wearing his and they were too small — his shirt off, and his pants hanging low on his hips. Everything about him oozed sex. The hellfire in his eyes was blazing, licking his cheeks, and his lips were quirked back in a wicked, hungry smile.

He leaned against the doorframe and I slowed my pace down just a little so he could watch me pump into her. The wickedness melted from his expression and turned into pure hunger.

Fuck. He desired her as much as I did. He had to, because he didn't need to feed. If that little wakeup call they'd given me hadn't brought him up to full, the frustrating hours of waiting for her to heal herself so I could be buried inside her would have finished the job. There was no reason to want her so strongly other than pure, hot desire.

"Pull your wings in, sweetheart," I said to Amiah, my voice thick with my fight to not go out too soon. "I want you to see this."

Her wings melted back into her body with a flash of white light, and while still inside her, I urged her to sit up and straddle me, her back to my chest. Now she could watch Hawk watching me fuck her.

I ran my hands over her belly and up to her breasts, cupping them, and with a sigh, she leaned back, wrapped her arms behind my neck, and gave me her body. No questions asked, no struggling to maintain any kind of control. She just gave herself over to me, trusting I'd make her feel good, and locked gazes with Hawk.

His breath picked up and I dropped my hands on her hips to steady her and slowly pushed myself in deep.

She moaned, maintaining eye contact with the incubus, and his hellfire sparked, tiny flecks snapping free and drifting to the floor.

Yeah, I know exactly what her eye contact does.

I pulled out, slowly pumped back in, and drew another moan, and my balls grew tighter. Fuck if I wasn't going to lose it. If Hawk wanted in on this, he was going to have to join now or it would be too late.

"Are you going to join us or what?" I asked.

Another spark of hellfire and Amiah moaned.

"Kiss me, Hawk," she said, her voice breathy, her body trembling against me. "Make love to me with Sebastian."

"Anytime anywhere," he murmured. He dropped the boots, took off his pants and boots, his cock standing at full attention, and pressed his lips against hers in a slow passionate kiss that left her gasping.

He started to draw away but she tangled her fingers in his hair and pulled him back to her, deepening the kiss, showing him with her lips how she felt, how much she wanted us. His hands trailed to her breasts and I struggled to keep a slow pace, to build her desire as tight as possible before crashing her over the edge.

But Hawk urged her to grip the back of my neck again then moved his mouth to her breasts, and her breath grew ragged, which turned my breath ragged. Fuck, that was hot. Seeing him turn her on like that, making her arch into his mouth, gasping and moaning with every brush and caress and thrust between us.

Then Hawk dipped lower, flicking his tongue on her clit. The shudder of a climax inside her clenched my cock. Oh, fuck. I lost all sense of control, unable to hold myself back any longer. I thrust into her, faster and harder, striving to bring her crashing over the edge before I came as Hawk suck and licked and teased her clit with his mouth and tongue.

Her nails dug into the back of my neck, her breasts heaving with her wild breaths, and with a scream, she came hard. Her whole body tensed, clenching me tight, making me explode inside her.

For a glorious moment we were locked together, our muscles contracted, and that connection that I'd felt before pulsed again through my veins. If we'd been married and she fae and not an angel, I would have gotten her pregnant right there. Hell, even if I'd worn a condom it would have been torn to shreds.

I collapsed back on the bed and Hawk captured her lips again in another slow kiss, making love to her mouth while I was still buried inside her. But I didn't care. The two of them were so damned hot together. I'd been wanting to watch him have sex with her since he made her come in his tent while we'd all watched, and now I had a front row seat.

He worked her desire back up with a kiss that was starting to get me hard again then pulled her off me, rolled onto his back on the bed, and slowly slid her onto his cock. She released a satisfied moan, captured his gaze again, her desire simmering in her brilliant blue eyes, and started to move with the confidence of someone who'd enjoyed that position before.

The hellfire in Hawk's eyes snapped again sending more sparks drifting around him, going out before they hit the blanket, and he helped her find her rhythm, letting her take her pleasure from him.

Her breath quickly picked up again and her eyelids slid shut as she fully gave in to the sensation of him moving inside her. It was mesmerizing to watch, her body moving with his in perfect rhythm, getting faster and faster as her desire grew, her breasts heaving with each gasp and moan, and her long blond hair swaying around her.

Hawk never looked away, more sparks bursting from his hellfire, and a strange, soft awe filled his expression. No, not just awe, adoration, raw, honest, dangerous adoration.

Then her breath caught and I watched her orgasm sweep through her, starting at her hips where she and Hawk were joined and rushing up her body physically with her muscle contractions and magically with her fae glow.

It tipped her head back and drew a long throaty sigh of pleasure. It wasn't the hard, screaming orgasm I'd given her, but it was somehow more powerful, deeper. It lit up her skin like the first time we'd had sex and turned her into a radiant goddess.

Hawk released a satisfied groan and came seconds after her, his gaze never leaving her, the raw adoration still in his eyes.

"Oh, Hawk," she murmured and her body went completely limp, his magic making her pass out.

He caught her, lying her on his chest with his arms around her and his lips pressed against her forehead, that soft awe in his expression growing stronger.

Oh, shit.

He was in love with her.

It was blatantly obvious. I didn't know how I hadn't seen it before. Maybe because he'd been hiding it really well or I hadn't been looking for it, or he wasn't even aware of it—

And if he didn't realize what he was feeling, then he needed to know before things went too far. He probably didn't even know he was falling in love, didn't recognize the emotion for what it was. He wasn't supposed to be able to do that. But I'd recently seen the same expression on four guys who were madly in love, one of them an incubus, and without a doubt, love was what I was looking at now.

"Hawk," I said, keeping my voice low, hoping not to wake Amiah. If she knew the truth, she'd do everything to save him, which meant sacrificing her sexual awakening to protect him, and deep down a part of me knew that would be very bad for her.

There was something about the way we connected that a part of her needed on a fundamental level because she hadn't just connected with me but with Hawk as well. Except I couldn't recall what and needed to search my library for the answer. And again, a problem for another day.

Hawk shifted his gaze to me and offered me a sad soft smile.

Fuck. He knew exactly what he was feeling and exactly what it meant.

"It's already done. Just let me have it while it lasts."

"Maybe it'll work out." Maybe she would pick us. Hawk wouldn't go crazy if she never left him, and he wouldn't starve or kill her if I stuck around. I'd happily share her with Hawk. The things the three of us could do together...

But my soul knew she belonged with Cassius. She always had. She just hadn't realized it. If she'd still had her partially formed mating brand it would only have been a matter of time before their souls were bound together. She'd needed to accept something in her soul, something about who she was, likely about the way she connected with us through sex, and then her brand would have awakened.

Of course, she hadn't wanted her brand, had suffered agonizing pain and permanently damaged her soul to get rid of it.

Maybe she would pick us. Maybe she'd ask us to make this arrangement permanent. God, I *wanted* her to make this permanent.

Fuck. Had I fallen in love too?

AMIAH

I woke in Hawk's arms, fully satiated, my body wonderfully limp, but with a strange cold pressure in my chest as if Sebastian had gotten too far away and had activated the leash spell. Except I could feel his life force, icy, bright, and writhing against demonic darkness close by, as well as his body pressed tight against my back, and when I cracked open an eye, one of the arms on top of me was pale, glowing, and covered in thick black tattoos.

"Hey, gorgeous," Hawk murmured.

Sebastian hummed low in his throat, snuggled closer, and pressed his lips against the back of my neck. "Go back to sleep. I don't want to get up just yet."

"How long was I out?"

Hawk flashed me a wicked smile, but I got the sense he was hiding something deeper and softer with that look. The awe that I thought I'd imagined the first time we'd had sex had definitely been there this time and my connection with his life force had been stronger, turning my orgasm into something that swept through both my body and my soul.

"You were out for about half an hour," he said.

"Half an hour. Is your magic supposed to do that?"

"No," Sebastian said, his warm breath washing over my still-sensitive skin making me shiver with a hint of renewed desire. "But you were well and thoroughly fucked." He snorted. "It's a good thing you screamed at Cassius that you and Hawk were doing it because you're glowing again."

"Again?" I dragged my still sleepy attention to my hand pressed against Hawk's chest. Radiant light pulsed from my skin in time to my heart, brighter than it had ever been before — even after the first time I'd had sex. "But I'm not a virgin anymore." Jeez, there wasn't going to be any way to hide my sexual activities if I lit up like the sun every time I orgasmed.

"Some high fae get glowy when they're deeply satisfied," Sebastian chuckled.

"Swell."

"Did you really scream at him that we were having sex?" Hawk asked.

I bit back a sigh. "I still don't want to talk about it."

"Oh yeah?" Sebastian's tone turned dark and seductive, making my thoughts jump to the last time I'd said that.

"And yes, I'll happily put your erection back in my mouth to avoid talking about it."

He huffed. "Just to avoid a conversation? No other reason?" He sounded upset and I wasn't sure if he was teasing me or not.

"Sebastian," I said, shifting so I could meet his pale gaze. His eyes sparkled with mischief as if he were daring me to take him in my mouth right now. "If I could fully move, I'd finish the job you wouldn't let me finish. But maybe I should give Hawk a turn. Maybe he'd be more interested in completing the act."

"Maybe I *want* to watch you suck Hawk's cock." His mischief shifted into that hot desire I'd seen when I was on my knees and the idea made my insides throb. Oh, yeah. That was definitely on the list of things to try.

The cold pressure in my chest swelled and I frowned, struggling to get my next breath. Had Sebastian's spell easing the Winter Court's cold stopped working? And why could I barely breathe?

"Hey, if you're not into it," Sebastian said, mistaking my change of expression, thinking his suggestion didn't turn me on.

"It's not that. It's just—" Another swell and now the pressure was almost as crushing as the original leash spell and the cold suddenly bone-deep. And just like the last time, it wasn't anything physical so my magic couldn't tell me what was wrong or fix it.

"God, Amiah. Just look at me and breathe." Hawk pulled his arm out from under me and cupped my cheeks with his burning-hot palms. "You're freezing again. How are you suddenly freezing?"

"Do you know what's wrong?" I gasped, my teeth chattering.

"That's what I'm about to find out." His hellfire flared and slick sensual heat unfurled inside me, drawing a throaty moan.

I fought to keep my gaze locked on his like he'd asked and strained to draw a breath that was picking up with desire.

"Speed it up," Sebastian said, his voice somehow far away even though he was right beside me. "She's having trouble breathing with your magic in her."

"Working on it." Hawk's magic swelled, rushing around my heart, filling me with aching desperate need.

Oh, God. Now that I knew what it felt like, I wanted him back inside me. Now.

The world darkened and spun and my focus narrowed down to Hawk's unusual blue-gray eyes and the hellfire flickering inside them. There was only him, his seductive magic, and the now soul-freezing pressure.

His eyes narrowed and he pressed a hand against Sebastian's shoulder. "Do you know what this is?"

Sebastian tensed and jerked away from him. "Shit. You can let her go. That's the key inside her responding to another key."

Hawk pushed his power through me instead of pulling it away, giving me a soft, satisfying orgasm — *thank God* — and drew me back into his arms as if he didn't want to let me go. Except his body heat against the frozen pressure was too much to bear.

"Too hot," I gasped, pushing out of his grip. "I'm sorry, but you're too hot."

"Amiah—" His eyes widened with surprise then he jerked farther away, the absence of his heat making my teeth chatter. "You need to get dressed."

"And we can't stay here," Sebastian added, rushing off the bed and grabbing our clothes from the floor.

"Another key has become empowered. Titus will be compelled to go to it whether he wants to or not and we can't let him go alone."

"Agreed," I said, struggling to sit up.

"How strong is the compulsion?" Hawk took our clothes, looked at me, then handed mine back to Sebastian so he could help me get dressed.

"I have no idea," Sebastian said, helping me stand. "Any idea where the others might be?"

His full-body glow dimmed for a second and a whisper of his magic caressed the inside of my thighs, cleaning me up.

"Stop unnecessarily using your magic." I clung to him, his normally cool body temperature hot against my skin, my legs shaky, and each breath getting harder than the next one. Sure, I still had air to breathe unlike the first version of the leash spell, but this wasn't much better.

Hawk closed his eyes. "Cassius is in the kitchen and Titus is coming our way."

"He probably smells the sex," Sebastian groaned as he set me back on the bed, laced himself back in, having not lost any clothing during our lovemaking, and helped me put on the pair of soft, calf-high boots that Hawk had brought me. "I really hope he doesn't punch me in the face again."

"That shouldn't be a problem," I said, hugging myself in a useless attempt to warm up. At least I hoped it wouldn't be. Titus had said he could give me the connection I craved with him but that he needed to get his beast to settle first... except I had no idea how long that would take.

Titus stormed into the doorway, his life force snapping across my senses powerful and wild. His breath was fast and shallow, although it looked like he was breathing a little better than me, and his golden gaze jumped to me even as he dug his claws into the stone on either side of the entrance as if he needed to hold himself back.

"You can feel it too, can't you?" he growled, his expression desperate.

"Yes." I pulled the blanket on the bed around me but it didn't ease the chill.

"Guess that answers that," Sebastian said. "The compulsion is strong."

"We need to join Sparky in the kitchen. Now." Hawk reached to pick me up but hesitated. "Bane, your body temperature is colder than mine."

"Right." Sebastian picked me up, blanket and all, and we hurried to the end of the hall to the kitchen.

The kitchen was bigger than I expected, although I wasn't sure exactly what I'd expected. The kitchen area proper had lots of counter space and cupboards, and beyond was a dining room area with long tables and benches.

Cassius sat backwards on the end of a bench closest to the kitchen, staring out another long wide-open window. But his attention jumped to us the moment we entered and he stood, his fire snapping over his skin, a sudden flash of light before it turned into billowing smoke and drifted off.

"What's wrong?" he asked, thankfully not commenting on my glow or restarting our argument about my sex life.

"Another key has become empowered," Titus said, his body tense and his pupils slitted.

The muscles in Cassius's jaw twitched and he met my gaze. "And of course you can feel it too."

"Really wish I couldn't," I gasped, leaning into Sebastian's heat and clinging to the blanket. "This is like the first leash spell only with a bit more air and a lot more cold."

"I can fix that. Well, the cold at least," Sebastian said, and he, with Hawk and Titus right behind him, carried me to Cassius and sat me on the edge of the table. "I'll just add more power to the spell diminishing the Winter Court's chill."

"Just wait a second," Hawk said. "Will this go away when someone gets the key?"

"Most likely." Sebastian placed a hand over my heart. "The magic of the key is strengthening the Winter Court's hold inside you. But then I'll just pull the power back out of the spell when you get too warm."

Hawk's hellfire flared and his expression darkened. Every time Sebastian used his magic, he hurt himself and his demonic infection got worse.

I pressed my hands above his, savoring a warmth he shouldn't have had, and met his gaze. "I can manage."

"I can't fix the breathing problem, but you don't have to be freezing," he insisted.

"Just do it," Titus growled, jerking to face the window then jerking back to us, his body tense with a compulsion I could relate to. When my magic locked onto someone, it was almost impossible to ignore it, and from Titus's expression, his compulsion was just as strong.

"No. It isn't worth it."

"Amiah—"

"We don't have time to argue about this. Titus, where's the key?" I wasn't sure if I'd be able to zero in on it, but even if I did, I might not know where it was since I knew nothing about Faerie, and the best way to stop the cold and not let Sebastian hurt himself was to get the key.

Titus closed his eyes and frowned.

His life force snapped, stinging under my skin as if it was trying to get out... or in... or I don't know what.

He sucked in a breath with an effort I more than understood and clenched his hands.

"I can't find it."

"What do you mean you can't find it?" Sebastian asked. "Amiah, can you?"

Another snap, this time around my heart and the cold and pressure swelled. "I don't know anything about Faerie."

"Just try," Hawk said, his expression filled with worry.

"And hurry," Titus growled.

"Okay." I closed my eyes but couldn't manage much of a breath, let alone a calming one.

The cold and pressure heaved, angry and blue slicing through the darkness behind my lids as if I could see its magic when I wasn't capable of seeing magic otherwise, and the sense of Titus's ferocious life force grew stronger. It pulled at the cold in my heart, drawing it out like an elastic band before it *snapped* out of Titus's reach and slammed back into my chest. His life force was trying to connect to the key inside me.

"Titus, take my hand," I said, reaching out to him as

his life force stretched out the key again, tighter and tighter.

His big warm hand engulfed mine just before it snapped again and a wave of pressure crushed inside me. Titus tensed and then all sense of him, the others, and the room around me vanished. I was trapped in darkness, squeezed so tight I couldn't move, couldn't breathe, couldn't think.

My pulse roared through my body and soul. Trapped. I was trapped. I couldn't be trapped, please—

Except it wasn't me. At least I was pretty sure it wasn't me... No, that was wrong. It was me. The key was crushing me so *I* had to be trapped. *God, no.*

"Fuck," Sebastian hissed. "Get them apart she's turning blue."

The darkness squeezed tighter and the cold seeped deeper into my soul. Please. I couldn't do it again. I couldn't be trapped again—

Burning hot hands grabbed my shoulders and yanked me back, and both Titus and I cried out.

"Shit," Cassius hissed by my ear and the burning hands vanished.

My vision cleared, but the cold and pressure didn't go away. Titus knelt on the floor in front of me, his chest heaving with desperate gasps. Hawk and Sebastian each held a muscular arm, while Cassius stood a good ten feet behind me, black smoke billowing around him, waves of heat radiating from him and washing over me.

Titus's gaze met mine, his expression fierce and sad. "I'm sorry."

"Sorry about what?" Hawk shifted toward me. I could

see in his eyes that he wanted to hold me, reassure me, but knew he couldn't because of his body temperature.

"I can't find the keys now without connecting with Amiah," Titus replied.

"But you know where the next one is," Cassius pressed.

"Only that it's in the Autumn Court. I won't know exactly where until we try again inside the court barrier."

"Shit," Sebastian hissed. "That means Amiah has to come with us."

Fire snapped over Cassius's arms, sending a painful wave of heat sweeping over me, and he sucked in a deep breath and turned the flames to smoke again. "Absolutely not."

"I don't think we have a choice," I said. The pressure swelled again and Titus's life force painfully *snapped* inside me. I really didn't want to go into the field, not while in agony and my power at full. If my magic locked onto the wrong person, I wouldn't stand a chance against it. There'd be no way I'd be able to fight its compulsion to heal.

"And we don't have the time to argue about it," Sebastian said.

His glow flickered for a second, revealing the gray complexion that I now knew was a result of being infected with demonic magic. "Not to mention I still need to deal with the leash spell. I'm not sure how comfortable it would be for Amiah to stay here while I'm in the Autumn Court."

"So deal with it," Cassius growled.

"No," Hawk said before Sebastian could respond.

"Breaking the leash spell will take a lot of magic and we might need it to get the key."

Sebastian ran a hand over his spiky white and silver hair. "I really hope we don't."

"Fine." The light in Cassius's eyes flared and an icy mask swept over his expression. "What do we need to know about the Autumn Court?"

"That it's going to be a problem," Titus said. "Let's go."

Sebastian rolled his eyes at him. "All the courts are a problem."

Titus snarled back, his canines extended. "You know what I mean. The court is unstable and shattered. Come on."

Fire flared from Cassius. "Not until I know exactly what that means and how it endangers Amiah."

"Amiah is coming regardless." Red-gold scales rippled over Titus's neck and he strode toward the open window and pulled off his shirt, revealing his massive muscular chest and arms.

"He's right," Hawk said not sounding at all happy about the situation.

"We can discuss it on the move." Titus yanked off his boots and pants and my pulse stuttered at the memory of him kissing me, his erection pressed against my belly, his desire for me ferocious as he begged me to be his mate. "Someone grab these for me."

He didn't wait for a response and jumped out the window and shifted, his body turning to liquid and rapidly expanding into his stunning dragon form.

I hadn't gotten a good look at him the last time he'd shifted because he'd flown away too quickly, but now I had a spectacular view. The late afternoon sunlight shimmered on his red-gold scales, the color shifting from dark red along the top of his head, back, and tail and melting into a pale gold on his underside. Horns swept up and back from his temples and spiky ridges trailed all the way down his spine to his tail. The spine ridges along his neck flexed up then settled back down and he flapped his massive leathery wings, sending air rushing into the dining room. With a hot huff of air from nostrils almost the size of my head, he gently set his back feet on the railing and his front feet on the closest stone table.

Everyone up, he said in my head — and presumably everyone else's as well.

"Okay, problem," Hawk said, gathering Titus's clothes. "How are we going to get Amiah on you without her seizing again?"

"Maybe the connection is only made when it's flesh to flesh," Cassius said.

"Maybe," Sebastian replied. "But you should carry her anyway. Just in case."

"Not a good idea." His angel glow flared and he jerked his attention away from me, his quick refusal stinging. He was still so mad at me that he hadn't even thought about it. "Let's get Amiah and Titus together with that blanket in between them first. Maybe it's nothing to worry about."

"How about I just fly," I said through clenched teeth, trying to get them to stop chattering. "I have wings.

Four dark glares snapped to me and Titus huffed smoke to punctuate his anger. Wow, that was one way to get them to all agree on something.

"You're shivering so hard you can't stand and you can

barely hold the blanket shut," Sebastian said, lifting me off the table and back into his arms. "You can't fly."

"And you might be able to ride on Titus," Cassius added, his expression frigid.

Sebastian leaned in and pressed my blanketed side against Titus and before we'd even touched, his life force painfully snapped and a wave of pressure crushed me back into that darkness, trapped, unable to even move.

No. Get me out. Get me out get me out get me out.

Sebastian jerked me away and I sucked in a painful desperate gasp.

"You're up, Sparky," Sebastian said.

Cassius heaved in a deep breath, his expression turning colder than the chill inside me, his body shaking with pent-up rage. With a low growl and a burst of fire, he released his wings and held out his arms. "Okay. Hand her over."

Jeez. Was he really that angry that I was having sex with Hawk? Or was it that I didn't want to take his advice? Maybe he was sick and tired of me being a burden. He didn't want to protect me or carry me around but his angelic honor wouldn't let him say no, just like he felt he *had* to help me heal my broken heart.

And really, what did it matter? He'd made himself clear. The man I'd known was gone, taken away by the war, it'd just taken me twenty years to realize that. Just like it had taken me over a hundred to realize the truth about my angelic mating brand.

"Let's just get through this," I said to Cassius as Sebastian handed me over. "When this is done, you'll never have to deal with me again."

The light in his eyes flared but his gaze remained locked on Titus as Sebastian and Hawk climbed onto the dragon's back.

This way, Titus said and he turned, diving out the window and catching the air currents sweeping around the mountain with his massive leathery wings.

Cassius followed, his grip on me so tight it hurt, and we soared away from the mountain, the Wilds a vast green jungle radiating a thick moist heat instead of the dry desolate wasteland it had been when we'd arrived.

"How long until we reach the Autumn Court?" Cassius asked as he glided into a position beside Titus's neck, close enough to have a yelled conversation with the others but not too close for the key to affect me or Titus.

Faerie wants me to get there, so not long. I can see it on the horizon, Titus replied.

A spark of white Faerie magic burst from Sebastian's cheek, making him wince in pain. "Thank fucking God."

"Then start talking. What are we flying into?" The light in Cassius's eyes blazed brighter and for a second his hands were too warm. "You said the court was unstable and shattered. What exactly does that mean?"

"It means be ready to catch me or Hawk if we fall off a land mass." Another spark burst from Sebastian's skin and whooshed down into the jungle. "The land is literally shattered, its pieces floating around the court barrier with magical pockets that slow time, speed up time, move you to the other side of the court, tear you to pieces, that kind of thing. Think, not just side to side and front to back but also up and down."

Titus's life force snapped in my chest, the cold sinking

deeper into my bones, and now something heavy tugged at me, pulling me in the direction we were flying.

When the Autumn Court's ancient queen let herself be consumed by Faerie's magic, her heir wasn't strong enough to hold the court together. Titus heaved in a breath, still struggling to breathe in his dragon form. *Faerie ripped through most of the Autumn Court's high fae as well as the court itself until it found its new king.*

I shuddered at the thought. Back in the Winter Court Titus had said a court monarch needed to be strong or the court would be in chaos. He didn't say it killed high fae and broke the land until it found someone strong enough, but he also hadn't gone into details.

The new king isn't strong enough to put the court back together. All he can do is hold it as is.

"Which is probably why my mother is crazy for another heir," Sebastian said. "If the Winter Court doesn't respond to Padraigin then all the high fae in court could be killed if someone from another court manages to assassinate her."

"So she's crazy with a good reason," Hawk drawled.

"Still doesn't make what she did to Amiah right," Sebastian replied.

"Or you," I said, even though I was sure none of them could hear me, my teeth still chattering despite the blanket, Cassius's body heat, and the heat rising from the jungle.

Fire popped inside me, painfully hot against the ice, and a flash of white Faerie magic exploded from my body, a reminder that the Winter Court had claimed me and turned me into a high fae.

The muscles in Cassius's jaw flexed, but there was nothing he could do about it, he couldn't even try to fly faster because we were already racing toward the horizon as fast as we could.

"So watch where you step," Cassius said. "Got it. Are the dangerous magical pockets identifiable?"

"For the most part, yes. Even if you're not a Sensitive, you should be able to see them," Sebastian replied, which was good since only he and Hawk were Sensitives which would have left the rest of us walking blindly into potential danger.

"Anything else I need to know?" Cassius asked, as another fiery pop seared through me.

Amiah stays safe. You abandon me and the key if you have to.

Oh, hell no.

"We're not abandoning you," I yelled back making sure they could all hear me this time.

I glanced at Sebastian to get his agreement, but he wasn't looking at me. Neither would Hawk.

"Are you kidding? You agree with him?" God, they'd leave Titus behind just to protect one person. "That's not acceptable. I don't care what kind of macho agreement you all have. We're not abandoning anyone. Certainly not for me. Besides, I can take care of myself. I have the Winter Court's magic." Except I'd yet to feel a single gust since we'd gotten out of there.

"Sorry, sweetheart," Sebastian called back as another burst of light flew out of his body. "If you're not the queen or king, the Winter Court's magic only works for you in the Winter Court."

So I was powerless again.

Just great.

"You're the healer," Hawk added. "You're more useful than any one of us."

"But we can only get the keys with Titus," I insisted.

If I'm dead, no one can get the keys.

His life force snapped hard again and the pull in my chest grew stronger. I bit back a moan of pain, fighting to draw more than just a shallow breath. There was no way I was going to leave him behind. I didn't know how I'd stop the guys from dragging me away, but God damn it, Titus wasn't dying. No one was.

AMIAH

THANKFULLY IT DIDN'T TAKE LONG TO GET TO THE AUTUMN Court's protective barrier, but by the time we'd reached it, the pressure and cold and pull inside me was agonizing. It took everything I had just to stay focused on what was around me and not succumb to the dark prison threatening my consciousness even with the fiery pops of Faerie reclaiming its magic from my body.

On top of that, the reek of rotting flesh started to fill my nose, and I couldn't figure out if it was my imagination, my brain overloading on everything else, or real.

Then we reached the Autumn Court's barrier, and I knew the reek wasn't in my head. The Autumn Court was sick and dying with a gangrenous disease that oozed through its magical essence.

I didn't understand how the court could smell like a corpse, it didn't have a physical body to decay, but my magical senses, the sense that connected with the guys' life forces knew the moment I saw the court's dull gray-brown barrier, that the smell came from the court itself.

And the reek was overwhelming, making my stomach heave and my eyes water as we passed through.

"Holy fuck," Hawk gasped. "Look at that."

I quickly blinked away my tears to see what had made Hawk gasp, and my mind stuttered at what I saw, unable for a second to fully comprehend what I was looking at.

It was like we'd flown into a surrealist painting with broken chunks of land consisting of dead and dying meadows, thick, dead leafless forests, hills, low mountains, and putrid lakes and rivers floating all over the place. Below us, above us, right side up, upside down, on their side, at strange angles. Water poured down from one chunk to another, but also up and sideways. Birds flew in strange patterns as if pulled by gravity coming from one direction and then another, dipping and swirling and gliding upside down then back to right side up.

My stomach heaved again as my brain tried to figure out where the horizon was and what was right side up.

But the horizon was everywhere and nowhere.

I couldn't see a sun, but it shone "down" on the ground with the beginnings of a dark ominous sunset regardless of the ground's orientation.

Titus landed on the closest land mass, a floating meadow directly below us about the size of a football field with ragged dead grass. Above us, a flock of birds darted toward us, hit a patch of shimmering air — like air over hot asphalt on a summer's day — vanished, and reappeared sixty feet to the left.

Beyond them stood a city, its walls a deep earth tone like it was made from bricks or adobe with towers spiking out at every angle as if the city was as shattered as the land.

Hawk scrambled off of Titus, leaving Titus's clothes behind, dropped to his knees, and pressed his forehead against the ground. "I think I'm going to throw up."

"Well do it fast," Cassius said, his voice hard and cold and in command, "then pull your shit together." He landed beside Hawk. "The less time we spend here the better."

"Agreed," Sebastian said, not getting off of Titus. "Bring Amiah close and let's find this key."

At the mention of the key, my attention jumped past Cassius's shoulder. It was that way. That was where the agonizing pull was coming from.

You ready for this? Titus asked in my head.

No, but I'd rather not put it off. And Cassius didn't even give me a chance to say anything. He just stepped close and pressed me against Titus's side.

The weight and cold slammed into me and I was gone again, trapped in darkness, squeezed tight, unable to move or breathe. My soul screamed. I had to be free. Get me out. Someone. Anyone. Please. But no one could see me, no one was looking for me, and no one could hear me.

"Did you get it?" Cassius asked, jerking me away.

Yes, Titus replied, as I fought to get my breath back. But I was shaking so hard from the cold, my muscles clenched so tight, that all I could manage were desperate shallow gasps.

"Good. Then let's go." Cassius set me on my feet, the dead grass crunching with my weight, and held me at arm's length. "Hawk, stay with her. We'll be back when we get the key."

I opened my mouth to argue then snapped it shut. I wasn't sure I had the breath for an argument and even if I did, I was still a serious liability if we ended up in a fight. It was safer for all of us for me to stay where I was.

A screeching flock of crows popped into existence above us, dipped low, and skimmed the ground, then soared up into the patch of shimmering air the other birds had flown through.

But instead of appearing sixty feet to our left like the previous birds, they appeared way above us and upside down, skimming the three dead trees crowded on a small island drifting overhead like a cloud.

Sebastian jerked his thumb at them. "You honestly think we'll be able to find our way back here? You can't even count on the fractures to go to the same place every time."

Cassius frowned. "She can't come with us. Look at her."

"I'll be fine here," I gasped. "Take Hawk, he's too heavy for me. When you get the key, I won't be cold and I'll be able to breathe. I'll fly back into the Wilds and wait for you."

"And if we get caught in a time bubble?" Sebastian asked. "You could be waiting for us for years, and without Titus, his ancestral nest will remain hidden to you."

Fire sparked from Cassius's wings and his hands grew painfully hot for a second then vanished as his expression grew even harder.

"Fine." He yanked me back into his arms and leaped into the air. "Let's get this damned key."

"Everyone keep an eye out for any shimmering air," Sebastian said as Hawk scrambled onto Titus's back. "We can't afford to be separated by a fracture or get caught in a magical bubble."

"Just great," Cassius huffed and he glided back into position by Titus's neck, close but not too close, while I fought to relax my clenched muscles and draw deeper breaths.

But the gravity of another dead meadow yanked us off course, tipping us upside down, and my heart leaped into my throat at the sudden loss of right side up.

Cassius's grip on me tightened and he jerked us "down" which was the new "up" narrowly missing a shimmer with three emaciated deer caught in it, frozen in mid-leap.

I shuddered at the thought. "Are they in forced hibernation?"

Or was it something worse given their physical condition? Forced magical hibernation didn't slowly starve someone, it just froze them, stopping time. Even if they'd been starving or on the brink of death before they were frozen, they wouldn't have been dying now, not until someone outside of the hibernation spell dispelled it.

"Time bubble," Sebastian said, clinging, like Hawk, to Titus's spine ridges while the dragon quickly turned to the new right side up. "They're not frozen or dead, they're just moving very slowly."

"For how long?" Hawk asked. He had Titus's clothes captured between his arms, while he clung to the dragon's spine ridge with his head down and his eyes squeezed shut. His complexion was getting paler and paler, and while he'd managed to not throw up when we were on the meadow island, it was clear his hold on his stomach was slipping.

"It's different for each bubble. If you look at it, Mr. Sensitive, you'll be able to see just how much it's slowing time."

"Ha ha. Your shield muting my magical sensitivity only blocks out so much. Not only is the landscape fucking with my stomach, but everything is still just a little too bright," Hawk said. "You really want to risk me throwing up all over you and Titus to take a peek at the bubble?"

Just give me a heads up, Titus said. *I'll turn to the side so none of it hits me. Oh, and don't get anything on my clothes.*

"Gee, thanks," Hawk groaned. "You're too kind." But he didn't ask to stop and I didn't think Titus would even if Hawk begged because the key's pull was overwhelming.

I could barely breathe or think and from Titus's rapid, labored breaths, he was struggling as well. The pressure and cold grew so strong it overwhelmed the painful snaps of Titus's life force in my chest, and I was shivering uncontrollably when we reached a cluster of small islands butted up against each other and the source of the pull.

The terrain was mountainous with cliffs and jutting rocks mostly covered in dead trees, their twisted blackened branches reaching into the sky like skeletal fingers. A fast-moving river, too wide to jump over, sliced around the jutting rocks and tumbled over the cliffs. It started at the far island from an unknown source in the ground, swept off a cliff and twisted midair to run along an island standing sideways, and finally ended at a large roaring waterfall that crashed down onto large jagged rocks and disappeared through a shimmering patch of air.

And there at the edge of the waterfall was a sharp blue pinprick of light as bright as the sun. The key. It wrenched on my soul, begging me to become one with it and twisting with the other key inside me with a crushing, agonizing force.

"It's down there," I gasped, "by the waterfall."

I see it, Titus said and he dipped forward to dive closer.

But a mass of writhing darkness exploded to life above us and slammed into us, knocking the air from my lungs.

The world went black, the air tearing at my hair as we careened down? Up? I had no idea. Even if I hadn't been desperate for breath, I wasn't sure I'd be able to tell which way was up. Cassius squeezed me against his chest. Far off, past the howl of the wind, Hawk yelled, and Titus roared.

Fire sparked through the darkness for a second and I caught a glimpse of blue sky and ominous red sunset, then we smashed into the trees, ricocheting off thick branches and smashing through rotted ones. They sliced my face, yanked my hair, and tore at the blanket.

Cassius curled his body around me, his temperature skyrocketing.

We crashed onto the hard, rocky ground, and I was

thrown out of his grip, across jagged rocks, into a solid tree trunk, and showered with dead, rotting branches.

Something hot and sticky oozed down the side of my face.

Blood—

I was bleeding—

I struggled to catch my breath against the pressure and the cold, praying the world would stop whirling... except it wasn't just whirling. What lay ahead of me, across the turbulent water of the river, was the ground side of another island, its "down" perpendicular to the "down" of the island I was on.

And even as I tried to wrap my mind around it, the key's pull tugged my attention to my right, to the blazing pinprick of blue light through the thick dead trees and underbrush and past the jagged rocky landscape.

We were close. We just had to climb that five-foot ridge jutting up from the ground, watch out for those two shimmers, and go through those trees... which also meant the roaring in my head wasn't just because I was still reeling, but from the nearby waterfall.

Cassius was on his hands and knees between me and the glimmer, his breath heaving and his wings trembling. Some of his feathers were damaged, but not badly enough to require my healing magic if he pulled them back into his body. With a groan, his fire burst from his hands and along his wings, and he heaved himself to his feet. Blood rushed from a cut above his right eye, down his cheek, and dripped off his chin onto his thin cotton shirt that had been ripped in numerous places and was now plastered to his body with more blood.

My whirling thoughts lurched, zeroing in on his blood, and my power roared into my palms, painfully hot. Once again a thread of my magic connected with him even though I wasn't touching him and told me nothing was broken. He just had dozens of lacerations, some of them deep.

I breathed a sigh of relief as his piercing blue gaze landed on me, making my pulse pound, and his flames ignited the dead wood around him.

"Shit." He jerked away from me, sucking his flames — and the accidental fire — back under his skin.

Behind me, someone moaned and my magic jerked my attention toward the sound. Hawk sat propped up against a trunk with Titus's clothes scattered around him and a shimmer only a few feet beside him. He held his left arm tight against his chest, blood gushing from a compound fracture of his forearm, his expression tight with pain.

Beside him, Sebastian lay face down in the dirt... and wasn't moving.

My magic snapped to him and my compulsion to heal added to the cold and pressure and pull. I hadn't locked onto him, he wasn't dying, but he was in rough shape with four broken ribs and three broken vertebrae paralyzing him from the waist down.

He groaned, waking up, and his breath turned sharp and fast with the pain from his injuries.

"Just hang on, Sebastian," I gasped, using the tree beside me to help me stand, the cold making me tremble.

"What's his condition?" Cassius barked, the soldier fully taking over.

"Manageable." I clung to my ripped blanket and staggered to his side.

"Hawk?" Cassius's gaze swept through the dead trees searching for danger instead of looking at us. "Titus?"

"I'll be okay in a minute," Hawk groaned, his broken bone already sinking back under his skin.

"Are you sure about that?" an all-too-familiar dark masculine voice asked.

My pulse stalled with fear. Thick shadows rushed in surrounding us in complete darkness and a cold lifeless essence surged close. Deaglan's demon-vampire hybrid.

I tried to jerk away, but I wasn't fast enough.

A warm hand that shouldn't have been warm, grabbed the back of my neck, and a strange barely-there life force shivered across my senses. It was a writhing mix of life and death, frozen and burning, wild and too still, and in pain. So much pain.

Except I had no idea what to make of it, and it didn't eliminate the fact that if Deaglan told the hybrid to kill me he would. He might have hesitated before biting me back in the Winter Court, but he'd still ended up obeying Deaglan, and I'd seen the hybrid decapitate a man with his katana in the blink of an eye without any emotion in his black eyes.

"Don't fight him," the hybrid said in his soft low voice, so quietly I was sure I was the only one who'd heard him. "You don't have to become collateral damage."

AMIAH

SOMEONE SCREAMED, THE SOUND SHARP WITH AGONY. MY senses jerked back to Sebastian, my compulsion to heal him growing stronger, and the shadows melted away, revealing Deaglan with his foot on Sebastian's broken back.

The King of the Shadow Court sneered, the expression turning his beautiful face ugly. He wore the same black leather as before with his black shoulder-length hair pulled back at the nape of his neck, and thick shadows undulating under his skin.

Someone crashed through the dead underbrush coming toward us and the nightmare, his hellfire hair writhing around his tall thick horns, and the other shadow fae on Deaglan's assassination team who was still high-fae-beautiful but nothing compared to Deaglan or Sebastian, dragged Titus into sight.

Titus was in his human form, barely conscious, and completely naked, giving me a perfect look at his mostly unharmed body — thank goodness. He'd probably tried to shift just before he hit the ground, his scales protecting him from the tree branches. But, from his barely conscious state, it was clear he hadn't been as successful with the sudden shift before landing as he'd been the last time when we'd tumbled into the Wilds.

"Well, Seireadan," Deaglan purred, pressing down on Sebastian's back and drawing a scream of pain that made my healing magic burn hotter in my hands and squeeze tighter in my chest. "I didn't think you'd bring the whole gang. Who'd have thought I'd get to kill you and the dragon, and then get to fuck your wife."

Deaglan raked his eyes down my body, his gaze growing heated despite me being covered up in a blanket, and I knew he was imagining me in the revealing dress the Winter Queen had made me wear. Then something dark flashed across his expression, drawing a frown, but a blast of heat billowed from behind me, and his attention jumped past my shoulder before I could figure out what it meant.

"Release your fire, angel. I dare you."

The demon-hybrid tensed. His pain flared and he extended his short, sharp vampire claws in my neck, making me whimper. Now blood oozed down my neck as well as from the cut in my temple, a strange hot contrast to the cold consuming me.

"If you kill Titus, you'll never get the Heart," Sebastian gasped, his pain growing inside me making my magic heave, desperate for me to go to him.

I couldn't stay connected to him like this, knowing I could help him but unable to touch him. I had to heal him, had to ease his suffering.

"You really think I'd kill the last dragon without a way to find the keys myself?" Deaglan snapped a shadow whip around Titus's neck and yanked him out of his men's grip down to his hands and knees. "I just needed him to find the first key so I could confirm that my tracking spell worked."

"So you didn't track us here? You tracked the key," Hawk said, his left arm covered in blood but now no longer bleeding.

"Which means I no longer have a use for Titus." Deaglan rammed his foot against Sebastian's back.

Sebastian screamed and my power surged, painfully hot in my hands, up my arms, and around my heart. It exploded through the thin thread connecting us, and roared into his body in a sudden, vicious blast, using up almost everything I had.

He screamed again and Deaglan's eyes flashed wide with surprise. Sebastian grabbed his left forearm, yelled a sibilant word, and a massive force-wave slammed into Deaglan and his men but not us — a testament to Sebastian's incredible ability that he was able to select who the wave hit.

The hybrid's claws scraped through my neck as he was ripped away, thankfully before he could tighten his grip and rip out my spine. Blood spurted from my neck and I shoved the remainder of my power into me before I passed out and bled to death. I barely had any power left, but it was just enough to heal my nicked arteries — and thankfully they'd just been nicked — leaving me with still bleeding gashes, but no longer on the verge of dying.

Deaglan went flying, crashing through rotted

branches and careening off still-solid tree trunks, and the nightmare and the other fae tumbled toward the edge of the island, were sucked up by the sideways island's gravity, and crashed onto the banks of a swamp.

A cloud of greenish-gray air wafted around them, hit the gravity of our island, and was sucked toward us. It billowed around Cassius and his fire ignited the bog gasses with a sudden flash and *pop*.

"We need to get the key," Titus said, grabbing his pants and boots before standing.

I sagged to the ground, exhausted at having spent my power, shivering, and barely able to breathe. I yanked the blanket up and held it tight against my neck to slow the bleeding, but I couldn't do anything about the cold or pressure inside me.

"We need to get out of here," Hawk said, rushing to my side.

He pressed his hands over mine to help add pressure, but his flesh was so hot it felt as if the back of my skin was being burned.

I yelped and he jerked his hands away, his expression filled with worry.

"We can't let Deaglan get the key." Cassius raked his gaze over the thick brush where Deaglan had disappeared.

"What about Amiah's safety? Didn't we agree?" Hawk shot back.

"That was before Deaglan could find the keys on his own. Now we don't have a choice. Hawk, protect her. Sebastian, we need to stall Deaglan long enough for Titus to get the key." Cassius snapped out a fire whip, jerked around, and seized the hybrid by the throat mid-lunge somehow knowing he was about to be attacked.

The hybrid drew his katana and sliced through the whip in one quick move and continued barreling toward Cassius with his faster-than-most-supers vampiric speed. Cassius twisted out of the way at the last second and wrenched up his fire whip, knocking the hybrid's slice off target.

Titus — with pants and boots on but not bothering with his shirt — turned toward the brilliant blue pinprick of light, and grabbed the edge of the ragged five-foot ledge to climb up and head toward the waterfall, but a tendril of shadow shot out of the underbrush and smashed him face first into the rock.

"Ah fuck." Sebastian scrambled to his feet and sent a blast of light into the brush, his fae glow shuddering and his complexion turning gray before it flared back to life.

Hawk reached for me, hesitated a second, then grabbed my arm over top of the blanket — his hand still painfully hot through the thick material — and yanked me to my feet. He bent to pick me up when the other shadow fae swept out of the shadow of the rock beside us and slashed his long knife at us.

"Shit." Hawk shoved me out of the way and grabbed the fae's arm, yanking him away from me.

I stumbled, hit a tree trunk — showering myself with more rotting debris — but thankfully didn't fall to the ground.

"The shadow fae can jump from shadow to shadow between islands," Hawk yelled, heaving forward to keep his grip on the fae's arm and preventing him from being able to fully attack.

And we were surrounded by shadows. The invisible sun sat low on a blood-red horizon that was everywhere and nowhere, slicing thin beams through the trees. But even if it had been midday we'd still be surrounded by the forest's shadows and there wasn't a large clearing in sight. The widest open space was the rushing river and the hole in the canopy — if you could call the lattice of dead branches a canopy — where we'd crashed through.

More of Deaglan's shadows pinned Titus to the ledge while also lashing out at Sebastian who looked like he was barely holding his own, his fae glow weak and his chest heaving with strained breaths. Cassius had split his whip in two, forcing the vampire to draw his second shorter sword, but it didn't look like he was winning either.

An inferno raged around them with billowing waves of heat, making sweat instantly slick my body despite still being frozen on the inside, and I staggered to the next tree, trying to get farther away from the fire and Hawk's fight with the shadow fae.

A part of me was furious that I no longer had the Winter Court's wind. I'd be able to help all of them and Sebastian wouldn't have had to risk his life by channeling magic while infected with demonic magic. But the only thing I could do right now was get out of the way. At least I was out of magic and there wasn't a chance that I'd be forced to heal one of Deaglan's men or worse, Deaglan.

Deaglan's writhing shadows shoved through the trees, breaking the trunks with sharp cracks, and sending them tumbling into the fight toward everyone with resounding *booms*. Everyone scrambled to get out of the way, and Titus wrenched down, the edge of the ledge breaking the fall of the trunk crashing toward him. A reeking cloud of debris and fine particles filled the air and swirled with the black smoke billowing from the fire started by Cassius's inferno. Some of it gusted into a shimmer and froze, a mix of fire, smoke, and particles, caught like smoke in volcanic glass.

Deaglan stormed through the passage he'd made and sent another flurry of shadows at Sebastian and Titus, as well as snapping a shadow whip to the sideways island and yanking the nightmare back onto our island.

My pulse stuttered. The guys were barely holding their own. Adding the nightmare could tip the battle in Deaglan's favor.

And there still wasn't anything I could do.

I couldn't help them. I couldn't heal them anymore. I—

I *could* try to get the key. No one was paying attention to me and with my exhaustion and the key's pressure and cold I couldn't move very fast... which wouldn't help if getting the key turned into a mad dash, but it would help if I didn't want to make any fast movements that could draw someone's attention.

I staggered to the next tree trunk over. Titus was trying to climb an outcropping protruding from the forest floor and there was no way I'd be able to haul myself up, especially while still trying to maintain pressure on my neck wounds, but the outcropping turned into a steep hill the closer it got to the river. If I could ignore the pull of the key screaming at me to go directly to it, and slip between those two large shimmers at the top of the hill, I should be able to climb that slope.

The shadow fae heaved free of Hawk's grip and yanked his blade across Hawk's gut. Hawk jerked back far enough to not be completely gutted, but the blade still sliced flesh. It made him scream and stumble and the shadow fae lunged in, his blade aimed for Hawk's heart.

I cried out, unable to do anything, and a blast of fire slammed the shadow fae into a nearby rock and knocked his knife from his hand.

Hawk dove for the blade, his rapid healing having already sealed the laceration in his gut shut, and grabbed it before the stunned shadow fae could regain his senses. My incubus slashed at the shadow fae who scrambled out of the way, closer to me, and Cassius snapped a fire whip at the man, yanking him away from me. But that opened Cassius up to the hybrid who sliced down at his head.

Cassius wrenched out of the way and for a second it looked like the hybrid had missed. Then blood rushed down the front of Cassius's shredded shirt, the katana's tip having sliced a deep line from Cassius's collarbone to his hip.

With a howl of pain, he turned his fire inward and cauterized the wound, and shot a massive blast of flame at the hybrid, sending him tumbling into the inferno behind him that was growing by the second and starting to threaten Deaglan, Sebastian, and Titus.

Everything within me screamed to help them, heal

them even though I had no power left. But the only way I could help was to get the key.

I yanked my attention away from them.

Get the key. The fight wouldn't end if I got it, but Titus and I would no longer be in pain and we could all escape.

Shivering and stumbling, I staggered from one tree to the next, then to a large rock, and another tree trunk, the ground's slope getting steeper and harder to climb. My breath sawed in my chest and my hands were getting tired from holding the edge of the blanket against my neck. The guys yelled and grunted, trees crashed to the ground sending up more clouds of debris, and Cassius's inferno sent waves of heat washing over me.

I just needed to get up this hill. I just needed for them to keep ignoring me.

Someone screamed, the sound sharp, filled with pain, jerking my attention back to the fight.

Hawk yanked the knife from the shadow fae's shoulder and kicked him into the side of the hill where the ledge just started to form, while Deaglan with ragged shadow wings tore through gnarled tree branches overtop of Titus and Sebastian and flew toward the key. But Cassius seized his ankle with his fire whip and slammed him back to the ground.

The hybrid sliced at Cassius's side with his katana and Sebastian sent a force-wave crashing into, knocking him off his feet toward the sideways island. The gravity yanked on him and he dug his sword into the ground and clung to it with both hands, letting his shorter sword fly into the bog.

Cassius sent a blast of fire at the hybrid, breaking his

grip and sending him hurtling toward the bog, but Deaglan grabbed the hybrid with a shadow whip as Titus jerked himself onto the top of the ledge and seized the front of Deaglan's leather jerkin.

With a roar, Titus smashed his fist into Deaglan's face and the Shadow King lost control of his whip, tossing the hybrid into a tree at the top of the ridge, twenty feet away.

Sebastian scrambled up to join Titus, wrapping bands of light around Deaglan, but the nightmare lunged up beside him, slashing a knife the length of his forearm at him and forcing Sebastian to release his light and dive out of the way.

Cassius half flew half dove to the top of the ledge and, yanking his wings inside his body at the last second, tackled the nightmare. They tumbled over the ragged ground and slammed into a tree which burst into flames.

It didn't look as if anyone had noticed me, or at least realized I was heading to the key, but they were still getting closer. If I wanted to get there first, I was going to have to hurry up.

I released one hand on my blanket and heaved myself over a stony outcropping overhanging the river and avoided a shimmer. Below, the water churned and frothed, crashing against rocks and spraying me with a putrid mist before plummeting over the edge of the island.

The pressure and cold pounded inside me, the key's pull tearing at my insides and blood oozed down my neck from the side I'd let go. Just a little farther. That was all.

I staggered the remaining few feet up the hill, each breath a shallow agonizing gasp.

The trees gave way to uneven barren rock, and the key, a miniature blue sun, blazed at the edge of the waterfall about fifty feet away. And between me and it, two shimmers, one with the ground blackened beneath it, and the other small unlike any of the other shimmers I'd seen so far. This one was more like liquid, the air undulating instead of shimmering and quickly growing.

My thoughts stuttered.

I'd seen that before.

That wasn't one of the Autumn Court's dangerous shimmers, it was a portal. The same kind of portal that had yanked us all into Faerie in the first place.

The portal swelled to double a man's size and the Winter Court high fae with the red and silver hair who'd pleasured the queen, along with her werepanther, and a group of ice guards stormed out.

"Get the dragon, Prince Seireadan, and his wife," the winter fae commanded, his gaze jumping to me the second he was through.

I staggered back, hitting a tree trunk before falling on my rear or worse tumbling down the hill or into the river.

"You can sense the key too?" I gasped.

"What key?" the man asked. "I'm tracking your connection to the Winter Court."

"Stop looking at the angel, Noaldar," the werepanther yelled. "Freeze that fire."

The winter fae, Noaldar, jerked his attention up and his eyes flashed wide as if he hadn't noticed there was an inferno blazing around us.

"Hold her," he snapped to an ice guard, then bolted a few feet across the hill, heading toward the ledge. His full-body glow flared and he raised his hands, sending a frozen blast of wind roaring through the trees and putting out the fire.

All eyes turned to Noaldar, the fight momentarily forgotten for a heartbeat.

"They've got a tracking spell on Amiah," Hawk yelled.

"I can see that," Sebastian snapped back as a blast of cold magic swept through me making my teeth chatter. "Track her now, assholes."

"I don't need to. I'm dragging you back to the Winter Court," Noaldar replied as Deaglan shot a shadow spear through Sebastian's shoulder, drawing a scream of pain.

"Protect the prince," the werepanther commanded, running toward the fight, his fingers extending into claws.

All the ice guards turned toward Sebastian.

"No, one of you secure the prince's wife." Noaldar turned back to face me but didn't make it all the way around, his gaze landing on the key instead.

The ice guard Noaldar had originally commanded to hold me, grabbed my arm, and Noaldar took a hesitant step toward the key.

I heaved against the ice guard's grip, but even if I hadn't been weakened by the key or the loss of my magic, I wouldn't have been able to break free.

A ball of fire shattered the guard's arm into ice chunks, releasing me, and it stumbled back, tumbled into the river, slammed into a large rock, and shattered, its pieces tumbling over the waterfall.

"Amiah," Hawk yelled, running toward me.

"No, protect the key." I pointed at Noaldar bolting toward the key.

But the shadow fae popped up from a shadow in front of Noaldar and attacked, slashing his knife at the winter fae's gut and making him stumble dangerously close to the shimmer with the blackened earth.

Deaglan tossed two of the ice guards onto the sideways island, sending up another cloud of bog gasses that hit the fire pouring from Cassius's arms. It exploded with a violent *whoosh,* stunning three more guards still in the middle of the fight as well as the nightmare.

Hawk changed directions, stabbed the nightmare in the back, and wrapped an arm around his neck, seizing the opportunity to attack the man while he was stunned, while Titus rammed his fist into the chest of one of the ice guards, shattering it. I wasn't sure why he hadn't shifted, although he was still trapped in the trees and even if he made it to the clearing where the key and the waterfall were there still wouldn't have been a lot of room for him and anyone else. He was just as likely to knock a friend off the island as he was an enemy.

I wrenched my attention back to my goal. Noaldar and the shadow fae fought directly in front of me beside the shimmer and I wasn't stupid enough to head closer to the fight with everyone else, which left me the narrow ledge running alongside the river.

I staggered toward it, clinging to the rocks to keep my balance, and inched my way to the other side. If I could make it, I'd be right there. I could get the key and we could escape.

"Secure the prince's wife," Noaldar yelled, sending the shadow fae tumbling back with a blast of frozen air.

But the fae hit a patch of shadow, vanished, and popped up beside Noaldar, and sliced at his ribs.

The closest ice guard jerked toward me and grabbed for my arm. I heaved back, but I wasn't going to be fast enough, not without losing my balance so I shoved the last desperate glimmer of my power into my back and release my wings.

They manifested through the blanket as if the blanket was a part of my clothing and I didn't have time to fix the problem.

I leaped in the air to escape and the ice guard lunged at me. He missed my foot but seized the edge of the blanket and yanked me down, using his enormous strength, to bring me crashing back to the river's edge.

"Amiah." Cassius scrambled toward us, blasting the ice guard into the river.

Behind him, Sebastian sent a force-wave at Deaglan, sweeping up debris and ripping more branches from the trees, but Deaglan sliced through the wave with his shadows and flew closer toward the key.

"I don't think so." Cassius seized Deaglan with his fire whip and wrenched him to the ground.

The King of the Shadow Court snarled and his shadows swept around Cassius's fire, rushing down the whip and crashing into Cassius.

With a scream, Cassius dropped to his knees, and the shadows surged under his skin then ripped out of his body, taking his inferno with them in a brilliant, fiery blast. Now not even a hint of smoke curled from his hands.

My pulse stuttered. He was out of fire. Deaglan had taken Cassius's fire.

On instinct, I jerked toward him as Noaldar shoved the shadow fae into the shimmer with the blackened ground, drawing a heart-stopping howl. The shimmer's magic tore through the shadow fae at the cellular level, disintegrating him in the blink of an eye, making Noaldar's eyes flash wide in fear for a second. Then the winter fae bolted toward the key and slammed his shoulder into me to get past, knocking me back. My foot hit uneven stone and debris and I tumbled into the river.

The blanket was instantly soaked, weighing me down. A small part of me knew I had to pull my wings in to get rid of the blanket, but the rest of me was screaming for air, and then I crashed into a rock and my thoughts scattered.

Strong hot hands grabbed me and jerked my head out of the water long enough for me to catch a breath before we crashed into another rock and another.

Cassius's brilliant blue gaze met mine for a second. He'd jumped in and saved me without thought to his own safety. Like he always did.

And then we plummeted over the waterfall, crashing against the jagged rocks and through the shimmer.

SEBASTIAN

Noaldar, a trusted member of my mother's harem, body checked Amiah into the river and my heart froze. Everything froze. My thoughts, fears, even the agony of the demonic magic consuming me from the inside out. There was only that horrific moment where Noaldar collided with her, the blanket tangled around her wings, and she went under the water.

Cassius, without a hint of fire, dove in after her with no hesitation, while Hawk screamed and started running toward her.

My thoughts lurched back into action and I started running too. But just like Hawk, I was too far away to save her. Titus howled and his beast took over, shifting him into his dragon form despite the trees caging him in, his wings crashing through the rotting wood, his tail thrashing trying to break free as he strained to get to her.

Noaldar didn't even glance over his shoulder. He just grabbed the key, created a portal, and disappeared, leaving behind the guards and the werepanther —

someone my mother must have acquired after I'd left court because I didn't recognize him or know his name.

I scrambled to the river's edge and caught a glimpse of blond hair and green blanket crash against the rocks then tumble over the waterfall.

Oh, God, no.

"Titus, catch them." I raced to the waterfall's edge and the pressure of the warped leash spell filled my chest, heavy but not painful. It was already too late. They'd already tumbled through the shimmer and gone to wherever the waterfall emptied out, which could have been one spot or many spots.

Titus spat fire at Deaglan, clawing through the shadows holding him down, broke through the trees, and careened to the front of the waterfall as Hawk scrambled up beside me, his chest heaving, his clothes covered in blood.

She's gone. She can't be gone. Titus pulled his wings in to dive into the shimmer after them.

"Titus, wait. It might not take us to her," I gasped. We couldn't afford to be separated anymore than we already were, and frankly Titus was my and Hawk's only way off the island.

Titus snarled at me but didn't go after them, and Deaglan snapped a shadow whip around my neck and yanked me away from the edge.

The werepanther lunged at him, severing the shadows with his claws before I fell over, but I barely managed to keep my balance.

"Secure Prince Seireadan," the werepanther yelled, and one of my mother's ice guards barreled toward me.

The demon-vampire hybrid rammed his shoulder into the guard, sending the construct flying into a shimmer that disintegrated it like it had disintegrated Deaglan's shadow fae assassin.

But I didn't have time to catch my breath. More ice guards raced toward me along with the hybrid and the nightmare.

I turned to face them as the demonic magic surged, searing through my whole body, and my knees gave out.

God damn it. I couldn't afford to go down, not with Deaglan determined to kill us, or in the very least determined to kill Titus. And while my mother's werepanther and constructs would protect me and Titus, they didn't stand a chance against Deaglan. Hell, the three of us with their help didn't stand a chance right now.

God. I couldn't believe Deaglan had figured out how to cast a spell that would track the keys. The kind of power he'd have needed to cast something like that would have been a hell of a lot more than he'd had the last time he'd tried to kill me.

But then, I'd grown in power in the last three hundred years. Deaglan probably had too.

And right now, he wasn't being consumed by a foreign magic.

Hawk grabbed me, slung my arm around his neck, and hauled me back to the waterfall's edge.

"Titus, get us out of here," he said, throwing us over the edge and just trusting that Titus would catch us.

Titus swooped in, snatching us in his claws. He dove around a cluster of nearby islands, hit the gravity of an upside-down island, jerked to the new right side up, hung a quick left, and darted around another large island, all the while keeping something between us and Deaglan.

I tried to keep an eye out for Deaglan's shadows, praying he was also exhausted and wouldn't bother chasing us, but with Titus's erratic flying and the sudden jolts to new right-side ups, it became harder and harder not to squeeze my eyes shut and pray I wouldn't throw up.

After a few minutes, with the key's island long out of sight, Titus landed on the edge of an island with a meadow large enough for him to land and a copse of dead trees big enough for us in our human forms to hide.

He gently set us down, and Hawk, on his hands and knees, promptly threw up. I dragged myself a little farther away to avoid any splatter in case he wasn't done, and Titus did one of his amazing almost about to land shift into human forms just before touching the ground.

"We have to go after her," Titus said, grabbing Hawk by the arm, hauling him to his feet, and helping him stumble into the trees. "She's weak. Even with the key's pressure gone, her angel glow was weak. She used all her power healing you." He glared at me as if her using her power on me was my fault. "She'll be exhausted."

At least he hadn't just left us.

I staggered after them, clinging to the trees to keep my balance.

"Cast a spell like the one your mother's man did to track her," Titus said, "or highjack it or something before he casts it again."

"I destroyed it and Amiah's concealment charm is still working. Noaldar is a decent enough sorcerer but the only way he'd managed to track her was because my mother crafted a complicated spell using Amiah's connection to the Winter Court. Noaldar can't cast it at all, and my mother won't be able to repeat it quickly."

"And you can't cast it?" Titus growled.

"Even if he could, he shouldn't," Hawk said, clinging to a tree trunk looking like he was going to throw up again. "And don't you dare try."

Titus jerked toward Hawk, seized his tattered shirt, and yanked him nose to nose. "So what, you have sex with her but you don't care what happens to her?"

Hawk's hellfire flared and while I doubted Titus could see it, it was clear Hawk was barely holding himself together. He was just as crazy to save her as Titus was, maybe more so, and the only reason he hadn't just run off to find her was because he couldn't fly.

"She's not alone. She's with Cassius. She'll be okay long enough for us to figure out something that doesn't kill Bane," he replied as if he were trying to convince him of that.

"I can try casting something," I said as the demonic magic burned hotter.

I had to.

Yes, she was with Cassius, but she was also without magic and injured. That hybrid had sliced up her neck and she'd still been bleeding when she'd fallen into the river. Not to mention Cassius had been seriously injured. For all I knew they were lying helpless and unconscious and Deaglan was using the key finding spell to find her.

Except if he could have done that, he would have come after her in the aerie. Even if the aerie remained hidden from outsiders, it didn't mean outsiders who had a way to find it couldn't. It just usually took an extreme magical effort that very few fae possessed.

"Don't you dare cast anything," Hawk said, clinging to Titus's hand, his toes skimming the ground. "If the demonic magic doesn't kill you, the effort to channel any more magic right now will burn you up. Your aura is already on fire."

"What's he talking about, Seireadan?" Titus growled, dropping Hawk back to the ground and glaring at me, his beast barely under control.

"I'm infected with demonic magic," I gasped. "Long story."

"And your shoulder is bleeding," Hawk added.

I dragged my attention to my shoulder and the blood gushing out of it. I couldn't even feel that pain, and I had no idea if I had any other injuries.

"You should put pressure on that." Hawk yanked off his shirt and staggered toward me. "Just sit."

His shirt was filthy, but I was more likely to die from blood loss at the moment than I was of an infection, so I sagged to the ground, using the tree to prop myself up. Hawk bunched the tattered fabric on both sides of my shoulder and applied pressure behind me on the exit wound while I tried to press against the entrance wound.

Titus heaved in a big breath, blew it out, and crouched in front of me. "You need Amiah."

We all did. We barely knew her and I was pretty sure we were all in love with her.

Even Titus.

Except if Titus was in love with her, why hadn't he

ripped out mine or Hawk's throats? He'd seen us in that bedroom getting dressed, the room smelling like sex. He knew we were still sleeping with her and dragons were like wolves. They didn't share well with others.

And that was a question for another time.

"Fuck." I tried to focus my thoughts, but the demonic magic surged again, stealing my breath.

Fuck fuck fuck.

"How are we going to find her if we can't use magic?" Titus asked. "Can you track her through the leash spell?"

"No. It's too warped." And for a second a part of me wished I hadn't had to change it. If I hadn't, I could have found her... and she'd have suffocated to death by now.

"You shared a connection when the key called you," Hawk said to Titus. "Can I touch you, see if that connection is still there? I might be able to make it stronger so you can find her, but you're not going to enjoy the side effects."

Meaning Hawk was going to make Titus hard and frustrated with few options for release. Which was beyond cruel. The man hadn't gotten laid in over five hundred years. And while he could jack off, that wasn't going to be completely satisfying, just like the last two times we'd had Hawk's magic burning through our systems.

Titus dug his claws into the hard-packed earth. "Whatever it takes. Just do it."

Hawk helped me shift so the tree trunk kept his ruined shirt in place at the back of my shoulder and turned to face Titus. "Take a breath and try to relax."

Titus glared at him and his canines extended into fangs.

"Okay. Don't relax. Just don't punch me in the face, then."

"I can't make any promises," Titus growled back.

"Swell." Hawk pressed his hand on Titus's bare chest over his heart and closed his eyes.

Titus tensed, his breath suddenly fast, and he released a shuddering growl. "Make it quick."

A hint of sensual magic teased my senses, thankfully not overly strong, since Hawk wasn't my type. Sure, I'd happily share Amiah with him and not care about the closeness that came with that, but without Amiah, he didn't turn me on. Amiah, on the other hand, would have been instantly flushed with desire, her pupils dilated, her breath picking up, and her breasts pushed out silently begging for them to be sucked on.

The demonic magic inside me flared, stealing my breath and all thoughts of Amiah. For a second there was only the acidic burn coursing through my veins.

Fucking hell.

I needed to get back to the mortal realm and deal with this infection. And pray to God Sargos, the demon I'd hired to pull the magic out of me wasn't completely pissed that I'd stood him up for our first meeting. I wasn't sure what I was going to do if he refused to help me instead of just raising his price. There wasn't anyone else in the area that I knew of who could do it.

"Got it," Hawk said, his eyes still closed.

Titus groaned, every muscle in his body contracted and trembling. Then he gasped and his eyes flew open, wide with shock. "I can feel her. She's far away, but I can feel her."

Hawk sagged back, his breath too fast as well. With the burn of the demonic magic, I couldn't tell how low Hawk's magic was, but it was a safe bet that manipulating Titus's connection to Amiah had drained him.

"Fuck," Titus groaned. "Just feeling her isn't enough."

I couldn't have agreed more, and from the look on Hawk's face, neither could he. But we had a way to find her. We'd get her back. Safe and sound.

Please, God. Safe and Sound.

AMIAH

THE SHIMMER DUMPED US ALONG WITH A HEAVY BLAST OF water into a deep, surprisingly clean pool, and the blanket dragged me down. My lungs screamed for air and I tried to kick up and reach the surface but after having spent all my magic, I was too weak to swim against the blanket's weight. I needed to pull my wings in and get rid of it, but I didn't even have enough power to do that and wouldn't for at least ten or fifteen minutes.

Above, the water grew still like glass, and a small, far off part of my mind knew that meant the shimmer on the other end of the waterfall had switched locations and was sending all of its water someplace else. It was peaceful, and heavy, getting darker, and still cold. God, it felt like I was always going to be cold.

At least the agonizing pressure crushing inside my chest and the key's painful pull were gone, replaced by the weight of the leash spell — which was nothing in comparison. Someone had gotten the key.

I could only pray it had been one of my guys.

And that they weren't too badly hurt.

Because I wasn't going to be able to save them.

I couldn't even save myself.

Then Cassius's face swept close, his weak angel glow barely visible in the darkness, and he grabbed my wrist. He yanked me back up to the surface and hauled me to the pool's rocky edge, dragging me half out of the water before collapsing to his hands and knees, coughing and gasping for breath.

I lay face down against the cold rocks, drawing in desperate breaths and coughing up water as well, choking between the two. Exhaustion pulled at my limbs and the world whirled and lurched around me. Warmth oozed from my neck and across my temple.

I was still bleeding.

And I was too tired to do anything about it, let alone move... or think. My thoughts were spinning as quickly as my vision, and getting just as dim and far away.

"What were you thinking?" Cassius gasped, heaving himself up to sit back on his heels and scanning the area around us. "You ran straight into the middle of the fight. Again."

Really? Those were the first words he wanted to say to me after falling over a waterfall?

I tried to glare at him— *wanted* to glare at him. But I couldn't turn the thought into action and couldn't focus on his wavering form for a good glare. Even if I could, he wasn't looking at me so the effort would have been wasted.

A stinging wind gusted around us, rolling dead leaves across the rocks in front of me and rustling through the trees seconds before a sudden, violent rush of water exploded behind us, sweeping waves up from my waist to my cheek.

Cassius jerked his attention to the pond behind me. "We can't stay out in the open like this."

Right.

We needed to move.

I had to get up. But I still couldn't force myself to turn the thought into action. All I could do was lie there and shiver, and pray the world would stop spinning.

"If any of Deaglan's men or the ice guards come through the shimmer we're in trouble." His gaze finally landed on me and his eyes flashed wide. "Shit, Amiah. We have to get you someplace dry and figure out how to stop your bleeding."

Before I could say anything, he picked me up, holding me with one arm under my knees while bracing my chest against his, making it easier to wrap an arm across my back with my wings still out. He didn't even bother asking me to pull them in, which spoke to how bad I must have looked.

The sudden movement sent the world lurching, turning the living autumn forest behind him into a barely visible kaleidoscope of reds, oranges, and yellows, as if we were in the mortal realm and not in the dying Autumn Court.

I caught a glimpse of what could be a path and more large jagged rocks protruding from the ground like the dead island where we'd been, then Cassius turned, making the world lurch again, and headed in the direction of the path.

Now I could see the pond where we'd been dumped, its water trickling down a thin rocky riverbed and disappearing into the forest's darkness. Overhead, was a hint of opalescent glow from the court's barrier as if the gangrenous disease consuming the court hadn't yet reached wherever we were. And I was sure if I could focus past the cold and exhaustion, my magical senses would confirm that.

As I watched, water exploded from a shimmer thirty feet above the center of the pond and poured down, sending waves washing against the shore and a swell of water rushing down the riverbed, before vanishing a few seconds later.

"About thirty seconds," Cassius said, but I was pretty sure he was talking to himself and even if I wasn't sure, I couldn't form coherent words to respond to him.

We crashed through the forest — so maybe that hadn't been a path — Cassius not seeming to care if we left a trail or not, choosing speed over caution.

The forest grew darker, but I couldn't tell if it was because the sun had finally set or if it was because I was on the verge of passing out.

All I wanted was to close my eyes and go to sleep, but my shivering was so violent it kept jerking me awake, and a small part of me screamed that passing out was a bad idea.

Except I couldn't figure out why.

I'd get my power back faster if I slept.

And I wouldn't feel the cold if I was unconscious.

The world lurched and somehow we'd gone from the

forest to a cave and Cassius was crouching and setting me on the cold ground.

He leaned me sideways against a rough stone wall and cupped my face between palms that were barely warm. "Just hold on. I need to get wood for a fire. I won't be long. See if you have enough power now to pull in your wings."

He hurried into the darkness and I dragged my thoughts to my wings. I couldn't tell if I had enough power to pull them in or not. The magic flame in my palms that never went out no matter how much magic I used was barely there… or I was barely there. Perhaps my mind was the problem and I needed to concentrate harder.

I struggled to focus. I just needed to push a little bit of power into my back and flex my shoulder blades to pull them in. That was all I needed to do.

Just push a spark of magic.

Just move a fraction of an inch.

My thoughts narrowed down to that. Just an inch. Just a spark.

I strained against the cold and exhaustion and the emptiness in my palms.

Just. Pull. Them. In.

With a desperate ragged cry, I pushed every last scrap of power from my palms into my back and heaved my wings back into my body. The effort left me gasping, my shivers growing stronger, my body weak, and the weight of the soaked blanket slipped from my shoulders.

God, I just want to pass out. Everything will be fine when I wake.

My eyelids slid closed and I leaned my cheek against the stone wall.

It would all just go away, the pain and the cold and the numbness seeping through my muscles, if I just passed out. Just for a few minutes.

Then strong hands jerked me forward. "Come on, Amiah. You've got to stay awake. You *know* this. Open your eyes."

I dragged my eyes open and met Cassius's brilliant blue gaze. Just like I had that night he'd rescued me from the faith healer...

Except there was something wrong with his eyes.

I frowned and raised a trembling hand to his cheek. "Your angel glow is barely there."

"And yours is practically gone." He pulled off my boots, drew me forward, balancing my body against his, and yanked off my shirt.

I slid my hands over his bare shoulders, savoring the feel of his well-developed muscles as he worked to hold me—

Wait a minute.

"You're not wearing a shirt?" I said, my words slurred.

My gaze dropped, as he rose into a crouch, lifting me up with him, and I realized he'd stripped down to his boxer briefs.

He reached for the laces on my pants and my heart lurched.

I wasn't wearing any underwear—

I hadn't had underwear since I'd last been in Sebastian's apartment in the mortal realm—

And I wasn't wearing a top anymore—

I was going to be naked, and as much as I desired Cassius, our relationship wasn't anywhere near being naked together. I wasn't even sure if we were still friends.

"Cassius, wait—"

"You'll die of hypothermia in your wet clothes. If you were thinking straight, you'd know that." He pulled my pants down to my ankles and froze.

"Cassius—" I gasped again.

God, was that the only thing I could get out?

"It'll be okay," he said through gritted teeth, although I couldn't tell if that was to himself or me.

He carried me the few feet to a small fire and laid me on my side facing it, but the flames weren't nearly strong enough to thaw the cold inside me, and no matter how hard I hugged myself I couldn't stop shivering.

"Tell me what else I'm supposed to do," he asked, wrapping his body behind me and holding me tight.

My lids started to slide shut again. Not even the flesh to flesh contact could draw my thoughts beyond the cold and exhaustion.

Cassius gave me a squeeze and my lids flew open. "Amiah. What else am I supposed to do?"

"You don't know?" I frowned, my eyes closing again. "I was sure you knew."

"So tell me." He gave me another squeeze and pressed his palms against my chest discretely high enough that they wouldn't hit my nipples.

My thoughts stuttered at that and I realized his hands were getting warmer, his arms too.

"Amiah. What do I do?"

"What do you—? What were we talking about?" God,

I couldn't get my thoughts to focus, and I was sure I should be thinking something or blushing or aching with desire, or being mortified that I was naked in Cassius's arms, but I couldn't keep a thought in my mind long enough to fully register on it.

"Jeez," he huffed, his breath warm against the back of my neck. "Fine. What the hell were you thinking running into that fight like that?"

Really? He was going to reprimand me now when I could barely think?

"Of course you'd want to bring that up," I mumbled back, angry one second, then drifting again as a little flame in the fire, fluttering at the edge of a piece of wood, caught my attention. "Right when I'm exhausted and can't think straight."

"Yeah, I'm a real asshole right now, but—"

The flame sparked, jolting me closer to consciousness. "Did you really just say asshole?" I think I'd heard him swear more times in the last few days than I had in the hundred years I'd known him.

"Bane and Hawk have been a bad influence," he said. "And right now I'm happy being an asshole to find out why you're a complete idiot. You could barely walk and barely breathe, and you thought what? Hey, I'll just saunter into the middle of a fight and risk everyone's lives by distracting them?"

"That wasn't at all what I was thinking." The little flame shrank and grew darker, my lids starting to slide shut again.

Cassius jerked me awake. "Then what were you thinking? You're smarter than that."

God, just let me sleep.

"I was thinking if everyone was busy fighting, I could get the key and we could get out of there." I would have gotten it too if that high fae from the Winter Court hadn't shown up.

"How could you even think that was a good idea? The key had practically incapacitated you, the fall left you bleeding, your neck had been sliced up and somehow you used up all your magic." Cassius jerked me again, and my eyes flew open. "And it wasn't to heal yourself. Your neck is still bleeding."

"Sebastian's back was broken." The little flame flared and joined a bigger flame and the tip of the piece of wood broke off, falling into the heart of the fire. Falling, falling. It was only a few inches, but it sent me spiraling down toward blissful darkness.

"But you didn't touch him," Cassius said.

"I know," I mumbled. *Everything will be better if I just give in.* "It's like when you stepped away from me and I still healed you back in the aerie. It uses up a lot of power and I don't really have control over it."

"Well that's just great," Cassius snapped, his tone cutting through the exhaustion, and jerking me out of my downward spiral. "Something else to worry about."

"I never asked you to worry about me." Of course he'd think that. He wasn't amazed my power had grown, that I could now heal someone without touching them — which if I really thought about it should have been terrifying since at my age, I should have been at my full magical ability already. Angels my age didn't just suddenly become stronger. Only if they branded a mate and formed a soul bond.

No, all he could think about was how it made things difficult for him, how he couldn't be overprotective of me if my magic locked onto someone and drained me without touching that person. I would have thought me not needing to run into danger to save someone was a good thing.

"If you hadn't turned into an idiot I wouldn't have to worry," he said, his tone sharp. "It's like you lost all common sense when you started sleeping with Hawk."

Oh, no. I wasn't going to justify my sex life to him again. I was too tired and, God damn it, it was none of his business.

"We're not having this conversation again." The fire snapped and the wood shifted, sending up sparks into the darkness above us. Up up up. Now I was spiraling up with the smoke, drifting, hazy, swaying. I didn't want to argue with Cassius. I just wanted to pass out—

And yet I couldn't seem to help myself. Words just kept pouring out of my mouth even though I wasn't really sure what I was saying. "Just because I'm not behaving the way I used to doesn't mean I've lost common sense or become a fool. It just means I'm different. People are allowed to change, aren't they?"

"People don't suddenly become different overnight."

They did if their beliefs had suddenly been shattered or their hearts broken like mine had. I hadn't known who I was or what I believed in. I'd never really known. I wasn't sure I knew now. But at least I was making an effort to finally find out instead of waiting for my destiny.

And I'd go back to that after I'd slept.

"It's like you've lost your mind."

God, just let me sleep.

"I realized I'd been a fool over my br— over my Marcus—" *No. Not mine.* My thoughts stuttered. "Over Marcus." That was right. "Not my Marcus. Just Marcus. Because I'd—"

Jeez, just stop talking.

I pressed my lips together. There was no point in telling Cassius about my partially formed mating brand. He wouldn't understand how horrible it was, even after he'd thought his brother had been branded to a weak human who endangered his life. Cassius still believed the angelic mating brand was beautiful and sacred, and he'd be horrified to learn I'd gotten rid of mine.

"So you decided to sleep with Hawk?" Cassius pressed.

"Yes, I did." And I was thoroughly enjoying it. My lids started sliding shut again.

He barked a bitter laugh. "Jeez, I'm an idiot." He gave me a jerk but my eyes didn't open this time. "You're sleeping with Bane too, aren't you? That's why you wanted him to help you change in the healing pool."

"I wanted him to help me because Balwyrdan kidnapped me without any underwear and you were guaranteed to freak out over that." Which was the truth, although I had no idea why I hadn't just come out and told Cassius I was also sleeping with Sebastian

"I wouldn't have freaked out." His embrace tightened, belying his words.

"Yeah, right," I replied, my words slurred, sleep tugging me deeper toward unconsciousness.

Just let me pass out.

"I wouldn't have," he insisted, his back growing gloriously warm and his body heat starting to soothe my shivers.

Oh yes.

The peaceful nothingness of unconsciousness swelled, dragging at my limbs and drawing me in.

"—underwear?"

Cassius jerked me again and my thoughts snapped back to him and the cave, but it was like he was a dream, a frustrating, bad dream, and the soothing darkness was reality.

"Amiah, why didn't you have underwear?"

"Because I'd just slept with Sebastian." There, now he knew the truth. *Now let me pass out. Please.*

"For the love of God! What's wrong with you?"

"What's wrong with me?" I tried to turn my head so I could glare at him but didn't have the strength to move. "What's wrong with you? Why are we arguing about this again? I thought I made myself clear. My sex life is my sex life. And please, I just need to go to sleep."

Cassius gave me another jerk and my lids fluttered open again. I hadn't even realized they'd closed.

"Not until your body temperature is higher."

"Not until what?"

"Your temperature. If you were thinking clearly, you'd know we need to get your temperature up before you can pass out. You were probably suffering from hypothermia before you were even dumped in the river and from the blood and growing bruise on your temple you have a concussion. That and it would be best if you pushed a little more power into your neck and maybe stopped that bleeding a bit more before you passed out."

My thoughts stuttered at that. "So you're arguing with me to keep me awake?"

That didn't make any sense.

"Asking you for detailed medical instructions didn't work," he said, pressing his lips to the top of my head. "But I knew restarting our fight would get you going."

"I'm that predictable?"

"You're that adamant. Especially when you're right."

The fire snapped, sharp and bright, jolting me back to the cave, and I struggled to focus on it and my surroundings and fight the seductive lull of exhaustion. Cassius was right. If I concentrated, my magical senses told me my body temperature was still dangerously low, I did have a mild concussion, and my neck was still bleeding. All of which could get worse if I let myself pass out.

Except focusing on my surroundings made me hyper-aware of Cassius's hot flesh against mine, his muscular arms wrapped around me, pulling me tight against his sculpted chest, and his hands so close to my nipples he'd brush them if he just shifted them the right way.

Not to mention his erection pressing against my rear.

I didn't know if Sebastian was right, that Cassius loved me, but he certainly desired me. And while yes, we were both naked — or in his case mostly naked — I was a battered wreck. I doubted I looked attractive so it had to be something deeper than just a physical attraction.

And I had no idea what I wanted to do about that.

My thoughts jerked back to the last thing he'd said.

"I'm right?"

"Who you sleep with is none of my business," he said, his tone soft and suddenly sad.

"But it bothers you that I'm having sex with Hawk and Sebastian."

"It just surprises me. Hawk can't love you back and Bane is looking for a good time with anyone and every-one. He's been adamant about never wanting a commitment."

"Probably because his ex-fiancé tried to murder him. I wouldn't want to commit to someone after that either," I replied. "Hawk and Sebastian are generous lovers, with lots of experience. They're exactly what I want right now. I'm not looking for love."

Except as soon as the words came out my heart squeezed, not necessarily because I wanted Hawk and Sebastian to love me or make a commitment, but because that statement meant what we had would come to an end and I wasn't ready for that.

"And that's what you're looking for. Just experience and no commitment?" Cassius asked. "Just because Marcus wasn't the one, doesn't mean he isn't out there."

"I'm sure." Horribly sure. There *was* someone out there fated to be my mate, and if I met that someone now I might fall in love or I might not. But now, at least, it was my choice. "Someday, yes, I'd like to settle down and have a committed relationship."

Cassius might even be that guy. Right now, in this moment, this was the Cassius who'd rescued me... except this was more than just the Cassius who'd rescued me.

This was the Cassius I'd started fantasizing about when my sexual restraint had started to slip. Strong, sexy, and naked.

He could very well have been my soul mate. Or at least this version of him, not the hardened icy soldier he'd become after the war, and if he didn't go back to bossing me around, I could fall in love with him.

He'd always been my rock, my safe place to land. I knew him, knew he loved cricket — of all sports! — hated onions and pineapple on his pizza, liked to go stargazing, and protected those he considered family with a passion verging on obsession.

Maybe I would fall in love with him.

Maybe Sebastian was right and I already had.

At least now I could allow myself to feel whatever I really felt for him without the fear that my brand would force me to fall in love with someone else.

"But I'm not ready. Not yet. I need to figure out who I am first. I wasted too much time waiting." My pulse picked up with a mix of fear at the thought of losing Hawk and Sebastian, and desire for the naked man behind me. My senses, still weak, connected with Cassius's life force and filled me with a hint of what I knew was a raging inferno on the verge of breaking free.

Except it wasn't breaking free at the moment. It was weak, his flame barely lit.

"Waiting for what? For Marcus?"

"No, not Marcus."

"Then passion," Cassius said, sounding certain in his conclusion. "The only man I've ever seen you set your sights on in the hundred years I've known you was Marcus. You want the unrestrained passion of a shifter."

I opened my mouth to argue with him that I didn't want Marcus because of his passionate shifter's nature, but a part of me had been thrilled at the idea, thought it made perfect sense. I needed him to loosen up my reserved angelic nature.

Except if I didn't deny that desire, I might not be able to move my friendship with Cassius to anything else.

And God, even weak and dizzy, the idea of moving our friendship to the next level was starting to seem like a great idea. I wasn't nearly as cold as I was before. Cassius's now gloriously warm body was melting the ice inside me, and his deliciously hard muscles were changing that ice into a soft, aching heat.

But if I didn't tell him the truth, he'd never understand why now, after so many years, I was interested in him.

A hint of the ice returned, this time as a sour churning fear in my stomach at the thought of what his reaction was going to be.

Except my soul yearned to connect with his life force in the same way I connected with Hawk and Sebastian, and in the way it yearned to connect with Titus. I needed that closeness with them.

But did that mean I needed a committed relationship with them?

When we got back to the mortal realm, Hawk was going to return to his other lovers. He said he'd still have sex with me, but he couldn't survive on just me alone, and Cassius wouldn't be able to see the difference between sex and a committed relationship. That was just the kind of guy he was and he'd want me to give up the others. Sebastian, given how he flirted with every woman he came across, would move on and not give me a second thought.

And yet I still wanted to have what I could with them. With all of them. Even Cassius.

Which meant if I ever wanted the hope of having more with him, I had to be honest about why I'd never looked at him that way in a hundred years. I had to tell him about my brand.

AMIAH

I SUCKED IN A SHARP BREATH, TRYING TO STEADY MY RACING heart. "I was waiting for my soul mate. I had a partially form mating brand, so I was waiting," I said in a rush.

Cassius stiffened, his muscles flexing around me. "You what? You *had*? Amiah—"

"It's my life. My body," I said before he could reprimand me or try to tell me how amazing a brand could be. "I got rid of it recently and even if it could come back, I'd never want it."

"Why would you do that?" Cassius shifted, sliding me to my back, his body pressed tight against my side still keeping me warm, but allowing him to stare down at me, his expression strange. He wasn't furious like I expected, but I couldn't figure out what he was thinking. "A mating brand is an amazing destiny. For there to be two angels with branded mates in this century is incredible."

"It's not incredible. It's a nightmare," I insisted. "You weren't conscious for it, but I saw what it did to Essie. When her guys were seriously wounded and she couldn't get to them, she was literally on the floor begging for someone to help them."

"But Amiah—"

"And Gideon was a wreck when Essie had been shot and nearly died," I pressed on. Cassius had to understand the truth about the brand. I wasn't crazy. I hadn't made a horrible mistake. "The brand nearly tore him apart when he tried to ignore it because he knew Essie was in love with Marcus." My throat tightened at the memory of their fear and pain. The image of Essie on her knees, screaming for help, of Gideon clinging to the wall outside Essie's hospital room trying desperately not to give into the brand's compulsion and go to her because she wasn't in love with him. "It's just another prison. I can't do that again."

"But to get rid of it you'd have to have damaged your soul."

"I can't be trapped by someone, my life ruled by them again. I just can't." Tears burned my eyes and my breath turned into short sharp gasps, the fear of being trapped, held prisoner, and hurt by someone again overwhelming me. "Cassius, I can't."

Cassius cupped my face with an ever-so-slightly too-warm hand, his eyes filled with a strange mix of grief and something else.

Probably judgment. I was a horrible angel. I'd ripped out a piece of my soul just to avoid the possibility that I'd fall in love with a stranger. For all I knew, Cassius could have been my soul mate.

Except if he was and I'd kept the brand, I wouldn't

ever know if I was really in love with him or if it was the brand making me love him.

"I want to fall in love like everyone else. I don't want some brand to force that on me. I put my life on hold for a lie." A tear broke free and trailed down my temple. "I don't even know who I really am. I had no idea that I need sex."

His eyes widened.

"You, ah— You need—" He cleared his throat. "You need sex? You sure that's not the euphoria of Hawk's magic?"

"No, there's something that clicks inside me, like a circuit being completed. It happens with both Hawk and Sebastian, and now that I know it's there, I feel... strange when I've gone without for too long... empty..." I didn't know how to explain it. "It's like I need physical contact like a shifter, my soul settles like a shifter and is stronger afterward, but it's deeper than that, something about needing to connect with their life forces."

Cassius swallowed hard. "You sure they're not your mates?"

"You really think those two are a match to my soul? I know the brand could bond me with a stranger, but it wouldn't be with someone so completely different from me. Essie might have been a being created in a laboratory intended for evil purposes, but her values, her sense of right and wrong, her goodness, perfectly aligns with all her guys."

"And you don't think Hawk and Sebastian share your values?"

I opened my mouth to deny that then closed it. Hawk

and Sebastian weren't the men I'd thought they were. They were generous and kind and compassionate, and they were willing to risk their lives for what was right. Just like I was. "I had sex with both of them before my brand was removed. It would have fully woken if either of them was my mate."

Unless I hadn't been ready. No one really knew why a brand formed. Sometimes it formed after years of knowing someone and being intimate with them, and sometimes right away, at first sight.

And none of that mattered anymore. The brand no longer controlled me.

"So you thought your brand would awaken if you and I— if we—?" Cassius's breath picked up and that ache between my thighs, the desire to be with him, swelled again.

"My brand didn't do anything when we first met, so I didn't think you were the one. But Cassius, you're my rock, my best friend. A part of me would be broken without you." Had been broken since he'd returned from the war and had been withdrawing from me. "When I decided to stop waiting, decided I wanted to fall in love like a normal person, I didn't want to risk my brand waking if we ever…" I stared into his eyes, able to clearly see just how brilliantly blue they were with his angel glow so weak.

"If we ever," he prompted.

"If we ever had sex," I said, my voice breathy.

His gaze dipped to my lips as if he wanted to kiss me.

God, please kiss me.

"And you've thought about that?" he asked, his pupils dilating, his voice husky. "About us having sex?"

"Recently. A lot."

I caressed his cheek with a trembling hand — although not nearly as shaky as before — and his expression turned pained.

"Amiah, this isn't right."

"Because I'm having sex with Hawk and Sebastian?"

Because I didn't want to make a commitment and he did.

Or was it because he thought I was a fool? He might have agreed that who I slept with was none of his business, but that didn't mean he had to join my growing list of sexual partners.

Which was actually kind of ridiculous since the total number of guys I'd slept with was two.

"Because I know you're not thinking straight. Your body has warmed up a bit, but you're still losing blood, it's a trickle now, but you're still losing it, and you still have a concussion."

"And if I was thinking straight?" God, I didn't know why I was pushing this. Even if I could see desire in his eyes and feel it from his body, that didn't mean he wanted to act on it. I needed to respect that.

"I wouldn't be able to give you what you want." The strange look in his eyes solidified into sadness, soft, heartbreaking grief. "And I certainly can't give you what *I* want."

"Because you want a commitment?" Which I couldn't give him. Not yet.

"No— well, yes. But I'd wait for you. I've been waiting

for you since before the war." He huffed a bitter laugh. "I think I've been waiting for you from the moment I saw you in that tent. I was just too dense to realize it."

He captured my hand against his cheek with his and leaned into my touch.

"God, you don't know how much I've wanted this, wanted to be able to show you that I was in love with you —" His gaze met mine again, the depths of his desire making my pulse stutter, and something in his eyes changed, a realization, a decision. "I've always been in love with you."

He leaned in and brushed his lips against mine, sending a swirl of emotions rushing through me.

Finally.

Yes.

Were we really going to make love?

How would that affect our friendship?

"Cassius—" God I wanted this. It was like his life force called to me, and just like my compulsion to heal, my soul was compelled to connect with him, complete the circuit. "Are you sure? I'm not going to stop having sex with Hawk or Sebastian right away."

"Do they make you happy? Give you what you need?"

"Yes."

"Then when we meet up with them, go back to them. Figure out who you are. I'll wait."

A shadow of sadness flashed across his expression so quickly I wasn't sure I'd actually seen it, then he pressed his lips against mine again.

His kiss was slow and sensual as if he wanted to put the desire of his hundred years of waiting into that one kiss. It reached all the way to my toes, seeped into my cells, and sank into my soul.

There was something so right about it, about finally taking the next step in our relationship. It reminded me of all the warm comfortable times we'd had together, laughing over bad jokes, watching the stars, just being comfortable in each other's company.

And yet there was a new sensation, a thread of heat, of fire, of need growing in my heart. His life force thrummed against my magical senses, and I thrilled at the feel of him, of his magic, his power, his naked body pressed close to mine.

It made the soft ache of desire within me warm and grow, and I kissed him back, sighing with pleasure, letting him know I wanted this as much as he did.

He brushed his warm fingers across my collarbone to the divot at the base of my neck then trailed them to the inner swell of my left breast.

My heart pounded at his touch and I slid my hands over his buzz cut, capturing his head and deepening our kiss.

A part of me couldn't believe this was really happening, that Cassius and I were kissing, while the rest of me thrilled at it.

I slowly teased my tongue against his lips and tongue, something Hawk had done the last time we'd kissed and it had driven me crazy.

Cassius moaned, rewarding my forwardness, but my thoughts scattered as his fingers traced the inside of my breast and his thumb brushed my nipple. Just a whisper of a touch, but it shot a spark of sensation straight to my core and made me gasp.

He did it again, drawing the same spark and another sharper gasp, and I pushed my breasts up, urging him for more than just a teasing touch.

"I wondered what that would sound like," he murmured against my lips.

"What?"

"You letting go." His fingers skimmed across my ribs. "Enjoying yourself."

"If you want me to enjoy myself, go back to my breast," I said.

He chuckled. "But you're still bossing me around."

"Pretty sure you're the one who keeps trying to boss me around."

"Pretty sure I've been failing."

He trailed kisses along the same path his fingers had taken, collarbone, divot, inner swell of my breasts, slowly, oh so agonizingly slowly, as if he wanted to memorize my body not just with his eyes, but his hands and lips too.

I was squirming by the time he flicked his tongue across my nipple, snapping more sensation through me, a mix of my desire and his fiery life force. He worked my nipple into a tight aching bud, then the other one, his pace slow, the building anticipation a glorious torture that made my breath fast and my heart race.

Then his hand shifted from my ribs to my hip where my partially formed mating brand had been and heat swelled in my skin.

My pulse stuttered and a flash of icy fear returned to my stomach.

Oh, crap.

But the moment I thought that, I realized the heat wasn't my brand reforming. The brand was gone. I could feel the hole left in my soul from ripping it out. The heat came from Cassius's palm. His whole body actually. His temperature had skyrocketed, hotter than the most powerful demon I'd ever encountered and his life force blazed against my senses.

This was just me and Cassius. No destiny, no soul bond, no fear. I could let everything go with him like I did with Hawk and Sebastian, and fully embrace my connection with him, a connection that was growing stronger by the second.

He trailed his lips over my belly, his hand skimming down my thigh beyond where the brand had ended, the heat from his skin continuing to grow, along with the heat of desire within me. He raised a gaze filled with need and awe, the look strangely similar to the look Hawk had given me, and captured me body, breath, and soul.

This was the way it was supposed to be between us, where we'd have been headed before the war if my brand had started to wake, and what had been missing in our relationship. I hadn't even realized just how deeply it had hurt me when he'd returned from the war cold and icy.

I knew now, with absolute certainty that I'd been in love with him for a long time too, and had used angelic propriety to keep him at arm's length to protect myself for when I'd met my soul mate.

But maybe that's what he was.

My soul mate.

There were still things I needed to figure out, desires I

wasn't sure I could explore with Cassius or not. I wasn't sure how he felt about having sex with more than just me.

But now that we'd realized the truth, that we were in love, we had a lifetime to figure it out. There was no need to rush. We could take it as slowly and explore our relationship as deeply as Cassius was exploring my body now... and I wouldn't have to give up Hawk and Sebastian right away.

Cassius nudged my legs open, shifting his stunning body between my thighs, the honed muscles in his shoulders and arms bunching with the movement. He teased kisses and licks across my skin, his breath hot against my folds before finally — God, finally! — he flicked his tongue over my clit.

More amazing sensation snapped through me. I bucked against his mouth as a throaty moan escaped my lips.

"God, that's the most amazing sound." He captured my hips, holding me steady, and slowly, reverently, as if he was worshiping my body with his mouth, worked me into a gasping, writhing frenzy, until my muscles contracted and a shuddering orgasm swept over me, sending my senses spinning, reminding me that I was still weak.

I clutched his head, riding the wave, and he raised his gaze back to me. His angel glow was brighter, his emotions heightened, and he held me safe and secure in his brilliant blue eyes. I'd always be safe with him, always be protected, he would move heaven and earth to ensure my safety, and I'd move it to keep this Cassius, the one I'd fallen in love with.

"I love you, Amiah. I've always loved you." He pulled off his boxer briefs and captured my lips in a searing kiss, his lips hot, his passion overwhelming, making my desire that hadn't been satiated with that first orgasm surge stronger.

His erection teased my folds, his hands roughly kneaded my breasts, and his warm flesh pressed deliciously against mine.

I curled my hips up, taking his tip inside me, letting him know how much I wanted him, needed him inside me.

"I'll always love you," he said, his voice thick, low.

Slowly — God he was going to drive me crazy with this pace! — so damned slowly, he pushed inside me. The heat of his life force flared and that piece of my soul that needed whatever it was from him, shifted and clicked into alignment, making my muscles tremble around him.

Our gazes locked, completing the circuit, and for a second he froze, his eyes ever-so-slightly too wide, as if he, too, felt the connection.

Then, with a masculine groan, he started a slow sensual rhythm, withdrawing and pushing back in, building my desire.

God, it felt so good, and I held nothing back. I freely gave myself to him, letting the feel of him moving inside me twist my need tighter until my whole body was throbbing, desperate for a release. My breath had become ragged. So had Cassius's.

His pace grew frantic, his body was blazingly hot,

smoke curling from his shoulders. Light and love blazed from his eyes, filling my heart, and my muscles contracted tight, my orgasm starting to sweep through me.

"Oh, Cassius," I cried.

Cassius gave another few hard fast thrusts then tensed and gasped my name.

I crashed over the edge. The sensation was glorious, breathtaking. It sent me whirling, tipping my head back and filling me with light and fire. My body lit up again, and his life force roared across my senses, filling me as completely as his erection did.

Fire flooded into every cell inside me and swept into my soul. I was strong like Cassius, a living inferno. My fae glow blazed brighter than ever before, and the connection with him was the strongest I'd ever felt.

I was complete. Whatever it was I needed from him, filled me.

God, I wish I knew what that was, what I needed from all of the guys.

But Cassius said he'd wait. I had time to figure it out before he'd want a commitment, and before Hawk and Sebastian went their own way.

And right now, in this moment, everything was perfect. I was in love with my best friend and I'd finally gotten him back.

CASSIUS

AMIAH HEALED HER NECK WITH THE LITTLE BIT OF POWER she'd managed to recover in the time it had taken us to make love — or maybe *because* we'd made love, I wasn't sure. She shrunk the cuts into something that would quickly scab over then passed out.

I pulled her back into my embrace, not bothering to put my briefs back on, savoring the feel of her slightly cool flesh against mine.

I didn't want to let her go.

Ever.

But I wasn't going to have much of a choice in the matter. I could already feel my fire building inside me and had maybe a few hours before I'd have to actively lock it and my emotions back down. And even after I'd locked it away, I didn't think I'd be able to keep holding her. It didn't matter if I put everything into keeping my fire controlled, my feelings for her were too strong and I wouldn't be able to hold it under my skin while touching her.

This was it. All I was ever going to get. I wouldn't ever be able to hold her again.

A satisfied sigh slipped from her lips and my heart twisted tight.

I wanted this forever, wanted to listen to the sounds she made and see the look on her face when she finally let it all go and she let me see the real her.

She was mesmerizing. Her angel's soul radiant.

I'd felt that connection she'd talked about and seen it in her eyes. Those brilliant blue orbs, so like my own in coloring, had blazed bright even though she hadn't recovered most of her magic, and her gaze had reached deep into my soul, capturing me.

I'd never felt anything like it before.

And she was right. It wasn't a soul bond.

After she'd come, her unnatural fae glow had lit up her whole body and the connection had vanished. If we'd been destined for each other— or rather if she'd still had her brand, the connection would have stayed and a matching brand would have formed on my body.

My heart clenched tighter, making it hard to breathe.

I never would have gotten this moment if Deaglan hadn't ripped out my fire.

God, I'd been terrified, helpless against him, afraid my fire was gone for good and without my magic, I'd be unable to protect her.

But my fire wasn't gone, and he'd unintentionally given me the greatest gift I could have asked for: a moment with the woman I loved, had always loved, and would continue to love until I died.

And while yes, she needed to move on, stay with Bane

and Hawk or commit to someone else, whatever she desired because she deserved to have the life she wanted, I never would.

I knew I should.

It'd be healthy to.

But she was my one.

Not because our souls were destined to be together, but because I'd completely fallen in love with her, with her determination and kindness and brilliant spirit. I'd fallen in love in the normal way, the way she wanted to fall in love. I'd even share her with Bane and Hawk if that was what her soul needed — what she seemed to think she needed because of the connection she made during sex — and I'd comfort her when they moved on. Because they would. That was their nature.

Except with my inability to hold back my fire, I wouldn't be able to comfort her very well, not the way I really wanted to.

I pressed my lips to the back of her head, trying to get closer, to touch more of her while I could. I needed to memorize how this felt, seal it in my mind so I'd never forget this one amazing moment.

God. There had to be a way to keep this, to fix me.

But the only being I'd ever heard of who had the power to heal an angel's magic had been the archangel Michael, and that bastard was thankfully long dead.

Maybe Bane would be able to help. He'd been able to put my fire out before.

Except that had been by encasing me in ice and my fire had quickly reignited and melted it. Although he hadn't been trying to fix my control over my magic or even remove it—

If Deaglan could pull out my fire, maybe Bane could too. They were both sorcerers able to channel raw Faerie magic and weave it into almost any kind of spell or power they wanted. They just needed the willpower to keep it controlled or they'd burn up and die.

That could give me a few hours with Amiah—

Hell, maybe Bane could take my fire altogether.

Then I could always be with Amiah and I wouldn't have to worry about burning her or anyone else. The war was over and I no longer had to be the Salamander. I didn't need to have magic to live my life.

Sure, I'd have to leave my job as a JP agent, but I'd do that in a heartbeat if it meant I could be with Amiah.

But first I needed to protect her until the mess with Faerie's Heart had been dealt with. Being with her now was a taste of what I might be able to have in the future, but none of it would matter if Deaglan or someone else killed her.

My pulse picked up, pounding in my chest as fear twisted in my gut. Whatever I did, I had to keep her safe. Even if that meant never being able to hold her again.

She murmured in her sleep, soft nonsensical sounds, her skin still radiating a gentle white light. It added to the flickering illumination from the fire, brightening the cave, pushing the shadows into the crevasses between the rocks and deeper into the back of our shelter, and clearly lighting the cave's entrance.

We'd be easy to spot if anyone was looking for us and I

could only pray it would be Bane and the others who arrived first because while I didn't want to admit it to Amiah, I was exhausted and injured too. I had a huge burn down my chest and was still weeping blood from numerous cuts.

It actually spoke to how exhausted and out of it Amiah had been for her to allow me to make love to her while in my injured condition. And without a doubt, she was going to be furious with herself when she woke for not noticing that right away.

Which was something I'd deal with when she woke.

I closed my eyes, listening to her slow, soft breathing and savoring the feel of her body against mine, while I drifted on the edge of sleep, trying to stay awake and listen for danger. Her skin wasn't as warm as it should have been, but it was a lot better than it was before and some of her chill could be attributed to my raised body temperature.

At least her lips were no longer blue and she could breathe normally.

Someone had gotten the key and I had a bad feeling about who.

Bane had barely been standing when I'd jumped into the river and I doubted Hawk could have taken a lot more damage. The only one who'd been capable of fighting had been Titus and Deaglan had tied him up with shadows seconds after he'd shifted.

The best outcome was that Deaglan had the key, and everyone else had managed to escape.

Something crunched outside the cave and I cracked open an eye just wide enough to see who was coming. With very little power, my best move was to let whoever it was think I was unconscious and use the element of surprise to defend us.

Another crunch and another that quickly turned into heavy rapid footfalls.

"She's this way," Titus said, and the footfalls — a mix of Titus's heavy tread and lighter ones from the others — pounded close, crashing through the forest then came to a sudden stop.

"Well, fuck," Bane said.

I raised my head so I could look at them clearly. The forest behind them was dark, it was still night, but now they stood within the radius of Amiah's radiance.

Both Bane and Hawk looked like shit, their clothes torn and bloody. Hawk had lost his shirt, and while he wasn't bleeding, he did have bruises, which meant his magic was low. If he took another serious injury, he wouldn't be able to heal it. While Bane held a wadded-up piece of blood-soaked fabric — probably Hawk's shirt — to his shoulder which was probably only slowing his blood loss not stopping it.

Titus on the other hand looked perfectly fine — and I could tell every bit of him was fine because he was completely naked and sporting some massive wood.

"So Sparky finally got laid," Bane said. "It's about fucking time."

But his words felt forced as if he weren't really happy that Amiah and I had finally made love. Although perhaps that was due to his horrible condition. It was actually a miracle Amiah hadn't immediately woken and healed him.

And even before any of us could do anything, Titus growled and stormed toward me and Amiah.

Ah, shit.

"Titus." Hawk grabbed Titus's arm, but he jerked free without missing a step as Amiah's eyes fluttered open.

Her gaze jumped straight to Bane then jerked to Titus and she sat up, sliding my arms to her waist, not seeming to care that she was naked or my hands were now in her lap, and reached out to the furious dragon.

He dropped to his knees in front of her, cupped her face in his massive hands, and pressed his forehead against hers.

My thoughts stuttered at that. I wasn't sure if I was expecting him to beat the crap out of me like he'd beaten Bane, but I certainly hadn't expected for him to kneel before her. Although if I really thought about it, he'd been using her to calm his shifter's soul almost from the moment we'd dragged him back to Bane's apartment.

Titus huffed, a very dragon-like sound, and closed his eyes, the muscles in his powerful thick arms flexing. "You mated with Cassius."

"We had sex," she said. "We're not mates."

The hellfire in Hawk's eyes flared and he frowned. Guess he thought if Amiah and I ever figured ourselves out, we'd end up in a committed, monogamous relationship. And if I hadn't felt that strange connection when we'd had sex, I would have expected the same thing too. That was the way it was supposed to be, wasn't it? Sure my brother was mated to a woman with other mates and there were a handful of other angels who didn't practice monogamy, but I always expected it'd just be me and Amiah.

Except right now it couldn't just be me and Amiah. I couldn't give her what she needed. In a way it was good she needed whatever it was she got from the others during sex and didn't want a committed relationship, because I had no idea how I was going to explain to her that we couldn't have sex again. Hell, I wouldn't even be able to hold her again anytime soon.

Amiah shifted in my embrace, jerking my attention to her, and I realized my hands were smoking and the heat of my fire was building again inside me.

Shit. Too soon.

It was God damned too soon.

I jerked away from her and grabbed my damp briefs and Titus captured her lips in a hard, ferocious kiss, not seeming to care that Amiah had just been in my arms.

There was a frenzy to his kiss, as if he'd been trying to hold back and couldn't any longer. His fingers tangled in her hair, he tilted her head back to deepen it, and she moaned softly into his mouth, her breath picking up.

He growled back in response, wrapped an arm around her waist, and jerked her into his lap, her legs straddling his, her mound pressed against his cock.

God damn it. That's what I wanted again. I'd barely gotten to hold her and my fire was back.

"This isn't the place," I snapped, my voice icier than I intended. "We should get back to the aerie."

"Just because you licked her doesn't make her yours?" Bane said, clinging to the mouth of the cave to keep standing.

Hey!" Hawk said. "That's my line. I think he's just feeling left out. Don't worry, Sparky. I'll kiss you." Hawk batted his eyelashes at me.

For the love of—

"Fuck off," I growled at Hawk and grabbed Titus's shoulder.

He jerked his head away from Amiah, bared his fangs, and snarled at me.

"If you two want to have sex, at least wait until you're somewhere more comfortable," I forced out.

"Says the man who fucked her in this very cave," Bane drawled.

"No, Cassius is right," Amiah said, her cheeks turning bright red with embarrassment as if she'd just realized she'd been about to have sex with Titus in front of all of us. "We should go back to your aerie," she said to the big man. "But first—" Her gaze jumped to Bane and she eased herself out of Titus's embrace. "Sit before you fall over."

"I can last until you've recovered more magic," he gasped.

"I've enough to deal with your shoulder and ease up some of Cassius's pain." She pointed to the ground. "Sit."

Bane glared at her.

She glared back. Her angel glow was brighter than I would have expected for only being asleep for such a short period, but maybe that connection she made when we had sex had helped... or maybe I'd actually dozed and we'd been asleep longer than I thought.

With a groan, Bane gave in and slid down the wall, and Amiah knelt beside him. She peeled away the bloody fabric he had bunched against his shoulder and gave the hole in Bane's shirt a fierce tug, ripping it open more so she could get a better look at his wound. Then she tipped him forward to check out his back.

At least she was being smart about it and checking him out without using her magic. I could only hope she'd do just enough to close the wound and no more, since I didn't want her exhausted and dizzy again anytime soon. I wouldn't be able to handle that. My emotions were already running wild and it only got worse when she was in bad shape.

She placed her hands over Bane's wound, not caring that she was getting bloody, and closed her eyes. Watching her work always amazed me. There was something incredible about her power, the way she knitted muscle, bone, and flesh back together. Before Amiah, I'd never met an angel who had healing magic, and while I'd met a lot more during and after the war, there was something about the way she worked that always made my breath catch with awe.

White light flickered around her palms and Bane tensed, anticipating pain. But she wasn't in a hurry, which meant she could control how fast her magic healed him so it wouldn't hurt and after a second, he realized that as well and breathed out a heavy sigh, tipped his head back, and closed his eyes.

Hawk and Titus watched and I pulled on my damp pants and shoved my feet into my wet boots. I wanted to get moving the moment she was done. She could heal my burns after we'd gotten to the aerie and she'd had a chance to clean up, eat, and sleep.

I was going to insist on that.

Bane needed to be healed, but I didn't. Yeah, I hurt and the burn down my chest was painful, but, like I had in the past, I'd get by.

"Okay," she murmured, pulling away from Bane and turning her gaze on me, her glow not as low as it could have been which meant she'd remained smart and hadn't fully healed him. "Your turn."

"I'm fine."

"You're in pain. I've enough left to ease that up and it'd be easier if I touch you," she replied, reminding me that she could now heal me without making contact.

"Amiah—" I pulled on my damp shirt. "If you're barely conscious and we end up in another fight we've got a problem."

"And you're injured. I'd say that's a bigger problem." She raised an eyebrow, daring me to keep arguing, and held out her hand. "Just take my hand, Cassius. Don't make me work harder than I have to."

Meaning she was going to heal me whether I wanted her to or not and was probably going to end up hurting herself.

"Fine."

I sucked in a sharp breath and clenched at the inferno starting to build again within me.

I would not burn her. God, please don't let me burn her.

It had barely been a minute since I let her go and already my fire seared under my skin.

"You don't have to look so sour about it." Disappointment swept through her expression before she pulled up her cold mask of professionalism.

The look and emotional withdrawal made my heart clench, knowing she thought I was back to my old ways, that the moment we'd had in the cave hadn't really changed anything between us.

"Jeez man, that's cold," Bane said. "She lets you in and now you're back to being an asshole?"

Of course I was. Because I couldn't God damned touch her again. Not the way I really wanted.

Smoke billowed from my palms and fire snapped over my hands and up my forearms. A few sparks flew dangerously close to Amiah, and I jerked back, my inferno surging with the sudden fear that I was going to hurt her, which only made the fire on my hands bigger.

Shit shit shit.

Ice. Frozen ice. Cold. Hard. Frozen.

But the mantra didn't help anymore. It had barely been helping in the first place. My flames raged through me, burning away any kind of control I might have had, suddenly powerful as if Deaglan hadn't ripped all of it out of me a few hours ago.

"Cassius—" Amiah's eyes grew wide with concern and she stood.

God, she was going to come to me and I was going to hurt her.

"Stay where you are." I jerked my gaze to the others. Titus glared at me as if I was the enemy, Bane's expression had turned thoughtful — yeah, he was close to figuring out the truth — and Hawk looked grim and knowing — he'd already figured it out.

God. I hadn't told anyone the truth, hadn't wanted to

admit it publicly, but the only way to get her to back away was to confess my problem.

"I don't have full control of my fire," I said.

I wasn't sure if I had *any* control anymore.

I couldn't hold her. I'd never be able to be with her again.

Flames dripped from my hands and hissed against the damp stone beneath my feet.

"It's connected to your emotions, isn't it?" Hawk squinted as if he were trying to get a better look at something. And maybe he could. The man was a Sensitive. Between him and Bane, they were the ones most likely to figure out what exactly was wrong with me. Then he shook his head and frowned. "Sorry, man. I have to touch you to find its source."

"We can deal with this when we get back to the aerie." I sucked in a deep breath. The fire still raged, snapping over my arms, past my elbows, and curling over my shoulders.

Another breath. I had to pull it all back. But the inferno roared through my veins, boiling my blood, stronger than before.

Ice. Frozen. Control. Please, God, just give me some control.

At least I'd had a chance to show her how I felt.

"This is why I lost my best friend, isn't it?" Amiah asked, her voice soft, barely audible over the fiery roar in my head. "And I only got you back because Deaglan took your fire."

"You'll get me back again," I promised her, even though it was a promise I couldn't make.

There was no guarantee I'd ever be able to regain

control. In fact what little control I had was getting harder and harder to maintain, and there was no guarantee Bane or anyone else would be able to permanently take it away.

"Right now we need my fire," I forced out. "Eventually Deaglan is going to figure out you have one of the keys and come after you. I'm not going to lose another person I love."

I wouldn't let what happened to Dominic happen to Amiah. I'd protect her. I'd give up everything to keep her safe. And that included having a future with her.

"When this is done, if I have to, I'll get rid of my fire to be with you." In a heartbeat without a second thought. "I love you."

HAWK

My heart clenched at Cassius's words. I knew he loved her, knew she loved him, knew they'd eventually have a committed relationship. They were both angels. It made sense.

But just for a moment, when Amiah had told Titus that she and Cassius weren't mates, that they'd just had sex, I'd had hope.

I could keep what I had with her—

Only if Bane or one of the other guys joined us so I wouldn't kill her or starve, but I could keep her.

Then Cassius had said the words I was too afraid to say and her expression turned soft and sad and her desire for him swelled.

She loved him back. She'd wait for him.

Of course she would.

He was willing to give up his magic for her.

When this mess with the Heart was over, it would be over between me and Amiah as well. Cassius didn't strike me as the sharing kind. Most angels weren't. They weren't

as possessive as wolves — and by the looks of it dragons
— but they tended toward devout monogamy. It was actually a little shocking that Amiah desired multiple partners... although maybe that had something to do with
that connection that she formed between us when we
had sex.

Regardless, the end had always been inevitable for us.
I knew that.

I'd just hoped I'd have more time with her.

And while I sort of did, time while we were running
for our lives wasn't the kind of time I wanted. I wanted
normal time, date time, living together time, just being
together time without the fear of death. I wanted to have
the time to help her explore her desires, to figure out who
she was and what she liked.

And above all, I wanted to connect with her again and
again. The very thing I told her I'd never be able to do.

I wasn't sure I'd be able to go back to just being a
body. Now that I'd had a lover who saw me, desired me
and not just my magic, and connected with my soul, the
idea of sex for survival wasn't enough. The idea of sex
with anyone else made my pulse race.

Which was crazy.

I was crazy.

Because I was an incubus in love.

Fuck.

"Can you hold your fire back long enough for me to
heal you?" she asked, her eyes filled with worry for
Cassius.

And rightly so. His aura was a complete mess now.
Last time it had looked this way, he'd been furious and

terrified because Amiah had risked her life. The situation now wasn't nearly as emotionally heightened but his aura raged like it had before, angry and red and barely under control. Whatever was broken inside him had gotten worse, and I didn't know if it was because Deaglan had pulled out his fire during the fight, or because Cassius had let his emotions go to make love to Amiah and couldn't rebuild the wall that maintained what little control he'd had before.

Except I wouldn't be able to tell the exact cause without using my magic to find what was wrong, and giving him even a hint of my magic right now was a terrible idea.

"Let's fly back to the aerie," he said through gritted teeth. "Maybe by then I'll have enough control to let you touch me."

Amiah's eyes narrowed. She didn't like that suggestion. I wonder if she felt guilty for having sex with him while he was injured or if it was just her nature compelling her to heal him before she'd fully recovered.

"If you haven't gotten it under control by then, I'm still healing you."

"You'll burn yourself," Titus growled, grabbing her clothes by the cave wall, frowning at them, but handing them over to her anyway.

"I can do it without touching him now." She pulled on pants that still looked wet and slid her gaze to Bane then to Titus. "I can do it to any of you. I think I might be able to do it to anyone. I just haven't had an opportunity to figure that out."

Her gaze landed on me and my heart did a crazy little jump in my chest.

"You need more than what Titus and I generated with our kissing."

Yes. I get to be with her again—

Unless she picks one of the others.

Which made me irrationally angry and sad.

I was so completely fucked.

Incubi didn't get jealous.

I forced a wicked smile and let my gaze slide to her still naked breasts. "Are you making an offer?"

"Back at the aerie," Cassius snapped, his body rigid with trying to keep his fire inside him — along with a huge dose of sexual frustration.

Of course, if I couldn't even touch Amiah, I think I'd lose my mind too.

Titus marched out of the cave, shifted, and violently swiped his tail, sending trees crashing to the ground and making an area big enough for him to take off.

Amiah shoved her feet into her boots and pulled on her still-wet shirt. The material clung to her breasts, the light cotton almost see-through, showing her pert nipples, and a wave of desire washed off of Bane and Cassius, giving a small boost to my magic.

"Swell," Cassius grumbled, the muscles in his jaw flexing, and he released his wings with a burst of angelic light and fire.

"Come here, gorgeous." I held out my hand to her and she took it without hesitation, making my heart sing. "Cuddle with me while we fly. That'll help."

Bane climbed onto Titus's back, held out a hand, and together we helped her up.

The dragon's desire surged as I climbed up behind her, wrapped my arms around her waist, and pulled her tight against my chest. I was going to hate myself for suggesting it, but the smart move would be to push Titus and Amiah together to restore my magic. It wouldn't be as powerful a boost as having sex with her myself, but it would be more helpful given our current situation.

Her desire when they'd kissed said she wanted him as much as he wanted her, and he desperately needed to release my magic from his system. His desire was getting painful. The catch would be convincing him to control his possessive nature, because I didn't want to give her up, and neither, I was sure, did Bane — at least for the moment. Although in the end, it would just be her and Cassius.

Titus's body bunched beneath us. He swept his wings down in a powerful stroke and leaped into the air, then flapped his wings to gain altitude, flying away from the large, almost healthy island where we'd found Amiah and Cassius and back into the stomach-churning shattered limbo of the Autumn Court.

I was going to be so glad when we finally got out of this nightmare world. And while it was night and everyone else with their night vision only saw dark shadowy islands suspended in the Autumn Court's nothingness, I saw writhing magic, sharp and angry, and ominous and sickly. It wrapped around islands, drawn in and pushed away by unnatural gravities, and surged like visible wind currents all around us.

"So," Cassius said as he flew in close to Titus, closer than before, now that he was no longer restricted to keeping Amiah and Titus apart. His aura seethed and smoke billowed behind him, but he was managing to keep his flames inside him. "Deaglan has a key."

"Actually Noaldar, my mother's man, has it," Bane corrected.

"I'm not so sure he's your mother's man," I said. Yes, that high fae, Noaldar, had sat beside the Winter Queen in the throne room, but the last time I'd seen him he hadn't been wearing the same clothes as the Winter Queen's other men and had tried to kill Amiah. "He was the man I saw with your sister, the one who'd tried to stab Amiah with that poisoned knife. From the flavor of their desire, I'm pretty sure they're in love."

Although the queen's werepanther had also been involved in the attack. He'd still been wearing the queen's colors, but I didn't want to assume bumping into Amiah had just been an accident.

I shuddered at the thought of them actually succeeding. That poison had been so powerful it would have killed her in seconds. And from the acid that had burned through my veins, that death would have been agonizing. The only reason I was still alive was because Amiah had sacrificed all of her magic and her body to save me.

I slipped a hand under her shirt, needing to be closer, to feel her aura and her desire sliding through me. I could have lost her.

As if sensing my need for her, she turned and captured my lips in a tender kiss filled with gentle yearning, and my hand instinctually slid up to her breast, deepening that yearning and turning it sultry.

She sighed softly and let me take control of the kiss for a moment before pulling away.

"Don't stop on my account," Bane said, his desire pouring off of him in a thick wave and sinking into me. "I don't think I'll ever get tired of watching you two."

"Can we not talk about sex?" Cassius asked, fire rolling down his wings and falling toward a small sideways island and igniting the two dead trees on it. His desire was almost as strong as Bane's but for different reasons. He wanted Amiah. And while Bane wanted Amiah too, he also got off on watching someone else be with her.

"Fine." Bane dragged his attention away from me and Amiah, and I gently, subtly kneaded her breast, carefully building her desire so it wasn't overwhelming and she wasn't going to want to have sex while on Titus's back, but still enough to help restore some of what I'd lost in the fight.

"So Noaldar is banging my sister," Bane said.

"Really, Bane?" Cassius growled. "It's hard enough already."

"Shit. Sorry." Bane gave him an apologetic smile. "So if Noaldar isn't really my mother's man, then he may not tell her about getting the key. He might want to get the Heart for Padraigin."

Can Noaldar make ice constructs? Titus asked in my head.

"He is a sorcerer." The demonic magic in Bane flared, now almost fully consuming his fae essence, and he drew in a sharp breath and tensed, trying to hide his pain from the others. "But it depends on how much he's grown in strength."

"If he can, then maybe he was the one behind the attack at the healing pool," Amiah said, her voice breathy, the only indication that I was turning her on — likely out of respect for Cassius and Titus. "Whoever that was had been after the Heart as well. But why give it to Padraigin? Why wouldn't he keep it for himself?"

"He might end up doing that when he realizes just how powerful it is," Bane said. "But if he's in love with Padraigin and the Winter Court doesn't respond to her, then having the Heart will give her enough power to control the court by force and take the throne. And whoever is queen, has the queen's harem."

"So you're saying if I ended up as Queen of the Winter Court, I'd end up with all those guys?" Amiah asked. "Even if I was your wife?"

"Yep," Bane said.

And then I'd eat them, Titus said.

"Jeez man," Bane said with a chuckle, not in the least bit worried, or making the connection that Titus wanting to eat the queen's harem meant he might also want to eat Amiah's current harem — currently consisting of me and Bane right now.

That would make Amiah cry, Titus said in my head. *And she needs you. I've seen it in her soul.*

You what—? I wasn't sure what to make of his words. A part of me was thrilled that Titus recognized my connection with Amiah, while the rest was confused. And I wasn't going to think too hard about the fact that

Titus had responded to a personal thought. It was usually considered rude in the shifter world to eavesdrop on other people's thoughts.

You thought it very loudly. And please, stop seducing her. Wait until we get back to the aerie. All I can smell right now is her arousal and it isn't fun flying with a hard on that you're making harder by the second.

So you won't challenge me for her? I asked, almost afraid to hope, because he wanted her as much as the rest of us, and I had a feeling it wasn't just because he hadn't gotten any in the last five hundred years or because of my magic. *Would you share?*

That's what she asked for. That's what she needs. Titus tilted sideways, making me tighten my grip on Amiah — one hand around her waist the other still on her breast — and soared around an upside-down island.

Her breath grew faster even as she clung to Titus's spine ridge to stay straddling him, and her desire surged, liquid power rushing into my veins, easing the sudden jolt of nausea of no longer being right side up.

"She could just let them go," Bane continued, clearly not hearing the conversation between me and Titus. "Just because they're in her harem doesn't mean they have to stay."

I don't know how to explain it and I don't think she does either, Titus said, *but I've seen it in her soul. It's like she's a dragon, but she isn't, and it isn't just me her soul needs.*

His words whirled through my head.

Her soul needs.

She was an angel and angels, out of all the supers in all the realms, had the ability to create permanent, powerful soul bonds with one or more mates. It was rare. Rumor had it that it only happened every few centuries, but maybe Amiah was one of those rare angels.

"Come on, Titus, tell me you wouldn't eat them," Bane said.

Do you think we're her mates? I asked.

I thought she was mine. Titus huffed, sending smoke pouring out of his nostrils, and dipped below another island, riding a putrid green wave of magic that I knew he couldn't see. *But I'm not the only one in her soul. So I must be wrong.*

Maybe you're not. Maybe we're all hers. God, wouldn't that be perfect? Except that had to be pure fantasy, my desire to keep her. If any of us were her mates, surely she would have branded us by now. She'd known Cassius for a century and they were in love. Surely she would have branded him.

"Your silence is terrifying," Bane said, the muscles in his back bunching with another angry surge of demonic magic.

No I wouldn't eat them, Titus huffed. *Your hand, incubus.*

Right. I was just so stunned that Titus, after clinging to her in the Winter Court and beating the crap out of Bane, would so easily share.

There's nothing easy about it, he growled back.

I slid my hand out from under Amiah's shirt and her desire softened, although her breathing was still a little too fast and shallow.

"So the Winter Queen may or may not have a key," Cassius said, his gaze locked straight ahead, his body almost as tense as Bane's. "And Deaglan has the ability to sense the keys."

"But only when they first become empowered," Bane said. "If he could sense them after they'd been claimed, he would have gone after Amiah in the aerie or in that cave in the Autumn Court."

"So it's even more of a race to get to the keys than it ever was." Amiah let go of Titus to wrap her arms around me and pressed her cheek and chest against my naked chest, the wind rushing around us cooling her already slightly-cool skin even more.

"A race you shouldn't be a part of," Cassius said. "We need to figure out a way for Titus to find the rest of the keys without you."

"And if you did that—" She drew in a heavy breath. "Sebastian would still have a broken back—" Another heavy breath. "And Deaglan would have killed all of you."

Titus hit a seething red stream of magic, lost the air under his wings for a second, dropping us a heart-stopping few feet, and caught his balance.

Cassius's eyes flashed wide and fire poured from his wings as he dipped to rejoin Titus. "What happens in our next fight when we seriously injure Deaglan or one of his men and your magic locks onto them? You can heal without touching now. Do you honestly think your magic won't just drain you? That'll make you weak and dizzy and a dangerous distraction for all of us."

"I'm with Sparky," Bane said. "When we get back to the aerie, I'll see if I can cast something that will give Titus back the key without killing you."

"Don't you dare," she gasped, shivering.

Titus grunted, but I didn't know if it was in agreement with Cassius or Amiah. He soared around a massive waterfall pouring from one island to the next, and there, ahead of us, was the writhing putrid barrier and our way out of this not-so-fun funhouse.

"I have to agree with Amiah," I said. "You don't know how much power pulling the key out of Amiah will take."

Bane shrugged. "Maybe it'll be easy. Titus just gave it to Amiah, maybe she can just give it back."

Titus grunted again and put on a burst of speed, heading straight to the barrier and then bursting through into the Wilds, but he didn't let up when we were through and kept up the pace, shooting through the night sky over the Wilds' steamy jungle.

"You honestly think taking the key is going to be easy?" I asked, as Amiah's shivering increased and her body temperature grew colder despite the humidity rising from the trees below us. Jeez. We needed to get her out of the wind and her wet clothes. "How far to the aerie?"

"Depends on how Faerie is feeling." Bane tensed and a small ball of magic exploded from his body and was sucked down into the trees below. "And I fucking hope it's feeling generous. I don't have a lot for it to take right now."

"Go quickly," Amiah said as a white ball of magic exploded from her back, drawing a whimper.

Titus beat his wings again, gaining more speed. Except instead of the dragon's mountain on the horizon, it was the opalescent shimmer of another court barrier, and he was headed straight for it.

"Why the hell is Faerie showing us the Summer Court?" Bane asked.

"Go," Amiah gasped, straining to draw a breath, her body frighteningly cold just like when the last key had become empowered.

Oh, shit.

Another key? Already? We hadn't had time to recover from the last one, and Amiah was still with us, still in danger.

"Find a place to land," I said, my voice sharp with panic. "We can't take Amiah with us. Titus land."

But the dragon kept barreling toward the barrier, making my pulse roar through me and my breath quicken. We were weak. We couldn't protect her. We'd barely been able to protect her at full power. If Deaglan realized she had a key and got his hands on her, he wouldn't think twice about killing her to get it.

I could only pray because we'd already been on the move, we'd get there first and would be able to escape before anyone else showed up.

TITUS

I SPED TO THE SUMMER COURT BEFORE AMIAH FROZE OR suffocated or whatever it was that happened to her when a key became empowered and we were in physical contact. The key's call clawed at my insides, urging, begging, screaming at me to take it into my dragon body where it belonged.

The guys yelled at me, ordering me to stop, but I couldn't. Not with the compulsion tearing through me. Not for a second. That, and if I let Amiah get off, I'd have to stop and make contact with her again once we were inside the Summer Court.

She was strong. She could handle the pressure and the cold for a little longer. Her breath was labored, but if I concentrated, I could still hear it, and she hadn't pushed Hawk away for being too warm, not yet. We still had time. I could fly fast enough to get to the key before its call overwhelmed her, even if her thoughts were starting to scare me.

I can't be trapped. Not again. Let me out. Please, God. Let me out.

Her desperate mental cries tore at my heart. Whatever the key did to her, it dragged her back into the horror of being a prisoner. She'd been taken. Twice. And by saving me, I'd trapped her with a leash spell, one that still connected her to Seireadan, and now the Winter Court wanted her. She was trapped over and over again and right now her soul saw no way to escape, no hope.

Just hang on, I said in her head and only her head.

I will. Get us... to that... key. Don't... listen to them. Even her mental voice was gasping, fighting for air.

"Titus, slow down," Seireadan yelled. "Her lips are turning blue. Let Cassius take her."

You think he can carry her? He couldn't even look at her without fire pouring from his wings, and taking the time to figure out if he could hold her was time that Deaglan could be getting the key, and I couldn't let him get even one.

Not to mention if I managed to fight the key's compulsion and stopped, I might end up pounding the shit out of Cassius instead of handing Amiah over.

My beast was still raging that he'd stopped us from mating. It didn't matter that he'd been right and it was best to wait until we were back at the aerie and Amiah could clean up and get something to eat. We weren't going back to the aerie and my beast had finally agreed to not kill any of the others if she slept with me and then them again.

She needed them, not just me, and my beast wanted what was best for my mate.

And it didn't matter how many times I tried to tell it she wasn't mine. It wouldn't listen.

I'd been relieved when she'd made the point of saying she and Cassius had just had sex because it had taken everything I had to go to her instead of attacking Cassius and stay with her even with her soul calming mine. If they were mates, my beast would challenge him. My beast still wanted to challenge him.

She was my mate, who just so happened to need sex from the others.

Unless, of course, Hawk's theory was correct and she was all of our mates.

I crashed through the Summer Court's barrier, its magic clinging to my scales as I passed through, and beat my wings, flying as fast as I could over the vast, lush — manicured within an inch of its life — summer garden that surrounded the court's royal villa. The key's compulsion urged me on — *go go, claim me, bring me home* — even though I had a chance to land and let Amiah off. It was so close. I knew exactly where it was.

Except Amiah's thoughts were getting desperate and her shivering violent, and Seireadan had turned around and taken her from Hawk.

Please, let me go. Please, she sobbed, and I couldn't tell if her sobbing was just in her thoughts or not.

Hang in there.

Please. I want out. I have to get out. I can't stay this way.

"For fuck's sake, Titus. Stop," Seireadan yelled, his thoughts flooding me. *She's dying. She can't breathe. I have to save her, sever her connection with the key.*

Almost there, I snarled in his head and plunged down

a steep slope of mixed grasses and shrubs, groomed to look like swirling clouds, and landed at the mouth of the Summer Court's luminous cave garden, its entrance too small for me to enter in my dragon form.

It took everything I had to hold myself steady as Seireadan pulled Amiah from my back and Hawk hopped down.

The key's call grew stronger by the second and the moment they were off, I leaped toward the fae-sized opening, shifting between one stride to the next into my human form before my dragon form slammed into the intricately carved pillars on either side of the entrance. It didn't matter that I was naked. I barely felt the flagstone path leading into the cavern under my bare feet. I had to get the key.

Now now now.

"Titus, wait," Cassius called. "Be smart about this. We don't know if Deaglan or Noaldar is already here."

"All the more reason to hurry." Even if I wanted, I couldn't resist the compulsion. It didn't matter that Cassius was right, that it was foolish to run headlong into the cavern. I couldn't stop. Not with the key screaming for me to get it and not with Amiah's desperate begging to be free still gasping in my mind even though I didn't have telepathy in human form.

"Titus." Cassius snapped a fire whip around my biceps and jerked me off balance.

"What the hell," Hawk said. "You'll burn him."

"My fire doesn't burn him, he's a fire dragon," Cassius replied and stormed toward me. "Take a breath. Running headlong puts Amiah in danger."

At the mention of her name, my gaze instantly jumped to her. She huddled against Seireadan, drawing in strained, shallow breaths, shivering so hard she couldn't keep her balance.

I'd done that. I'd hurt her.

She met my gaze, the glow in her eyes barely brighter than the glow from her body, and captured my soul, like she always did.

Mine.

Not. Just. Mine.

Still makes her mine.

"We go in cautiously," she said.

Cassius glared at her. "You're not going anywhere."

"And you'd leave me out here to be found by Deaglan or Noaldar?"

His fire snapped and black smoke billowed around him.

"Even if one of you stays, neither of you are well enough to face either man alone. It'd just end up with the two of us captured or dead." Her angel glow flared and her shivering increased. "And neither is an acceptable option."

Her words made my beast heave inside me, not just because it hated either option, but because both of us knew she'd pick death over capture again.

"God damn it." Cassius shot a blast of fire into the ground. "You hide the moment there's trouble."

He jerked his attention to the garden's entrance and heaved his wings back inside his body. "Anyone know what this place is?"

"The Summer Court's luminous cave garden,"

Seireadan said, lifting her into his arms and cradling her against his chest.

Something I needed to do.

Except I also had to get the key. Now.

"Sounds pretentious." Hawk rolled his eyes then closed them.

"Everything about the Summer Court is," I snapped.

Go now. Claim me. Bring me home.

I ground my teeth against the compulsion. "Unless you can fly, and you're smaller than a dragon, this is the only way in or out."

Now. Go now. Come on.

Cassius stepped past the pillars and peered down the long tunnel leading to the garden. "Can you smell anyone's scent?"

"I don't smell anyone who's been here since the key became empowered," I replied, "and nothing that smells like Deaglan, shadow fae, or Noaldar."

"I can't sense anyone inside, either," Hawk said. "Although that could mean they're shielded or having little to no sexual desire at the moment."

"It's a single passage in, and while there might be a few places to hide, it's mostly one big cavern with glowing rocks and moss," Seireadan added.

"Okay. Eyes open everyone." Cassius squared his shoulders. "Titus, you've got the lead. Stay cautious."

I jerked forward before I fully realized what I was doing, then forced myself to pay attention to my surroundings. Cassius was right. Running headlong put Amiah in danger.

The walls and ceiling of the passage into the luminous cave garden were carved with intricate swirls that looked like flowers and clouds. It was similar to the carving in the Winter Court, although softer, swirlier. Hints of luminescent moss and moonstones glowed throughout the decoration, providing just enough light for me with my night vision to see where I was going.

Ahead, the glow grew brighter, and it took everything I had not to race to the end.

Claim me. Bring me home. Now. Now.

I reached the threshold between passage and cavern and dug my claws into the wall beside me to stop and look for danger. Except my attention jerked to the blazing blue pinprick of light at the back of the cavern on the wide top shelf of three shallow rocky shelves, hovering a few feet off the uneven ground.

Seireadan drew up behind me and Amiah gasped, making my heart clench. I wished I could have taken her here just to show it to her.

The place was stunning, with its numerous stalagmites and stalactites softly glowing in yellows, blues, and pinks, and the patches of green and blue mosses that curled over the stones near the two fae-sized shafts that let light into the top half of the cavern during the daytime. In the center, surrounded by a mesmerizing pattern of softly glowing moonstones, was the cavern's luminescent pool, a deep pool with shimmering specks of glowing algae suspended in its clear water.

"Hawk? Bane?" Cassius asked.

Just get me. Bring me home.

I clenched my teeth. I could wait a few more seconds.

"I think we got here first," Hawk said. "I also don't sense any magical traps, just the power of the key."

"Good." Cassius stepped into the cavern proper and released his wings with a fiery burst. "Titus, get that key and let's get out of here."

Finally. I lunged forward, shifting with the movement and dove for the key. It wasn't practical to be in my dragon form, there were too many rocky protrusions barring the way, but there was enough space to get over the pond.

I jerked sideways to fly between two stalactites too close together for my wingspan, straightened and caught the air over the pond, and shifted, midflight, to land on the other side.

The key wrenched on my soul.

Bring me home. Bring me home.

I ran to it, easily leaped up the rocky shelves — they weren't even as tall as me — and lunged, my hand outstretched to grab the key.

AMIAH

Titus reached for the key, his hand inches from its blazing light, and a thick strand of shadow shot out from the cluster of stalagmites behind him. It seized his wrist and slammed him against the ground.

I gasped, barely able to draw that surprised breath against the frozen crushing pressure in my chest.

"I don't think so," Deaglan said, oozing out of the same shadow his strand had come from.

"Are you fucking kidding me?" Hawk groaned, and he bolted out of the cave entrance toward Titus.

Cassius shot a ball of fire across the cavern and burned through the shadow holding Titus, but Deaglan quickly reformed it, recaptured Titus, and tossed him off the rocky shelves, sending him tumbling over the rough ground to the edge of the pool.

"How could you possibly have gotten your fire back so soon?" He demanded as Cassius shot another fireball at him, making him jerk away from the key.

Except Cassius hadn't gotten all of his fire back. If he

had, he would have dropped a pillar of fire on Deaglan. The fact that he used a fireball, said he wasn't at full strength and was trying to be smart about how he used his magic.

"Kill them," Deaglan commanded and the shadows around Cassius and Hawk surged. Dozens of shadow fae jumped out of the darkness, their skin a mix of white fae glow and undulating shadows, their life forces dark and thick and suddenly there, thrumming against my senses.

Then my senses jerked my attention up. There were three more life forces in a large shadow descending from a hole in the ceiling. A fiery, sour force, a wild primal force, and a barely-there strange life and death, cold and hot, and filled with pain force. Deaglan's nightmare, a new shifter, and the vampire-demon hybrid.

The shadow deposited them in front of Titus and they immediately lunged into action along with their fellow assassins.

"Fuck," Sebastian hissed, leaning me against the cave wall. "Just stay out of sight."

He stepped into the cavern, the absence of his body heat making me shiver so hard I could barely keep standing, dropped to his knees, and pressed both hands to his chest. Brilliant white light flooded the space, blinding me, and from the grunts, gasps, and cries, everyone else as well.

"Take that, asshole," Sebastian yelled.

"Only makes you easier to kill, Seireadan," Deaglan spat back.

"Hawk, protect Bane and Amiah," Cassius called out

and the sound of another fireball exploded against the rocks.

I cracked open one eye, making it water, but forced myself to keep it open. Yes, I didn't need to see to fight, but I still needed to avoid being attacked and distracting the guys, which meant I needed to be able to see the danger coming.

Light filled the entire cavern, reaching into every crack and stretching all the way behind me to the garden's entrance not giving the shadow fae any shadows to hop between.

Sebastian still knelt, his eyes squeezed tight, his complexion gray, and his breath short and shallow. He needed to keep channeling magic to maintain the light spell and he wasn't going to last very long.

Hawk fought with three shadow fae, somehow already getting a knife from one of them, and three more fae rushed toward Sebastian. Titus also fought with a swarm of shadow fae, the nightmare, and the new shifter — although I couldn't tell what animal the woman shifted into — and was unable to get closer to the key, while Cassius flew across the pond flecked with light, and snagged Deaglan's wrist with a fire whip.

Deaglan sliced Cassius's whip with a shadow blade and lunged for the key.

But the air beside him burst into a shimmering liquid mirror and Noaldar leaped through and grabbed the key.

The brilliant blue light flared and sank into his skin and the frozen pressure in my chest vanished.

I gasped in a desperate deep breath even as my chill shifted into a cold dread in my gut.

Noaldar now had two keys.

I didn't know if he knew I had one or not, but I didn't want to bet he wouldn't be able to find out.

Noaldar flashed Deaglan a victorious sneer and jumped back into the shimmer, slamming into something and tumbling onto his rear instead of going through the portal.

Deaglan's shadows seized him and wrenched him into the air, his arms and legs stretched taut. "You really thought I wouldn't cast a one-way portal lock?"

My magic flared in my chest, jerking my attention to Titus and locking on a shadow fae gravely injured among other dead shadow fae lay in a growing pool of blood around Titus.

The fae gasped and died before my power forced me forward, but it continued to snap and heave inside me as my guys battled Deaglan's men.

I clenched my teeth and clung to the wall.

I will not let my magic run free or enter the fight. I'll keep my magic. I'll stay safe. Even if it means suffering backlash. I won't endanger my guys.

"You really think I'll let you have his keys?" Cassius said, and I wrenched my attention back to him.

He landed on the far end of the shelf, pulled his wings in, and sliced through the shadows holding Noaldar.

The winter court fae hit the ground and scrambled to the edge of the shelf behind him, but Deaglan's shadows exploded from his body, capturing Noaldar while also slamming into Cassius, just like they had when Deaglan had taken his fire.

My heart skipped a beat. We hadn't had time to protect Cassius from this attack. It hadn't even come up, and Cassius had to have known if he confronted Deaglan straight on, the Shadow King would take his fire again. He was smarter than that. He had to have a plan. Something that would stop Deaglan.

"Stop interrupting me," Deaglan screamed, and his shadows surged under Cassius's skin, extinguishing the flames roaring over his body.

Then fire and shadows erupted from his chest, drawing a heart-wrenching cry of pain and he dropped to his knees, his chest heaving, once again not a hint of fire or even smoke curling from his skin.

I jerked forward, my heart pounding, not because my magic had locked onto Cassius, but because he was suffering.

Except I couldn't help him. The best I could do was stay put and remain unnoticed.

Just stay put.

Deaglan sneered, turned his back on Cassius, and wrenched Noaldar within arm's reach.

"Those don't belong to you," Deaglan said and he grabbed Noaldar's jaw and forced the man's mouth open.

Noaldar heaved against Deaglan's grip and more shadows wrapped around the winter fae's neck, choking him. His eyes bulged and his fae glow flared bright even in the brightly lit cavern. The glow rolled up his body and focused into a blazing blue stream that poured out of his mouth along with a desperate scream.

Deaglan's sneer deepened and Noaldar wrenched and thrashed against the shadows, his breath wild gasps, his eyes filled with terror. His life force snapped against my senses with a terrifing frenzy, and Deaglan sucked it in.

My magic surged and locked onto Noaldar, my power bursting into my palms and racing up my forearms. I could feel Deaglan not just sucking out the magic of the keys, but the Faerie magic inside Noaldar that made him high fae *and* his life force. All of it. And without a doubt, Deaglan wasn't going to stop until he had every last drop of magic in Noaldar, killing him.

My magic wrenched me forward and I fought to stay where I was. More light than there should have been, given how low my power was, blazed from my hands. Everything within me screamed to save him, heal his rapidly draining life force. And if I didn't go to him, my power would connect with him anyway. There wasn't even a risk of suffering a terrible backlash for refusing. I couldn't refuse. I had no choice. I *had* to save him.

Except I didn't know how to heal his life force. I healed bodies. My magic knitted bone and muscle and flesh together. It didn't heal magic and it certainly couldn't restore someone's life force.

Noaldar gasped, a final desperate, weak breath, and the last drop of his life force swept out of him, leaving a gray shell without any hint of fae glow hanging in Deaglan's shadows.

It had only taken a few rapid pounds of my heart. One second Noaldar was alive and my power was howling through me, the next he was dead and I was released.

Then Cassius, without making a sound, leaped at Deaglan, a rock clenched in his hands aimed at the

Shadow King's head. So that was the plan. Get close and attack when the Shadow King least expected it. But Deaglan wrenched around to face him as if he was able to sense Cassius was attacking, and a massive shadow spear formed beside him.

Cassius hit first, the rock smashing against Deaglan's temple, but the shadow spear still lurched forward even as Deaglan dropped to his hands and knees. The spear missed Cassius's heart but still sliced a deep laceration into his side.

"Cassius." I could heal that.

I had to heal that.

It was deep and would kill him without medical attention, but I had enough magic within me to stop the bleeding. *If* I could get my hands on him in time.

I bolted out of hiding and raced toward him.

"Amiah, get back," Hawk yelled at me.

"He doesn't have fire. He can't cauterize the wound."

An assassin grabbed for me and Hawk tackled him to the ground.

"Amiah. Stop," Hawk screamed, his voice sharp with panic.

More assassins broke off their fight with Hawk and Titus and rushed toward me, but I wasn't going to lose Cassius. Not when I could save him. "Clear the way for me."

Cassius pressed his hands against the wound doing nothing to slow the bleeding and sagged to his knees.

I could reach him. I had to reach him.

I loved him and he loved me. We'd finally admitted the truth to ourselves and each other, and even if my feelings were still complicated, my desire for the other still strong, I knew in the depth of my soul that I was in love with Cassius.

And, God damn it, we were going to figure that out. We were getting that lifetime of being together that I'd dreamed of when we'd had sex.

Someone screamed, but I kept my focus on Cassius.

Deaglan groaned. Blood dripped from his temple where Cassius had struck him, splattering the rocky ground between his hands, and he swayed as if he were on the verge of passing out.

"Just hold on," I yelled to Cassius and his attention jerked up to me, his bright blue eyes, now fully visible because his power was gone, capturing my soul.

"What are you doing?" he yelled at me. "Get back."

"I'm saving your life, you idiot."

"Get back!" He staggered to his feet and one of Deaglan's assassins leaped onto the shelf behind him and yanked his knife across Cassius's throat.

Everything within me froze.

My body, mind, and soul froze then lurched into a desperate, soul-rending scream.

I couldn't stop screaming.

My soul was screaming.

Cassius's eyes flashed wide and he grabbed his neck, but arterial blood sprayed between his fingers, hitting Deaglan in the face.

"About fucking time," the Shadow King snarled.

My power exploded within me, making me stumble and fall to my knees at the edge of the pool. It locked onto Cassius and slammed into him without me even thinking about it. He collapsed on the ground and I scrambled to my feet, heaved my magic back inside my body, and started running again. But I was only halfway around the pool.

"Cassius!" I couldn't let him die. I'd just realized I loved him. We were supposed to have a lifetime together.

God, I wasn't going to get to him in time. I had to release my magic and heal him from afar. It was the only way.

Except I didn't have a lot of power to begin with. I wasn't sure I had enough to heal him while touching him. I certainly didn't have enough power to heal him from a distance. I had to hold it in, fight the compulsion raging through me long enough to get to him. It was his best chance.

I tried to push power into my back to release my wings, but my magic wouldn't move out of my hands and forearms. I was supposed to send it out, use it on others, use it on Cassius, and I couldn't even draw the miniscule amount needed to fly.

God damn it. Why did it have to do that? If I could fly, I could get to him faster. Save him.

Yes, save him.

My soul screamed at me to save him.

I pumped my arms, trying to run faster, my lungs and muscles burning with the effort.

Hawk screamed my name and out of the corner of my eye, I saw a shadow fae diving for me.

I jerked out of the way. I couldn't get caught. Cassius would die if I even slowed down for a second, and maybe, just maybe if I could get to him, I'd have enough magic to stabilize him.

Please let it be enough. It had to be enough. I had to save him.

My power burned so hot it felt as if my hands were on fire and the promise of an excruciating backlash squeezed in my chest making it harder to breathe.

I couldn't lose him.

Please. Please. I can't.

His fiery life force heaved and snapped against my senses, desperate to stay lit, but was growing weaker by the second.

"Amiah, stop, please," Titus roared.

But I couldn't stop. I had to save Cassius. I didn't know what I'd do without him. He was my best friend, my rock. I'd just gotten him back.

Save him.

My toe hit a ridge in the uneven floor and I fell, tumbling face first onto the stone. I was still fifty feet away from Cassius, and he lay in a massive pool of blood, his eyes glassy with death.

I could barely feel his life force.

I was going to lose him, and I couldn't lose him. I just couldn't.

A horrible frozen stone formed in my gut. I wasn't going to have enough power even if I reached him in time.

There had to be a way to get more power. I needed more power, more life.

My senses snapped to the shadow assassin who'd slit Cassius's throat, now rushing toward me. His life writhed with a similar darkness as Deaglan's, strong and sure. It slid across my senses, taunting me. Everyone's life force did.

I could feel all of them, the sense stronger than it had ever been before. Every one of Deaglan's assassins, his nightmare, his new shifter — a bear — his hybrid, and Deaglan himself. He had the most life force out of everyone because he had a life that didn't belong to him, and while I could feel the keys inside him as well, I didn't immediately connect with them and didn't have the time to figure out if I could.

My magic latched onto Noaldar's life force inside Deaglan, and the Shadow King gasped. He dragged his head up and searched the cavern to figure out who was attacking him. Then his dark gaze zeroed in on me and he sent a flurry of shadows at me, but I didn't care. I just needed more power to save Cassius.

I heaved on Noaldar's life force and Deaglan's shadows burst apart, his magic stuttering at the sudden withdrawal of power, and Noaldar's life poured into me and flew back out into Cassius.

Cassius's life force sparked, a dying flame given a speck of fuel to stay alive.

It was working. I could save him. I just needed more.

I grabbed Deaglan's life force. His expression filled with terror and a blast of fae magic ripped through my connection to him and created a wall blocking me from reconnecting with him. The wall was weak, riddled with fissures that I might be able to get through, but no—

No time.

There were other life forces that were easier to

connect with. I could feel them, feel every living thing in the cavern, my guys, Deaglan's men, the mice and rats and bugs hiding in small tunnels away from the light, even the moss growing on the glowing stalactites and stalagmites and the algae in the pond.

All of it thrummed against my senses, mine to take and use.

Except the moss, algae, bugs, and rodents didn't have a strong enough life force, and the cost for using the men's was the likelihood that I draw too much and kill them.

And the moment I realized that, I knew I'd pay any price to save Cassius.

Even if it meant staining my soul by killing someone.

And while these men were trying to kill us, and obeyed a man who'd held Titus, his friend, captive for five hundred years, and who wanted Faerie's Heart for his own gain, that didn't lessen the fact that I was going to kill them.

To save Cassius.

God, please.

I pushed my magic into all of Deaglan's men and seized their life forces. The power heaved in my grip and my magic clenched tighter.

I would save Cassius. I would sacrifice my soul for him.

I just needed more power.

I wrenched at the life forces, and every man that I could see collapsed and started screaming.

I didn't care.

I had to save Cassius.

Their life poured into me, burning through my veins and making my skin blaze with power, and streamed into Cassius, making his life force flicker stronger.

"I don't think so, little angel," Deaglan screamed, his eyes wild with anger and fear.

A wall slammed around the hybrid, cutting me off from him.

Fine. I didn't need him. His life force was strange and weak anyway. I still had the others.

But then another wall and another burst around the men and my power weakened and so did Cassius's life force.

Deaglan created shadow wings and flew up to the ledge near the hole in the ceiling where his nightmare and hybrid had come from.

"Kill the angel and get me her key," he yelled and those assassins who were no longer on the ground screaming picked up their weapons, and rushed toward me.

Titus and Hawk jumped into action to protect me, and I fought to keep a connection with the few men I was still connected to. But another wall went up and another.

I was losing all my power, and I hadn't saved Cassius. Healing from afar took an enormous amount of magic, especially something as serious as a slit throat and massive blood loss. I had to focus, and I couldn't do that and run at the same time.

I staggered to a stop about twenty feet from the shelves where Cassius lay, strengthened my hold on the life forces I was still connected to, and rammed my magic through the barriers of the half dozen of Deaglan's men who were closest to me.

Please let this work. Please let this save him.

With a scream, I wrenched on their life forces, drawing a horrific wail that echoed through the cavern before going suddenly deathly silent. Their life roared into my body and swept to my hands as another life force jerked close behind me.

A strange cold, burning, pain-filled life force, life and death at the same time. Deaglan's hybrid.

I wrenched around to see how close he was, and he slid his katana into my heart.

My mind stuttered unable to comprehend what had just happened.

Then agonizing pain exploded in my chest and he wrenched his blade free.

My connection with Cassius shattered and the life forces I'd gathered slammed into my chest, but it was too much, I couldn't control it, couldn't focus it to save myself. Agony roared around my heart, a ferocious fire, consuming me from the inside out. It swelled through my whole body before gathering, a searing inferno in my left hip, and erupted into a brilliant burning golden blaze.

My soul locked onto the hybrid's soul and horror stole my breath.

No, please, God, no.

His eyes widened and his hellfire burst into wild flames.

"What did you do?" he asked in that soft, terrifying, barely audible voice of his.

I'd branded him.

Oh, God.

He'd forced me to lose control of the power I needed to save Cassius and the angelic mating brand that I thought was gone, that I'd damaged my soul to get rid of, had awakened.

I was soul bonded to Deaglan's demon-vampire hybrid.

And I could no longer feel Cassius's life force.

Don't miss the next book in the series!

FATED DESPAIR
Angel's Fate: Book Four

There's no outrunning fate once it's branded her heart.

I'd thought I was safe, free of the horrible fate awaiting me. I'd never been more wrong.

Now I'm living in my worst nightmare. I failed my guys as we fought for our lives against the Shadow King and his assassins, and the mating brand I'd tried so hard to get rid of flared to life.

And only one thing can break its agonizing power without killing me. Faerie's Heart.

But we have no time to succumb to crushing heart-break and sorrow. Somehow, we must pull our drained powers and broken bodies together — and evade the Winter Queen's assassins — to find the final key needed to release the Heart before the Shadow King can get his hands on it. Failure means he will control all of Faerie.

And the brand will become a chasm — putting my guys and their love beyond forever beyond my reach.

OTHER BOOKS BY TESSA COLE

NEPHILIM'S DESTINY

Destined Shadows, prequel story

Destined Darkness, book 1

Destined Blood, book 2

Destined Fire, book 3

Destined Storm, book 4

Destined Radiance, book 5

ANGEL'S FATE

Fated Bonds, book 1

Fated Winter, book 2

Fated Fear, book 3

Fated Despair, book 4

Fated Resolve, book 5

Fated Heart, book 6

THE GRECIAN GODDESS TRILOGY

Kiss of the Goddess, book 1

Power of the Goddess, book 2

Bonds of the Goddess, book 3

ENSNARED BY THE PACK